PEEPING PAUL

John W A Roberts

CHAPTER 1

When he first saw the murderer, Paul thought he was going to a fancy dress party. The all white suit made him think of Elvis Presley but what the man was carrying wasn't a guitar. When he raised it up and placed it over his head Paul saw it was a white helmet with a large visor. The last time he had seen anything like it was at the chemical warfare exercise staged by the council in the summer.

He'd been standing in a back garden watching a woman at her dressing table in the bedroom of the house for several minutes. She kept looking at something on her left arm; he guessed it was a new bracelet or watch. She was wearing only a black bra and knickers. When she'd stood up he'd hoped she was going to take them off. She'd lifted a dress off the bed and put it in the wardrobe but she'd made no move to take off her underwear. He hadn't been too disappointed. She might be waiting for her partner to take them off. That would be exciting. He'd seen a teenager walking about stark naked only eleven nights ago. Perhaps, as the sports commentators were fond of saying, he was "on a roll"

The man in the white suit was advancing towards her with his arms wide apart. Paul felt himself tense. They must be going to have some kinky sex. He'd never seen anything like that, never. Once he'd looked through the back window of a car as it was rocking up and down but it had been too misted up to see anything. He'd heard them though. That had really excited him but this could be the sexiest thing he'd ever experienced. He could tell the woman was puzzled from the way she stood up and hesitantly raised her arms. She started to back away as the white arms reached out for...for her throat! What the hell was going on? He couldn't be going to kill her. People in Meldrum Avenue didn't kill one another. This was a very respectable part of town. This must be some sex game. If only he could get closer. But the window was so high that even a little step forward cut down his view. He moved back so quickly he slipped. He had to put his hand down to steady himself. When he looked up again they were still struggling. She was thumping the visor with both fists. They had to stop this. They must or she would really be hurt. They lurched

3

sideways; then straightened up and stood rocking too and fro like two grotesque puppets. Suddenly she was being lifted and carried across the room to the bed. Paul's excitement rocketed. Was he going to see...? No...No...No. The man was pushing her down, pressing her into the bed. He held her there for so long that she would soon be strangled or suffocated. This was no game.

Paul felt sick. He had to stop this. He looked for something to throw at the window. Seeing nothing he crouched down and felt around in the hope of finding some sort of missile. All he could feel was the grass and the thick coat of Kaiser, his German Shepherd. The dog gave a little whine. He knew something was wrong. He would bark if commanded, but if the man looked out of the window how could he explain his being here? He couldn't risk being caught. He had his position in the town and at work to think of. Perhaps it was only play acting after all. Perhaps it was some masochistic game where the woman was supposed to be abducted by an alien. It had to be something like that. It just had to be.

He stood up cautiously, just in time to see the back of the white suit leaving the room. There was no sign of the woman. She must still be on the bed. He'd stay here till she sat up. He'd let his imagination run away with him. Fancy thinking he'd seen a murder. That was ridiculous. It couldn't be. There had to be some other explanation.

Paul stood praying for the woman to reappear. He was rigid with fear and horror. When he at last had to move because his muscles ached he felt he couldn't deceive himself any longer. He must have witnessed a murder. Trembling he fumbled in his jacket for his mobile phone. He had only dialled the first 9 when he realised he didn't know the house number. He often came up here because the backs of the houses weren't overlooked; there was nothing but acres of open farmland behind them and people were careless about closing bedroom curtains. But he'd never taken any notice of the house names nor numbers. There was no way he could let the police know that he'd seen the killing from the back garden. He'd have to go round the front and tell them he'd heard screams as he walked by.

He hurried out into the alleyway and began to count his way along. He mustn't make a mistake counting the houses. But he wouldn't... Not a professional accountant like himself. No, he was ....Christ! Was it nine or ten back gates he'd passed? Had he missed one as he was thinking about miscounting? He couldn't afford to be wrong. He'd have to check. He must be able to identify the murderer's house from the front. He concentrated hard on recounting. He touched each back gate as he counted. It was the tenth from the end, he was sure of that now. His insides were churning and he was shaking but he made himself adopt a natural dog walking pace as he stepped out of the alleyway. The houses all had long front gardens and of course being Meldrum Avenue most identified themselves by name rather than number. *"Eriskey"* *"The Firs"* *"nothing"* *"nothing"*, *"Tralee"* *"Top S'il"* *"Dun Romin"* *"Billann"* *"Mandeley"* *" nothing!...* There was nothing on the tenth gate. The front door was too far away from him to see any name or number there. What was he to tell the police? He forced himself to bend down and pretend to tie up a shoelace while looking for anything distinctive he could use to make sure the police got the right house. The downstairs front room and the hall were lit. The fanlight above the door was heavily leaded with some sort of design but he couldn't make out what it was.

It was all such a mess. The murderer might come out any minute. He might want to put the body in one of the cars parked here. He'd better get out of the way. He stood up, being careful not to look straight at the house. He might be being watched from one of the upstairs windows. The next gate had a name on it but it was so faint he couldn't read it. Two more gates along was *"Bideawee"*. The murderer lived three doors down to the left from *"Bideawee"*. That would have to do. That was the left as you walked up to Meldrum Avenue from Marram Rd. Thank God he knew the names of all the roads here.

What could he write? "I have just heard a murder take place"...that was absurd. "I've just heard a lady scream loudly a few minutes ago. I think she's being murdered." No. That wasn't strong enough. How could he make sure the police would come? Of course with such an obviously well educated voice as his they must take him seriously. They'd want him to wait until they arrived but there was no way he was going to do that. Even if the police believed him and turned up at the house he described; the man would be under no obligation to let them in. He knew that from the Crime series he watched on TV they wouldn't have a search warrant. But even if the man didn't allow them in, sometime in the future he'd have to explain his wife's absence. When there was an investigation the police would remember

5

they'd been called to his house tonight. They had to write these things down, make a report. .

Crossing over to the opposite side of the Avenue and walking along until he was sure he couldn't possibly be seen by anyone in the murder house he took his mobile phone out and...and... The police? Hadn't he read somewhere that they could trace all mobile calls? He couldn't risk that happening. He shoved it back in his pocket and hurried out of the Avenue.

There was a Public Telephone box somewhere around here wasn't there? He'd not used one for years. But that wouldn't be any good. He couldn't use one now, it would probably be vandalised anyway. Drunks used them as toilets and drug dealers and people with AIDS used them for all sorts of things. No way was he going to put his mouth anywhere near a receiver that had been used by people like that.

Anyway there was nothing he could do for the woman now. She might not even be dead. There was no way he could be sure. It was well known that women fainted easily. Women were such peculiar creatures. His mother had warned him against them. Always fussing and complaining. Even at concerts up London you couldn't sit and enjoy the music because there was always some fat woman distracting you by fanning herself with her programme. On coach trips it was always the women who wanted the ventilation or the heating adjusted. Maybe...maybe the woman had been unfaithful and driven the man to do what he did.

But nothing could justify murder, if that is what it was. Just to be safe he'd write an anonymous letter to the police. A clearly stated grammatically correct missive in his literate hand wouldn't be ignored.

CHAPTER 2

As he sat in the kitchen cutting up the white chemical warfare suit he'd worn while strangling his wife, the grandfather clock that had been in Byron Fuller's family for four generations began its midnight chimes. For no reason that he could think of the sound reminded him of another momentous night in his life. Thirty years ago the chimes had interrupted him as he'd shouted at his father.

"Bankrupt. Bankrupt. How can you have been such a bloody fool?"

He heard once more his mother's plaintive whine and his response.

"Byron, don't speak to your father like that."

"Oh shut up and finish your gin mother. My whole life's ruined because he cared more about a factory full of bloody plebs than his own son."

His father's voice had been full of contempt as he lifted his head and said "These men you denigrate as plebs are skilled engineers, as were their fathers and grandfathers. They were the ones who made our family's money in the first place."

"And you've thrown it all away. Mortgaging our home to save a crappy factory that's been going down the drain for years. What am I going do now?"

"Oh I've no doubt you'll survive. You've always known how to look after number one."

"Ha. Ha. What about my University expenses? You know how many extras I've got to pay for on my Estate Management Course."

"I'm afraid all our financial affairs are now in the hands of the official receiver. I wouldn't think there's much hope of his allocating funds for your course."

"Fuck you"

His mother screamed as he took a step forward with his fist clenched. The noise made him hesitate; then with a final look of loathing he turned and rushed out of the room.

7

He'd thought that night was the end of all his hopes and dreams. How wrong he'd been. Two years later it was another voice that had rescued him.

"Byron? Byron Fuller?"

He knew it was his old Prep school headmistress even before he looked up. She was much greyer and smaller than he remembered but her voice had lost none of its authority and she was as ever dressed in a green speckled tweed suit.

"Miss Calleder. How nice to see you." He pushed the Sporting Record to one side as he rose to shake her hand. "What brings you down to Bellsea?"

"I'm moving down here into a warden controlled flat."

"You're leaving *Ferndale*? "

"It's far too big for me nowadays. Actually it has been for years especially since I closed the school."

"Oh." He didn't know what to say. Wendy the married woman he was meeting wasn't the type to cut and run just because she saw him talking to someone. On the other hand the sooner they got down into the cabin of her husband's cruiser the sooner he could begin to enjoy her charms. Praying Miss Calleder would refuse he said "Let me get you a drink?"

His prayer was answered. "Thank you Byron, but I just had one with my meal here. This pub does lovely meals. I've got to get home; I've a lot to think about."

"I understand. This is a lovely little town but you'll be leaving a lot of friends behind in Lamdon."

"I will but unfortunately no family. They've all passed on before me. However I do know a lot of people down here. No it's the money that concerns me."

"Really? I would have thought that the sale of a big four bed roomed house like *Ferndale* will more than cover your expenses of living here. "

"That's just it. There's so much money involved. I was shocked when I got over £500,000 for Ferndale. It needed so much doing to it, I never expected that much. It's knowing what to do with the surplus that worries me. There are so many different investments and saving schemes nowadays."

"Indeed there are, Miss Calleder. You really do need to take professional advice. This might be your lucky day. Profitable Investments are just what I've been studying the last three years at Cambridge."

"My goodness. Mind you as I remember you were always good with figures Byron."

"If I am it's thanks to you and Miss Tranter."

"How kind of you to say so. But then you were also a very polite little boy."

"Manners maketh man eh? Not much heeded nowadays I'm afraid. But to return to what you were saying. Do you know that it's possible to get returns of over ten per cent regularly if you know which trusts to invest in?"

"Ten per cent? I've never been quoted anything as high as that".

"Do sit down Miss Calleder. Let me get you something. A coffee perhaps? I was just going to have one myself."

"Well, I was going to wait and have one when I got home but perhaps if you don't mind I'll have one with you."

As he approached the bar he saw Wendy was already there with her usual pint of bitter in front of her. She wasn't a woman for half measures.

He ordered the coffees and when the barmaid turned away he whispered "Been here long."

"About five minutes. You didn't tell me you'd got another date."

"Good God woman. What's wrong with your eyes? She's my old prep school headmistress."

"Only joking Bry. You're good in bed but you've not got much of a sense of humour."

"Life's too serious for me nowadays. Anyway why don't you go on down to the boat when you've finished your drink. Get the heater going and warm up the cabin. I won't be long. Just giving her some financial advice."

"Oh yes and what's in it for you lover boy?"

He shushed her as the barmaid came back with the coffees. After he'd paid, as she turned away he whispered "Nothing compared to what I have in mind for you."

Her throaty laugh made heads turn but Miss Calleder didn't seem to notice. As they drank their coffees he told her briefly about some of the tax saving schemes and investments that all the big estates were using nowadays and concluded saying "Look Miss Calleder, this is something you need to see written down. If you like I could come round some evening and explain all this in detail."

"You're sure it wouldn't be too much trouble for you?"

"Not at all, I'd be glad to help."

After they arranged to meet in two days time she began to tell him about some of his old classmates' lives. He let her talk for a few minutes before looking at his watch and exclaiming "Goodness! Is that the time? I'm afraid I was supposed to meet someone down in the harbour five minutes ago. I'll have to fly. It's been lovely meeting you again. See you Thursday."

"Oh, yes indeed Byron. Thank you so much"

As he hurried along the pontoon to the boat he checked to see if there was anyone about. Sailors were a gossipy lot and he didn't want anyone asking Wendy's husband about who was on his boat midweek. There wasn't anyone in sight so it was with a light heart he hurried down the companion way and into the master cabin of the Moody 49. Wendy welcomed him into the double bed with open legs. They didn't talk until they had sexually exhausted each other.

"Was it just me who put that big smile on your face Bry?" she asked.

"You and…" he paused.

"And what?"

"I think I've found my career in life?"

"Con man?"

He slapped her backside playfully. "Investment Consultant."

"Same thing".

"So what? As long as it makes me lots dosh. That's all that matters."

She shook her head "That's what my husband thinks. He's a fool. There's more to life than money but I suppose you'll have to find that out for yourself?"

"What do you think I'm doing now?" he said as he rolled over on top of her.

CHAPTER 3

In October 1978 just after his twenty second birthday Byron opened his own office with the £36,000 commission he'd paid himself out of Miss Calleder's estate. A third of it he'd invested in blue chip stocks, a third in much riskier ventures, £2000 in Premium Bonds and the rest was in his business account; *Loiddes Investment & Insurance Ltd*. He'd told her that there was always some risks involved in High Yielding Shares but he'd keep a watchful eye on the market for her. She was so impressed with his assurances of a 10% annual dividend that she had already persuaded two of her friends to invest £5000 each with him. He knew that as long as he paid out his promised 10% return for a few of years all would be well.

Although there was nothing wrong with his eyes he had two pairs of spectacles with clear glass lens made to give him an air of gravitas. His dark hair was kept neatly trimmed and he bought the best quality suits he could afford to cover his athletic five feet eleven inches. He'd developed a sales pitch so persuasive that at times he almost found himself believing it. Always he took care to emphasise the hazards involved in investing in stocks and shares but he did so in such a way as to give the impression that if their ship ever did hit the rocks there would always be a lifeboat near at hand to save them.

Both his parents had been keen Foxhunters until the bankruptcy. He'd been "blooded" when he was seven. Through hunting, he became interested in National Hunt racing and began to gamble on it. Not being very successful, he'd answered an advert promising "Winning Tips" that had cost him £10 and produced no winners. When he discovered he'd no comeback against the advertisers he decided he'd recoup his losses by becoming an advertiser himself. He was amazed at how many ten pounds he received for his "Secrets from the Stables." If one of his selections won: he doubled his advertising for the next four weeks.

For himself a close study of form and equine pedigrees became the guiding lights that enabled him to become a serious gambler. He abandoned any idea of "Luck" but nevertheless soon learned that "Chance" played the biggest part of all in the outcome of races. To combat it he kept a detailed record of his bets with all the circumstances and outcomes of their running. In this way he built up an archive of invaluable information that brought him more winners than losers. The drawback was they were mostly short priced favourites. None provided the spectacular wins he longed for.

He loved hunting for the thrill of the chase. Privately his sympathies were with the foxes because of their cunning and ruthlessness. He never lingered at the kill. Now he hunted mainly for the social benefits it brought him. He hired or borrowed a horse for every meet because he calculated that was cheaper than buying and stabling one. That didn't affect the welcome he received at the houses of the rich. Women like Wendy enjoyed his company because he was a good listener and a virile lover. Whatever he learned from these women about their husband's business affairs he was quick to turn to his own advantage.

Over the next four years he accumulated an increasing pool of elderly investors. Two deaths among them resulted in angry confrontations with relatives over the amount of commission and fees he'd taken from their estates but their threats came to nothing.

In 1982 in what he considered a remarkable piece of luck his mother died. He inherited almost £46,000 from half of her estate. The other half had gone to Battersea Dog's Home. He thought of contesting her will but was advised against it. She'd never recovered from his father's death three years previously and her heavy drinking and medical care had been draining away her private funds at an alarming rate.

On that New Year's Eve he promised himself he'd be a millionaire before he was forty.

CHAPTER 4

Paul looked up from his computer when Kaiser whined. "My goodness, old boy, is that the time? Daddy's been so busy with this letter he hasn't noticed the time." He'd been unable to sleep and had got up before 6 o'clock and after a quick coffee sat down at his computer to begin writing. Now, two hours later, well after he usually took Kaiser for his walk, he was scrutinising his latest rewrite. "Just let me check it again and then we'll be off." He read through what he'd written with increasing pride.

Chief Constable Henry Deerfield MBE

Retshire Police Headquarters

Norland St.

Cleendon

M10 2BB   Saturday 8/7/2000

Dear Chief Constable Deerfield

Yesterday evening (Friday, 7th. July 2000) at approximately 11-15 pm. I was exercising my dog in the historic town of Lamdon of which I am proud to be a resident.

On my way home I was walking along the North side of Meldrum Avenue in a Northerly direction and as I was passing a property which I now know to be named "Sunset": I heard the most horrifying scream which startled both myself and my dog. I was so horrified by the fearfulness of this scream which I am certain was being made by a lady that I immediately said to myself, "Someone is being murdered in there."

I stopped and listened but could hear no further noise from this property although lights were on both in the hallway and the lounge. After waiting for some while I decided that perhaps I was exaggerating the import of this scream and walked on.

Subsequently however for all last night and this morning the horror of this scream has troubled my conscience and I feel that I must inform you of my fears for the well-being of the lady concerned.

I am certain that the scream came from a living individual and not from a radio or television programme. I have checked in my Radio Times all the channels on Radio and Television of both on the BBC and the Commercial Services at that time and I cannot see any horror or other programme that could possibly account for such a scream. I also think that as I have mentioned above how I stood and listened for a while afterwards and the fact there was no subsequent noise at all rules out the possibility that it was a broadcast programme responsible for this scream.

I am a person of over 50 years experience of this world and I can truthfully tell you that never have I heard so much terror in one sound.

I am not in the habit of writing missives such as this as your records will clearly show but as a concerned citizen I feel I must inform you that I am convinced some dastardly deed was perpetrated at that time at that address.

I did not know who resides at this property but to help speed your investigation I have subsequently checked the electoral register for Meldrum Avenue and the names given for the residents of that address are a Mr. Byron W. Fuller and a Mrs. Lucy Fuller.

I am sure you will treat this information with the seriousness it deserves.

Because I am not seeking any publicity nor credit for whatever horror your investigation may uncover I feel it prudent to leave this missive unsigned.

The chief constable was bound to be impressed. Look at the way he had used a colon after *"Sunset"* in the second paragraph. Few people were literate enough to do that nowadays. Satisfied it couldn't be improved; he folded it exactly in two and placed it in the envelope. He used the kitchen sponge to wet the flap and put it in a plastic folder where he smoothed it down. Not until then did he take off his rubber gloves. He wouldn't have to touch the envelope again because he would slide it out of the folder straight into the post box.

He posted the letter on the way to the fields beside the canal where Kaiser could have a good run. As he watched his pet enjoying his freedom he thought back to the fright he'd had that made him to get a dog. He'd been shocked that awful night some eighteen months ago when that common lout had confronted him at the back of the council flats. Thank God he'd had the wit to say he was searching for his dog. The fellow had been so suspicious. Wanted to know why he wasn't calling the dog's name and how vulgarly he'd asked "Where the dog's lead then?" Even when he assured him that the dog had seen a cat and had jerked the lead out of his hand as it dashed after it the lout had kept on at him: "Why wasn't you calling his name then?"

It was only the fact that the lout had kept repeating the question that had given him time to think up his excuse. In his most authoritative and professional tone he'd said "I'm afraid Rufus (that was the first name that had come into his head) not only chases cats, he is very food orientated. I know I'll always find him by a dustbin. If I call out his name he just runs off again. I've got to creep up on him and take him by surprise."

"You were doing enough bloody creeping about back there that's for sure" had been the insolent reply.

He'd asked the man to help him check the rest of the back garden dustbins. That had shut him up. When they'd found the end house's bin on its side and its contents scattered over the lawn he'd been the one who'd muttered "Looks as if he's been here mate."

Mate! Bloody cheek! Quickly he'd told the man "If he's got something like a chicken carcass or shin bone he'll have made his way straight home. I'd better get after him." For a few frightening seconds he'd been afraid the man would want to accompany him but after giving him a long stare as if he wanted to be certain he'd recognize him again he'd turned and gone back down the alleyway without a word. That's when he knew he must get a dog.

What a treasure Kaiser had proved to be. So loyal and obedient. Qualities sadly lacking in his staff at the Council. The Rescue centre had charged him £150 but Kaiser was worth every penny. Now Kaiser was his insurance. His *raison d'être* for being round back alleys late at night. He loved that foreign phrase. It sounded so sophisticated. He'd loved Kaiser from the moment he'd seen him. This was no runt of a litter. This was a real dog. A man's dog. You could see that just from the way he held his head. The centre had said he was too boisterous for the family who had him. Paul had taken him to obedience classes and he was a perfect pupil.

After feeding Kaiser when he got home he decided to look at all the letters he'd "saved" in his literary folder on the computer. It contained everything he'd written to the newspapers over the years. He also kept a scrapbook of every one published. He'd had many letters in both the national and local press. Most had been severely cut but he understood that was due to pressures of space. They still had his name on for all to see. Every time he pasted a new cutting of his work into his scrapbook he hoped that the teachers at his grammar school who still lived in the area remembered his name. He still resented the fact that he never got the proper marks for his English compositions. "Fair" and the occasional "Good" had been the most frequent comments on his work.

Perhaps when this murderer Fuller was caught, his letter would be published in the trial reports and in all the newspapers. He wouldn't have to stay anonymous then. That would show those stupid teachers how much they'd misjudged him.

CHAPTER 5

As Paul was writing and rewriting his early morning letter, in a house on the other side of town Serena Thoms was looking at her self in the mirror with increasing disgust She'd been deliberately overeating these last few months to pile on the pounds and she hated it. She'd acted the part of a fat woman once before when she'd been one of the ugly sisters in *Cinderella* but then she'd used lots of padding. Now Byron had insisted that she eat herself into the same shape as his wife. She'd put on twenty lbs. That was as far as she would go. Padding would have to take care of the rest no matter how uncomfortable it made her, Sod Byron and his fat cow of a wife. Her anger whelmed up inside her. She thought "My mother must have been out of her tiny mind when she called me Serena; 'Peaceful' I am not."

As long as she could remember she'd been angry. Angry with others for what they had and angry with her family and herself for what they hadn't. At school her anger was stoked by those who called her names like "Rusty, Ginger Nut, Carrot Top." She told herself it wouldn't be so bad if her hair was a rich deep russet colour but all she saw in the mirror was an anaemic red. She determined that if the world hadn't dealt her a favourable hand she wasn't going to be the one who would suffer for it. Her strong personality made her a natural leader for other rebels. She had a gift for mimicking teachers and delighted in making their life Hell.

She was born and grew up in Hastings but she never had any affection for the town. The monotony of the miles of hotels and lodging houses along its seafront depressed her.

She was 13 when she was "broken in to", the local way of describing a girl's first sexual experience. She'd only let 16 year old Tony do it because a girl she hated was boasting she was his girlfriend. He'd promised not to tell anyone, so when she found he'd told all his mates she beat him up so severely with a half a brick that he was kept in hospital for 48 hours. His parents threatened her with the police but soon backed off when she swore she'd say he'd raped her.

In the years that followed, Serena did not intend to be a troublemaker but trouble clung to her like chewing gum to the sole of a shoe. She never looked for trouble but was adamant she'd "take no shit from nobody" For a while she found an outlet for much of her aggression in Judo and later Karate but was asked to leave both disciplines because she often lost her temper and injured opponents. She continued to train with weights on her own. Her muscular five foot nine and nine and a half stone meant that when she hit someone they were often seriously hurt and she was three times brought before the courts on charges of GBH. She'd always been put on probation but in her mid –twenties she'd been warned that the next time she was before a court she must expect a prison sentence. "You absolutely have to stay out of trouble" her Probation officer Gertrude Gzerkivich told her

Serena admired Gertrude even though she was two years younger and had what Serena mocked as a "la de dah" accent. Ever since they'd met she'd thought; "Gzerkivich: what a monniker! And 'Gertrude' A name out of the ark. Yet the young woman radiated class and style. It made Serena think that if Gertrude could make a go of it in this world burdened with a name like that then she could do just as well as Serena Jane Thoms but what Gertrude had proposed to her six years ago was unbelievable.

"You want me to join a Drama group?"

"Yes."

"But why, Gertrude?"

"First of all, because you're a bloody good actress. I've watched you in court. You ought to have got an Oscar for your last performance as a put upon little innocent before that judge."

"You're joking"

"No I'm not. But there's a more important reason. You're intelligent enough to make your anger a positive force in your life."

"What do you mean?"

"This group I want you to join specialises in Social Realism. Several of them have done serious time inside. The plays they put on deal with things like gang warfare, family strife, rape, drug addition, alcoholism. You know all the everyday events of working class life."

"You reckon I'd get a part in plays like that?"

19

"Don't take this the wrong way Serena but I reckon you'd be a natural. It would be such a positive outlet for all that anger inside you. Why not give it a go?"

"Will I get paid?"

"No. You'll get something worth much more than money."

"Oh yeah. What?"

"Self –esteem."

"Give over. Nobody messes with me. I know who I am."

"Of course, Serena. But your present sense of worth comes mainly from things that put you at odds with Society. With this group you'd be praised for doing something positive."

"H'mm. I'll think about it."

"Smashing. Now here's some more good news. A friend of mine is opening a new theme pub and he's looking for barmaids. I've recommended you. Interested?"

"Yes, I'm boracic."

"Boracic ? What's that?

"Christ. Don't you know nothing? Rhyming slang. Boracic lint 'skint'"

Gertrude gave one of those huge belly laughs that made everyone in the café stare at her. But she wasn't in the least abashed. That was one of the reasons why Serena liked her so much.

"But you're not a Cockney, Serena."

"No, but lots of my mates are."

When she was interviewed for the theme pub job and accepted she was none too pleased to be told that it was going to be a 1940's wartime establishment and the barmaids had to look a bit "brassy" But the money was good and it was in the West End, somewhere she had never worked before. She took the job.

The pub flourished and so did little old Serena. She saw that it was the women who smiled the most and said the least that had the richest partners. At least once every week a customer would proposition her. She never accepted the first time. However, she was willing to reward persistence especially if it came from a wealthy punter. Also, since she had always believed that "The Lord helps those who help themselves" she discretely augmented her wages by taking small but regular amounts from the tills.

When she'd went to the Drama group she'd only intended to go for the one night just to tell Gertrude she'd tried it. She was very late because she had difficulty finding the hall where they met. The people who were already there were not moving around on a stage as she expected but sitting in a circle holding sheets of paper. The effusive welcome she got from Gordon, the hand waving producer almost made her turn around and leave immediately. But his grip on her wrist was surprisingly strong and he'd pulled her into the middle of the group and introduced her as "Gertrude's lovely friend Serena" before she could escape.

She'd hardly finished acknowledging all the welcomes she received when he asked, "You're not a Yorkshire lass by any chance are you?"

When she shook her head he made no attempt to hide his disappointment. "Oh my dear; it's like the number 50 bus. Never comes along when you want it. Take five everybody. I must have tea and a biccky while I think of what to do."

She found out that they were putting on a play about the 1982 Miners strike and in it a delegation of three Yorkshire women came down to London to seek financial support from local Trade Unionists. While only one had a major speech to deliver the other two had plenty to say, especially one who started an affair with a black communist. The Group's difficulty was they only had one Yorkshire speaker among them, a man.

Gordon summoned them all back to their chairs. "Right, we have decided…"

"Who the Hell's we?" a heavily bearded man whose clothes seemed too big for him demanded.

"It's the royal we, Daniel. What I'm saying is that I'm determined we're not going to let this dialect thing beat us. Now let's crack on. I'll take the boys through scene two where they discover and duff up the undercover policeman…. (Everyone cheered) while Mike will audition the girls to see if we can find our Yorkshire Threesome."

Mike was an angelic looking young man who didn't seem at all fazed at being surrounded by tough looking women She was amazed when he addressed them in a beautifully modulated Oxbridge accent. (She learned later that he was one of a number of University graduates who worked voluntarily for the Settlement who owned the hall.) "I'm afraid ladies I've travelled a rather long way from my Yorkshire roots but I shouldn't worry too much about the authenticity of your accents. I think it's fair to say that the closest that most of your audience will have been to Yorkshire is watching episodes of 'Last of the Summer Wine'."

Serena found it difficult to follow what he said about vowels and diphthongs. She was more at ease with the individual words he gave them to repeat like "tek", "mek", and "sek" for" take", "make," and" sake." After they'd practiced these for a while he said "Right, sorry, I mean 'Reet' let try 'summat longer'." Imagine ladies you're dressing up for an evening out. You look in the mirror and say "Ah shud like ter goa aht, bur ah've nowt ter wear" He got each of them to repeat the sentence. When they'd finished he asked Serena to say the words again. When she did so he smiled and said, "You've got a wonderful ear Serena."

Before she knew what she was saying she'd blurted out "I suppose that makes up for having small tits." The accompanying laughter did much to establish her popularity with the group. By the time of the next read through the following week she'd got the role of the leading Yorkshire delegate. She never missed a rehearsal and was very disappointed the play was only put on for a Friday and Saturday night. She found she loved being on the stage and it was a thrill to see her performance favourably commented on by both local papers

She had a happy three years with the group, usually playing one of the major character roles in their productions. She left only because Neil, a generous punter who'd taken her home several times, offered her the chance to manage an "English pub" he was buying in Ibiza. She liked it so much that she went there for eight months of the year for the next five years. Back in England in the winter months she went regularly to the Gym where her tanned athletic body made her attractive to men and envied by women. That was where she met Byron.

CHAPTER 6

Byron's hands ached by the time he'd finished cutting up his white protective suit. He knew the material wouldn't burn so he put it in plastic shopping bags and was going to dispose of them and the old bed sheet he'd spread out beneath him to catch any loose fibres in various bins on the way to the airport. He'd be glad to be rid of this bloody white stuff. Lucy had been wearing white the first time he met her,

It had been at Lincoln races and he'd lost a packet. He remembered his friend Trevor's insincere condolences just before he first set eyes on her.

"Hard luck old man"

Byron clenched his teeth into a "good loser's" smile, shrugged his shoulders and replied "That's life." Inwardly he was in despair. How could he of all people have ignored his own advice "never chase your losses?"

Of course he knew why. Because he was desperate. He'd been desperate when he came to the racecourse. Now he was desperate and broke. He'd lost £6000 in four hours. His world had turned completely upside down. In 1982 he'd been well on his way to being a millionaire; ten years later he was burdened with debt. Properties where he had invested of his money were now a disaster area. House prices were falling so fast that mortgage debts far exceeded the value of the properties. At dinner parties people talked of nothing else but "Negative equity."

He trudged to the bar behind his solicitor friend Trevor who if he was telling the truth was at was hundreds up on the day.

"The usual Bry?"

"If you don't mind I'll have double malt. Glenlivit if they have it. I need something special to pick me up."

"Good old Bry. Excelling at spending other people's money as usual."

"Bookies money. Trev. Buy it out of your winnings."

He stood listening as Trevor talked of how astute he'd been backing the 16 to 1 outsider winner of the last race, "Goodhaven" with £100 each way. Byron was getting increasingly annoyed with the man's boasting but he couldn't afford to antagonize him.

So he just kept nodding at the self congratulatory flow. He was relieved when Trevor said "Excuse me old fellow. Must go for a wee."

Byron stood nursing his drink and trying desperately to think of some way of alleviating his problems.

"Excuse me"

He turned to see a full figured blonde woman with flushed cheeks smiling up at him. She was adorned with so much gold and jewellery that as she moved she sparkled like a Christmas tree. She was dressed in white all the way down to her high heeled shoes. "Sorry, I was miles away" he said as he stepped quickly aside. There was something familiar about her. After she'd ordered her drinks he enquired "Excuse me, but I can't help feeling I've seen you somewhere before."

"Borthwick stables?" she answered shyly.

"Of course" he replied as the vision of her face above an immaculately turned out grey horse filled his mind, "You ride that beautiful Welsh Pony."

She nodded, "Paddy. He was a twenty-first birthday present."

"You lucky girl." He jumped at the chance to flatter her "You've only had him a couple of years then."

She blushed "And some. Eight years would be more like it."

"Never. You've got to be joking."

The barman interrupted their conversation by asking "Would you like a tray madam?"

"Yes please."

When he'd put the drinks on the tray Byron stepped forward saying "Here, let me carry that for you. I'm sorry I don't know your name. I'm Byron"

"I'm Lucy. You're very kind." She led him through the crowd to a table by the window where four people were sitting. It was immediately obvious that three of them were relatives, not only from their rotund features but from the amount of gold they were wearing. The fourth, a more conservatively adorned but very fashionably dressed blonde was also someone that he knew he'd seen before. There were so many empty glasses on the table that he had to move some on to the tray to make room for the new drinks.

"Meet my dad Danny, my mum Dot, my uncle Len and my best friend Vanessa. This is Byron" she said as she added some more empty glasses to the tray. Before he could speak she turned to her friend and asked "Recognize him, Van?"

"Of course. Rides out of the same yard as us. Looks a natural on a horse. You've been riding since you were young haven't you?"

"Yes, since I was a two. But I don't get out as much as I'd like nowadays. I've been snowed under with work these last few years."

"But you took a day off today "said the uncle. Byron immediately felt uncomfortable. The man looked like an ex boxer or wrestler. "Perhaps not so much ex" Byron thought as he noticed how the man's muscles strained against his suit.

"Sort of. Entertaining a client." He looked up and saw Trevor had returned to the bar. "There he is now. Afraid I must go. Been nice meeting you."

Lucy's father stood up and said, "No need to rush away Byron. Bring him over and get yourselves a good drink each while you're doing it. We've got a tab going. Tell the barman it's the Boothe's table. I'll get us a couple more chairs while you're about it."

Byron thought this might be his lucky day after all. If only he and Trevor hadn't come in the same car everything would have been perfect. He could have played a much stronger hand alone. They ordered a single scotch each and on their way back to the Boothes he warned Trevor; "These people look as if they've got money to burn. So we want them to think we've got the golden touch. We won a few thousand each today, Right? Tell them your 16-1 winner was because you'd won so much you could afford to take a chance on an outsider I didn't back it because I'm a cautious punter."

Trevor smiled maliciously "Don't worry. They'll think you're as pure as the driven slush after I've finished praising you"

"You'd better" Byron muttered.

After introductions had been made and they'd discretely established that they'd all lightened a few bookmakers' satchels Danny asked, "So what line of business are you two in?"

Trevor told him he was a partner in a firm of solicitors specialising in property development and Byron added "I'm an Investment Consultant."

"Know a lot about Tax avoidance then?" said Lenny.

"As a matter of fact I do, especially off shore tax havens. Can mail you some details if you're interested."

"No need. I get paid cash in my line of work." he answered.

Lenny's accompanying stare should have warned Byron not to pursue the matter but the whiskey had loosened his tongue, "What do you do then, Lenny?"

"He's in the personal protection business" said Lucy quickly.

"Yeah, and I do a bit of debt collecting as well."

Everyone laughed when Trevor said "Of course. You're the right build for it"

Anxious to get the conversation away from Lenny, Byron asked "Do you have any trouble with the tax man, Danny"

"Never" he replied with a wink "The scrap business don't make much profit. Never has."

"Can you men talk about something else instead of money" said Dot suddenly.

"Yes mum" Lucy answered "What are we having for dinner?"

In years to come Byron wished he'd paid more attention to her question. Instead he'd joined unthinkingly in the laughter when Dot replied "I don't know except I'm not cooking it. We're eating out tonight."

That got them all talking about favourite restaurants. When Byron mentioned he loved Greek food Lucy and Vanessa enthusiastically agreed with him. It turned out that they had all often dined at the same Taverna in Cleedon.

"I don't know how we kept missing one another "said Lucy.

"Neither do I" he answered "but with so many near misses it almost seems as if we were fated to meet one day."

Lucy blushed and looked down.

"Can't stand any of that foreign muck myself" Danny interjected. "You can't beat a good steak and chips." Lenny nodded in agreement.

Anxious to avoid any argument Byron asked "Ever been to Greece ladies?"

"I went there on my honeymoon" said Vanessa "and do you know what? When my old man buggered off and left me with three kids to bring up on my own, he had the cheek to go back there with his new girlfriend."

"You were well rid of him Van," Lucy said, "I've always wanted to go to Greece, especially the islands."

Nine months later she did, as Byron's bride.

CHAPTER 7

On Sunday night Paul told his father they would walk Kaiser the mile back home with him to his council house. The old man complained he was too tired to walk so far.

"You can't be tired. The only time you got up from that settee since we came home was to come to the table for your dinner."

"Being indoors for hours makes me tired. If today's match hadn't been rained off I'd have been out in the fresh air watching young Drake bat."

"And drinking more of the free beer Toringham ply you with. I've told them they're wasting their time but they keep doing it."

"It's rude of guests to spurn the host's hospitality."

"Not when the guest is umpiring their cup match it isn't."

"Come off it. You ate plenty of their salmon sandwiches and you had two big slices of that apple pie."

"The League Rules require the host club to provide food for the officials. Besides, it would have been a shame to let all that good food go to waste."

"And drink. It includes drink doesn't it?"

"Of course. Since you were counting you'll know I had three cups of tea."

"Tea? Gnat's piss more like. That Toringham ale has won awards. You're a fool not to taste it."

"You know I promised mother I'd stay tee-total. I'm a man of my word."

"You don't go to her gospel hall though. They'd hardly finished shovelling the soil on her grave and you were off to that nobs' church, St.Peters. Not that it done you much good."

Even though he knew that the old man was being rude in the hope of annoying him into wanting to get rid of him quickly by driving him home, the words still rankled. It had vexed Paul for years that his father had never shown him the proper respect that was his due. "You are well aware of the responsible position I hold at Council headquarters."

"O yes. And how long have you held this 'responsible position,'? Over fifteen bloody years that's what. They soon spotted you're not officer material."

"You mean I'm only a sergeant like you were."

"Colour sergeant. I've told you often enough that's a dammed sight higher than an ordinary three striper."

Paul reflected they were having this argument much more frequently than usual. Perhaps "Earl Haigh Thewell" was beginning to lose it. It would be good news if he was. The old man had only agreed to let him buy the council house if he promised to freeze the rent. He could get double what his father paid if the old fool was (as the Salvation Army put it, "promoted to Glory.") and new tenants moved in.

"Let's get walking instead of sitting here arguing" he said brusquely. "Remember how you used to make me march all round the living room, 'Hup, one, two, three, Hup, one, two, three."

Kaiser got up from his rug and came running over and rubbed against Paul's legs. Sometime if they needed to hurry home from a walk Paul would march along counting out like this as they strode along. He stroked the luxuriant fur. "Soon boy" he whispered.

"You'd have had a dammed sight better life if you'd joined the Royal Anglians. Especially with the middle name "Montgomery". It was me that insisted you be called that."

"I was in the Army Cadets."

"Two years that's all."

Paul fetched his father coat and held out for him. Reluctantly the old man rose "You don't need to button me up. These hands are as strong as when they held a Lee Enfield above my head for hours as we waded through jungle rivers and swamps."

"That's not what Dr. Murray says. He's just increased the strength of your pills."

"Slip of the pen that's all. Easily happens when you drink as much as he does."

Paul's voice rose in astonishment "Talk about the kettle calling the pot black!

He was glad when his father didn't reply. He led his father out of the house and they walked the mile in silence. "No need to come in, boy" his father said at the gate "I can take care of myself." Paul was glad to say " goodnight "and walked away but as soon as the front door closed he hurried back and stood just out of sight as his father drew the curtains. There had been a spate of burglaries on the estate in the past month. As soon as he was satisfied all was well he started to walk away but memories made him stop and take a few steps into the alleyway at the side of the house. He glanced up at the back bedroom window of what used to be the O'Flannerys' house.

It had been through that window he had seen his first naked female when he was 12. There were five sisters in the family; three shared this bedroom which was directly opposite his. He spent many hours in the dark watching them. They kept their light on till all hours and had no inhibitions about dressing and undressing with the curtains open. They had carried on their "shameful exhibitionism"" until the last of them left home when he was 27. Three of the sisters still lived in the town. He did his best to avoid them. They made him feel uncomfortable. He thought they talked about him and pointed him out to their friends when they saw him.

He took Kaiser the longest way home. Thinking about how his father had made him parade around their living room reminded him how often his mother had told him she prayed that he'd become a "soldier of Christ." How such a religious woman had ever married his father was beyond him. She had been a member of a declining East Anglian evangelical sect, The Peculiar People. Its heyday was in the 1850's when it's fiercely proclaimed teetotal message had helped combat the alcoholism prominent in the countryside. She had taken Paul every Sunday to one of the few chapels that remained. Along with their teetotalism they believed strongly in the sanctity of marriage. It was drummed into him that women were God's chosen creatures to help restore men to a state of grace. They had been selected by God to keep man from Hell through the sanctifying power of marriage. "There are many wicked women surrounding us but I know there's a good woman waiting for you. One specially chosen by God." was his mother's oft repeated assurance. Contrary to her purpose, her continual references to the mystery and sanctity of marriage had imbued the young Paul with a fear of women. He'd never outgrown it. He thought of women as a trap waiting to be sprung on him. Although he could mingle socially with women and work amongst them, he didn't like to be too close to them. He hated being accidentally touched by one. He enjoyed seeing their bodies only when he knew they couldn't see him. Then he was in charge, he was in control.

His mother's prolonged dying from liver cancer in his early 20s was a big blow to Paul. She was his refuge from the crudeness of the world. He owed everything to her. She was the one who had done his homework with him, enabling him to pass the eleven plus and go to the County Grammar School. He had found it a struggle and had been glad to leave and go to work in the town's rates department when he was 16. The Council had encouraged him to study for his accountancy exams giving him day release to College. It had been a long hard grind but eventually he had qualified as an Accountant. He bitterly regretted his mother had not lived to see him receive his diploma. He'd taken fresh flowers to her grave that day and spent a long time there telling her how well he'd done and what a bright future lay ahead if him.

CHAPTER 8

Byron and Lucy's honeymoon preparations had been a triumph of will power for both of them. She had by rigorous self sacrifice managed to drop three dress sizes and he had been "a real gentleman" of a suitor. They both managed to sustain their facades in Greece although Lucy was often hungry and found she had lost a lot of her vitality and "bounce" along with her fat and had been tired most of the time.

Byron told himself he shouldn't be surprised. As a bloodstock analyst he knew that "the filly follows the dam" and Dot's shape told him that Lucy would always be at war with her body. He thought it wouldn't bother him: he was more concerned about the size of her wallet than the size of her waist. Nevertheless the first sight of the folds of loose flesh that furrowed her stomach revolted him. Only by keeping his eyes on her ample breasts did he manage to think of her as sexually desirable. At least Lucy by her little screams and groans (which were not faked) had contributed greatly to his self esteem.

On their first night back in England they were staying in his flat until they moved into the house on which her parents had already paid a substantial part of the mortgage as a wedding present. He was anticipating another night of pleasure when she came storming out of the bathroom, banging the door behind her.

"What's the matter?" he asked.

"Those bathroom scales of yours, how long have you had them?"

"Don't know. Years I suppose."

"They're crap. I'll bring mine from home tomorrow."

"I've never noticed anything wrong with them, let me see." He got up from the edge of the bed and hurried into the bedroom. When he came out he said "Can't see anything wrong with them Luce."

"Never. You can't tell me they're not showing you've put on lbs."

"Four lbs actually. But that's not surprising considering how much we ate in Letsos. How much have you put one?"

She turned away from him and picked up her pearl backed hairbrush.

"How much?"

"Not much."

He knew she was lying. It wasn't that he'd noticed her eating excessive amounts of food at mealtimes. Rather it was all the nibbles and drinks she had while lounging by the side of the hotel pool. She'd told him he'd exhausted her by his sexual athleticism and she needed the rest to be able to participate fully in their next coupling. Although he was flattered by her words he couldn't enjoy just lying around reading and sunbathing. He liked to be active even in the sunshine. Fortunately he had met up with the husband of an equally indolent wife and on several afternoons they'd hired a Hobie catamaran and sailed it to its limits for hours around the bay.

He tried to jest the truth out of her; "C'mon, don't be shy. A couple of pounds…kilos …stones?"

Her face froze and then contorted into a bulging eyed madwoman's mask as she screamed. He had never heard a scream like it. It seemed to erupt from deep inside her, starting as a low moan and rising to an ear damaging screech before diminishing to a self pitying whimper. There was a brief silence before she began to sob.

Byron hated weeping women. He usually gave them a slap to shut them up but he didn't want to hit Lucy so early in their marriage. He hadn't got his hands on her money yet. At the wedding, her father Danny had taken him aside and told him while they were waiting for Lucy to change into her going away outfit, "My little princess ain't never been hit. I can rely on you to keep it that way Bry, can't I?" When Byron had reassured him that he was a gentleman "in every sense of the word" Danny had added "Only in our families we take care of our own. You know what I mean Bry?" Byron had seen enough rough justice meted out in the racing world to know exactly what he meant.

When he put his arms around her to comfort her, at first she shrugged him away, whispering repeatedly "You think I'm fat."

"No darling" he lied to her, "I like you just the way you are. He hadn't realised she was so neurotic about her bulk. She eventually allowed herself to be persuaded that she was just the shape he wanted her to be.

Once in bed they had sex as they'd done every night of their marriage. Her voluminous nightdress allowed him to enjoy the ample softness of her body without distraction and her moans of their climaxing together reinforced his belief in himself as a great lover. They lay in silence for a while. Then she began to tell him how she had been teased as a "fattie" right from infant school. "You must never call me 'fat' Bry. I couldn't stand it." He kept his word for almost two years but eventually the rollercoaster of diets broke his self control. He found that he was remembered his marriage not in months but in diets. There was The South Beach Diet, The Scarsdale Diet, The Cider Vinegar Diet, The Low Fat Diet, The Grapefruit Diet, The Mediterranean Diet, The Cabbage Soup Diet (He'd forced her to give that up after 10 days because of her flatulence) The Weight Watchers Diet, and lately The G.I.Diet. When she'd first told him about it, she'd screamed when he'd said "Does that mean you'll get an American soldier to fuck you thin?"

He always was profusely contrite afterwards. That was until he got access to her Safe Deposit Box. From the start of their marriage he'd put her on his firm's books as an employee and let her do some secretarial work on the Insurance side of the business. Eventually he convinced her that where he held securities like the deeds of Properties and the suchlike the safest place for them was in a safe deposit box. "It's silly for me to go through all the rigmarole of setting up on of my own when you already have one dear" had been his argument. He had also emphasised he wanted somewhere safe to hide cash from the Income Tax. Like her father,she hated the thought of money being given to the Government to waste. When she'd finally allowed him to be a co-key holder, he'd been astounded at the number of gold ingots she had in the box.

When Danny had his fatal heart attack four years into their marriage he left her two more deposit boxes but by then relations between them had deteriorated so much that she refused to let him have any access to them. Lucy had gone almost insane with grief when Danny died. Her body ballooned so much from comfort eating that he couldn't bear the sight of her. It was almost a year before she, as he cruelly put it "begun to let the air out of her tyres."

But it had been her threats to divorce him that had sealed her fate. She'd sworn she'd reveal all his insurance scams and how he used his high fees and commissions to rob the elderly of their savings. He had no compulsion about killing her. He took the view that you didn't let sick animals suffer. Lucy had been sick for years and her howls of misery had become more than any reasonable man could be expected to endure. Her wealth was wasted on her. She didn't know how to live. She didn't deserve to live.

When he sat down to plan the "perfect murder" he was amazed how easy it was and how long he must have had such a thing in mind. It was a holiday boating tragedy that gave him what he saw was the perfect way of getting rid of her. Lucy liked routine, she felt safest with what she knew. It was at her urging that they returned each year to the Greek Island where they had spent their honeymoon. He went along with her wishes for the first three years, then after months of subtle persuasion got her to agree to go to a neighbouring island for their fourth anniversary. Much to her surprise she enjoyed it and from then on she let him pick a different Greek island destination each year. The year of Danny's death was the only time they didn't go to Greece. That year Lucy insisted that they should have no holidays at all as a mark of respect for her father. He couldn't be bothered to argue, he'd met Serena by then and welcomed the chance to spend more time with her.

CHAPTER 9

Serena had been a shock to him. At first he thought it would be just the usual "fling" but the better he got to know her the more he wanted her. He didn't know why. It wasn't as if she was wealthy or well connected like the other woman he pursued. She had nothing to offer except her body and her ruthlessness. It was the way she gave her opponents no quarter at Squash that first made him take notice of her. One of his Squash partners actually said "She plays just like you do old man." When they were apart he was constantly thinking about her. Most amazing of all, he realized he admired her: something he'd never thought possible about any woman.

When he read about the boating accident off Letsos, the island they would have holidayed on but for Danny's death, it was the headline BODY STILL NOT FOUND that he remembered most. The report told of a dingy with four people aboard capsizing and how three of them had been found clinging to the upturned hull, but the fourth, a woman in her mid forties had been swept away. The accident had happened three weeks previously and despite extensive searches her body had still not been recovered. In the following months he kept a careful watch on the papers and the internet but there was never any news of the body being found. He made sure that Lucy never knew about the accident.

He always did some dingy sailing on holiday. Lucy was a reluctant sailor but for appearances sake he always talked her into a least one boat trip with him. She enjoyed being taken to a deserted island for a picnic and some open air sex. When a year had passed and a body still hadn't been recovered he knew he had found the perfect "accident" for Lucy. He could easily cause any dingy to capsize when Lucy wasn't wearing a lifejacket. He could feign injury or sunstroke to account for his inability to rescue her.

That had been his plan until the night he'd been dining with Serena and he'd tried to tell her a joke with a punch line needing a Geordie accent. She'd laughed and said "Not bad, Bry, you almost got the accent right."

"How should I have said 'I'm going home'" then?" he'd asked.

"Am gannin yem"

"That's great. What about Scousers ? What would they say?"

"Probably something like, 'Am go'n back ter me bricks.'"

"That's fantastic. How do you do it?"

"I've always been a nosey cow. Wherever I am I'm always earwigging And I love stand up comics, especially Northern ones."

"But that doesn't necessarily make you good at imitating them. Why do you think you're so good at it?"

"I don't really know. It's something I've always been able to do. I'll tell you something funny. One bloke, he was some sort of University lecturer. He was a regular in a pub where I worked. He told me "You're good at it because somebody you respect told you that you were good.""

"Was he right?"

She told him about her first night at the Drama Group and added "I was really made up when Mike said I had a wonderful ear."

He told her about the plays he'd been in at school and the good reviews he'd got for playing the butler in *The Admirable Crichton* during his first year at University. Much to his surprise she knew the play. "I used to listen to lots of plays on the radio when I was off in the afternoons" she told him.

They spent the rest of the meal talking about the theatre and plays they'd enjoyed.

Next morning at home, as he sat at breakfast, trying to block out Lucy's whining monologue about how much everything cost nowadays he suddenly thought, "If Serena can imitate all those other people, why shouldn't she imitate this moaning cow?"

From then on he'd listened closely to every word his wife said.

CHAPTER 10.

On Monday night Paul approached *"Sunset"* for the third time since the murder. He had walked past the house on Saturday and Sunday afternoon in the hope of catching sight of Mr. Byron Fuller. Both times he had parked his car at the top of the Avenue in case he got the chance to follow him. If Fuller wasn't concentrating he might not notice he was being followed and lead him to the area where he'd buried his wife. He might want to make sure she was safely buried.

He felt both thrilled and apprehensive as he turned into the Avenue. He wanted the excitement of seeing signs of police activity at *"Sunset."* Some striped blue tape across the gate or even a constable standing in the porch. But he was also afraid that he might be stopped and questioned by any officers who were there. He knew he sometimes got confused under pressure. He didn't interview well. He had long ago concluded that was the reason for his lack of promotion at the Council.

There was no sign of any police activity at the house. It looked as undisturbed as he'd last seen it. Worse still it seemed unoccupied. What if the murderer had slipped away to another country? Maybe one with no extradition treaty to Britain? Was it possible that his letter hadn't been delivered? The slovenly staff employed by the Post Office meant anything was possible nowadays. But it was only going to the next town, less than 15 miles away. It must have got there. Then another though struck him. The letter couldn't have gone astray. Surely not. No one would tamper with a letter addressed to the Chief Constable. Of course some minor officer would open all such letters first but even the most plodding member of the force just had to be impressed by the quality of the stationary and the eloquence of the message. Its startling contents demanded immediate action. At the council he always paid more attention to such letters than those in nondescript envelopes with second class stamps.

He decided to write another letter. It would be brief and to the point. He hurried home, made himself a coffee, took his usual two Bath Oliver biscuits from the tin and sat down to plan his letter. He didn't enjoy eating his biscuits while wearing plastic gloves but he wasn't taking any chances. When he'd finished he vacuumed the desk top and himself with the mini Hoover he used when valeting his car. If a crumb accidentally fell into the envelope they might be able to identify him from his DNA. After a further fifteen minutes of note making he booted up "Word" on his computer and got his Collins Dictionary and Roget's Thesaurus down off the shelf. He didn't trust the American spelling of the autocorrect.

An hour later he was satisfied he'd produced a trenchant missive that would galvanise the police into immediate action. He checked it one more time.

Chief Constable Henry Deerfield MBE

Retshire Police Headquarters

Norland St.

Cleeford

LM10 2BB   *5/7/2000*

Dear Chief Constable Deerfield

I am writing with reference to my previous correspondence of the 1st. inst. wherein I informed you of my well founded belief that at approximately 11-15p.m. on Friday 30th June, a murder had taken place at the property named "Sunset" in Melcott Ave. Lamdon LM9 5BQ

I realise that your esteemed force must get a goodly number of anonymous letters each year. Many of them will be I'm sure from cranks and busybodies whose ramblings it obviously would be a waste of your forces time to pursue.

However as an educated man yourself, I am confident that you are able to recognize an erudite message from a knowledgeable citizen whose only desire is to do his public duty

I have a twofold reason for sending this follow up letter:

1. In case my previous letter has been lost in the post. (The slovenly appearance of most post men and post ladies nowadays do not fill one with confidence that they would always be most conscientious in fulfilling their duties).

2. I am not aware of any action that has so far taken place to apprehend the murderer Mr. Byron Fuller. I appreciate that you may in fact be pursuing your enquiries in an unobtrusive manner but I am very concerned that Mr. Fuller may be using his continuing freedom to dispose of the body of his female victim in a location where it will be difficult for your force to find it.

So I am respectfully requesting you to treat this matter as one of extreme urgency and to visit this address with your forensic teams without delay.

I anticipate that your prompt action will result in Mr. Fuller's swift apprehension and that he will be prevented from fleeing the country. The resulting publicity if he did escape notwithstanding the warnings you have received would not reflect well on your force.

Yours truly,

A very concerned citizen

.

The implied threat in the last paragraph he considered a master-stroke. The police couldn't possibly not take notice now.

CHAPTER 11

Shortly after take-off Byron checked with the elderly female passenger behind him that she had no objections before he put his seat back. The more people that could testify that he'd been on this plane with his wife the better. Everything had gone to plan. Lucy was starting new career as a slow release fertiliser for rockery plants and no one had seen him bury her.

It was ironic she had chosen her own grave. It was she who had told him that old Mrs. Harrison next door couldn't find a gardener. He was quick to offer to help. It was obvious from the quality of her clothes that Mrs. Harrison had money. In the six years they'd been neighbours he'd not seen many visitors to her house. There might be a good chance she had neither family nor relations to inherit her cash. It would do him no harm to be in her good books. At the very least he might persuade her to invest in one of his "high yield" schemes.

As soon as he saw the decrepit rockery at the bottom of her garden he knew it was just the place for Lucy. It was far enough from the house for Mrs. Morrison not to see what he was doing. The only danger was that there was gazebo near the back gate and the old woman liked to sit there on warm summer days. He said he'd restock the rockery with a variety of brightly coloured plants that she could enjoy even with her poor eyesight. When he'd dug down far enough to make a deep grave for Lucy he got Mrs. Morrison to promise not to come down to the bottom of the garden again until the rockery was finished.

He'd never been an enthusiastic gardener but in the last month he reckoned he must have read every rockery book in Lamdon and Cleendon libraries. He was lucky that two nearby nurseries had a large selection of rockery plants and he made full use of the nursery workers brains. He'd bought a load of granite rocks to cover Lucy. No animal was ever going to able to dig down and disturb her. It was only right that she should rest in peace. The trolley he'd hired to transport the rocks would be her hearse. He'd removed a fence panel so that he could get directly to the rockery from his garden. He set the alarm for 3am, and dressed from head to foot in black he carried Lucy down to the trolley. She was in her grave in less than five minutes. It took almost an hour to finish the rockery and clear up thoroughly. He was washed and back in bed by four thirty.

The reason why he had so little time to bury her was because she phoned Dot, her mother four or five times a day. If he'd killed her the day before, Dot would be demanding to know where she was and why she hadn't phoned. He'd lied to Lucy about the time they would have to leave for the airport. She'd thought they had to leave before 7 o'clock in the morning and she never phoned her mother that early. The fact that the flight didn't actually leave until 11 a.m. had given him plenty of time to set things up with Betty Harrison.

It had been a masterstroke arranging for Serena to imitate Lucy. It removed any chance of Lucy being rescued or her body being found after he'd capsized the dingy. There was always the possibility of some idiot on a Jet Ski or motorboat coming roaring out of a nearby bay. That had been his greatest fear. He couldn't have killed her on holiday using any kind of force. They would hold a post mortem if her body was recovered. Getting her stoned before shoving her overboard was out of the question. Lucy would never drink alcohol when she knew she'd be on a boat. She was terrified of being seasick. Dot and Van knew that. That bunch of blabbermouths knew every bloody thing about each other.

Above all else, Serena's pretending to be Lucy eliminated any possibility of the fat cow spoiling everything by refusing to sail with him. Things had been so bad between them lately she might very well have done that. Then the whole journey to Greece would have been wasted.

The passport check at Gatwick had been as cursory as he'd hoped. The ex-con make up artist that Serena found had charged a fortune for his work but it had been well worth it. Fortunately Lucy's photo had been taken for their honeymoon when she'd been slimming for months. Both women were brown eyed and a prosthetic nose had changed Serena's pert upturned nose into Lucy's brutally straight one. Serena's reddish hair had been shaved and covered by a blonde wig. Her years in the Spain had given her a permanent tan that helped her look like Lucy. She was over two inches taller than Lucy but flat heelless sandals had hidden that discrepancy. Their vast difference in width had been overcome by layers of padding hidden under a long sleeved tent like dress.

He smiled at the approaching air hostess before turning to Serena and asking loudly "What would you like to drink Luce?"

She was listening intently to the tapes of Lucy talking on the phone. For the past four months she'd been studying how Lucy spoke and trying to absorb everything about her personal life and habits that Byron had told her. It had been demanding work practicing but it was twice as hard now it was for real. There was so much to remember. Lucy had lived in East London for the first eighteen years of her life and had never ever thought of changing her accent. She remembered Mike telling the drama group that East Londoners spoke with very "loose vowels." "Better than loose bowels" somebody had called out.

Byron squeezed her padded arm to get her attention. "A drink, Luce? Vodka O.K?" She nodded and returned to her tapes. She couldn't afford to get this wrong. Byron ordered her Vodka and a Teacher's for himself adding "If it's not too much trouble would you mind pouring them? I'm afraid we've got ourselves a bit cluttered here." He wanted the hostess to notice how the bulk of the woman beside him cramped his movements.

"Not at all Sir. Ice in both?"

"Yes thanks."

She poured the Vodka and ice into a plastic cup and handed it to him before beginning to open the whiskey miniature. He turned to offer the drink to Serena but as he did so his hand knocked against the side of the lowered tray on the back of the seat in front of her and the Vodka spilled into her lap.

She was so absorbed in her tapes that the shock of the spilled drink made her exclaim "Fucking Hell!" Byron cringed with embarrassment. This wasn't how he wanted their presence on the plane to be remembered. Lucy was if anything excessively polite. "So sorry" he said more to the hostess than Serena. He quickly moved out of his seat to give Serena room to mop herself down. She smiled apologetically at the hostess and said in what she hoped was a convincing Lucy accent, "Pardon my French, dear. Flying makes me terribly nervous"

The hostess smiled as she handed her a bunch of paper napkins. "Don't worry, it's understandable madam."

Serena started to wipe herself down but decided she'd take this chance to go to the toilet. She was dying to give her head a good scratch. The wig was driving her mad and the padding was making her sweat like a pig. Getting out of her seat was a performance. She had quite an audience by the time she managed to wriggle into the aisle.

Byron tried to insist on paying for the spilled drink as well as its replacement but the hostess wouldn't allow him. As she and her trolley moved further down the plane he began to think that maybe this accident was a stroke of luck. They'd certainly got themselves noticed. He was alert to Serena's return and stood well out into the aisle to let manoeuvre her bulk back into her seat. "Sorry Bry" she whispered.

"Don't worry; it's got us noticed hasn't it."

"Too fucking right it has." she whispered.

Their hands touched as he handed her the replacement Vodka. She hoped he didn't notice the slight shiver she'd given as their hands met. She was finding it more difficult than she'd expected to get used to the idea that the hand she had just touched was a killer's. She'd know from the moment that Byron had talked about getting rid of Lucy that he was capable of doing it. He was a passionate man and ruthless with it. Perhaps it was because of all the years she'd had to listen to so many posers on the other side of the bar that she'd been so quick to spot how different Byron was.

She'd taken plenty of chances herself in her 37 years but this was by far the biggest. She'd quizzed him thoroughly on how he planned to kill Lucy because she wanted to make sure what she was letting herself in for. She'd never thought she'd fall for any man as passionately as she had Byron. She certainly wasn't sharing him with some porky bitch. As far as she could see there were no flaws in the plan. Thank God she hadn't anything to do with the murder. If it all went pear shaped and they were arrested she couldn't be charged with anything more than being an accessory. She'd stayed well away from the killing; only arriving at the house fifteen minutes before they drove away next morning. In the car she'd played her part perfectly. Byron had been so clever arranging to leave a key with Betty Harrison the elderly next door neighbour as they left. The car had been parked so that Betty would see "Lucy" in the passenger seat. She'd waved and called loudly "Thanks Betty" to her.

So far all had gone smoothly. Only one more passport check on the island and they'd have cracked it. They would make for the queues with a man at the desk. One blessing of the "Lucy" padding was that it had greatly improved her bust size. She'd loosen a few top dress buttons to make sure he'd get a good eyeful. As a fellow barmaid once said, "Men preferred jugs to mugs any day."

Confident all would go well she went back to the tapes. It was strange listening to a dead woman's voice. Christ what a load of bollocks she talked! Serena had already phoned the mother from the airport telling her about the supposed flight delay. Dot seemed to have had no doubt it was her daughter she was talking to.

Vanessa's ("Van" Lucy called her) call was more difficult. She and Lucy had been friends since infant school and Serena had no idea what secrets and memories they shared. Like every other man she'd met Byron knew little about his wife's female friends but he'd been trying to remedy that in the past months. From the notes he'd given her she knew Vanessa had been the first to marry and move to the countryside and Lucy and her family had followed her two years later. Byron had also made sure that all Lucy's friends knew that Letsos was her Greek island destination this year. He'd sworn it would be a "second honeymoon" enabling them to rebuild their relationship. She'd had plenty of time to plan for the care of her animals and her house-plants. A neighbour in Meldrum Ave. was coming in regularly to water them. The two cats Becks and Vicks were going into kennels because they didn't get on with Van's greyhounds. But as always Lucy's biggest concern was "Paddy" her horse. Van was going to provide Lucy with daily reports on how Paddy was "bearing up" without his mistress's visits.

Serena found it difficult to keep the laughter out of her voice when she practised using these words. She couldn't stop thinking that the last thing Paddy had to do was "bear up" now he was forever relieved of Lucy's weight.

CHAPTER 12

Paul was in a hurry to get to work. He was glad to have something to do that would be a distraction from worrying about the murder. He'd seen Myra Williamson sneaking out of the council offices 10 minutes early yesterday afternoon and he wanted to have a word with her. He didn't tolerate that sort of behaviour in his department. The traffic was nose to tail as usual but it kept moving and he got to his office in plenty of time to wash his hands and arrange his desktop to his satisfaction before any of the others came in. Checking his department's e-mails revealed nothing out of the ordinary so he was able to concentrate on what he was going to say to her. Myra was a large bouncy Jamaican woman who'd worked with him for…it must be six years at least He considered she'd never shown him the full respect he deserved. Not that she was openly disrespectful; she was too clever for that. Since she'd been made assistant manager it seemed to him that she walked about the office as if she was in charge. He'd noticed the rest of the staff were in the habit of asking her for advice instead of him. She was far too familiar with them. Every day his ears were assaulted by her shrill piercing laugh. She needed taking down a peg or two. He'd do it in front of the whole office.

The first two hours of the morning were busy dealing with the "meanies" who didn't want to pay their Council Tax. What a pathetic bunch they were. He loved writing out in tortuous detail the exact reasons why they had been put in their particular Council Tax Band. Where there was the odd one or two that might have been wrongly assigned he put them aside to look at again in seven days time.

At coffee break he wandered casually over to Myra's desk and said loudly,

"What time do you make it Miss Williamson?"

She looked at him, then up to the clock above the door and back to him, "The clock's working, Mr.Thewell, why do you ask?"

"I am well aware of our office timepiece's accuracy Miss Williamson, I just wondered if you agreed with it?"

The sudden silence told him now everyone was listening. She looked puzzled. She knew him well enough to know that he was up to something.

"Is this some sort of joke?"

"No indeed, Miss Williamson. Would you agree with me that it is now twenty six minutes to eleven?"

She looked again at the clock and back to him and nodded her head.

Paul waited, hoping she'd speak, but when he saw she was determined to remain silent he said, "The reason why I ask is that as you well know we do not finish our labours here until five p.m. When the big hand is exactly on twelve and the small hand exactly on five"

She looked at him as if he was going mad. Such insolence!

"So?" she said.

"So indeed, Miss Williamson. I will proceed to tell you 'So' Yesterday evening as I was returning to this office from conferring with our chief cashier Mr. Thompson, I am sure I saw you leaving this building and when I glanced at my watch it was not quite ten minutes to five. Am I correct, Miss Williamson?"

The speed of her answer surprised him, "You are indeed Mr. Thewell. And if you had been here you would have seen from the time on that clock on the wall that I actually left this office at twenty minutes to five. I went to the toilet on my way out"

He was shocked. The brazen hussy. He'd take this further. Drawing himself up to his full five feet six inches he asked "Indeed. Indeed. I hope you have a good explanation for your unauthorised leaving work so early"

She had that faint sardonic smile hovering on her lips that he hated.

"I believe I have, Mr. Thewell. I was leaving at that time because I wanted to post a letter."

"Oh. Forgot someone's birthday had you?"

"No"

He waited...and waited. The cheeky cow was going to make him ask her for more details. He had no choice. He'd do it but he'd make her pay.

"So, may I ask what was so important about his letter that you had to leave work early to post it? Or is it a secret?"

She seemed to raise her voice so that everyone would hear; "It's no secret, Mr.Thewell. The letter contained all the details of the Hanny case that Buckinghamshire County Council has been pestering us about for weeks."

He felt a flush beginning to spread over his body. He could feel her eyes and the eyes of the whole office upon him. Desperately he looked up at the clock before replying, "Indeed. A most important letter. Most important. Why did it not go out in the three-thirty office collection may I ask?"

She didn't answer immediately. The silence became unbearable but before he could say any thing she said in a loud clear voice, "Because you hadn't signed it then, Mr.Thewell"

"I hadn't signed it? Why not? Didn't you give it to me on time?"

"I certainly did , Mr. Thewell. It was one of four that I gave you just after one o'clock yesterday. You signed three of them but you left the Hanney file unsigned on top of your desk. When it got so close to five and you weren't here I checked your desk and when I saw that you'd eventually signed it I thought it best to make sure it got posted immediately."

He remembered now. Because of its importance he'd decided to check it thoroughly before letting it leave the office. There had been ten different files associated with it. Some of them were very complicated but he was never one to rush things. He'd signed it just before he'd been called into Mr. Thompson's office.

He jumped at the chance to get away. "Very good, Miss Williamson. Very good. You know how thorough I am."

Head down he scurried back to his desk. She was far too clever for her own good that woman. She might have got the better of him now but things would be different when he was known to the world as the man who had solved the Meldrum Avenue murder.

CHAPTER 13

"Have you phoned her mother yet?"

"For Christ's sake Byron, you know I spoke to her last night. We've only just finished breakfast."

"Lucy's on the phone to her mother five or six times a day when we're on holiday, even in England. You'd best get another call in before we go out."

"What the sodding hell am I going to talk about? We haven't done anything since last night. Well, nothing I could tell Dot about"

"Tell her what there was for breakfast; tell her what funny things these foreigners eat at breakfast, ham and cheese and pepperoni and things like that. Tell her how clean or how dirty the knives and forks were. What the waiters are like. Say one of them is already making eyes at you. Luce was always saying that. ...Oh! And say how nice I'm being to you."

"O.K. But I'll go up to our room and do it. I've got to really concentrate, it's not as if you can learn the lines like. I'm shit scared she'll ask me something I don't know. Somebody's birthday or something."

"If anything like that crops up, make out the line's gone bad and you can't hear her. Cut the call if you have to. And call Van when you're at it"

"Van! Makes me think I'm calling bloody Pickfords. Vanessa's a nice name, why does she have to shorten it to a fucking truck?"

"She's been called that since she and Luce were at school together. You remember what school it was?"

"Yeah. But the line's going dead if we get on to that. I don't know the name of even one of the teachers."

"O.K. But remember, first you ask how Paddy's 'bearing up'"

"Don't Byron. You'll make me laugh."

"Don't even think about laughing. One wrong word could ruin everything. Remember to get things in the proper order when you talk to Van. First the horse, then the cats and then Van's animals and then her family. Make sure you get their names right, Larry, Molly and the youngest. Charlene. She's still at school. I'm sure there was talk a few weeks ago of Molly buying her own hairdressing Salon."

"Right. What does Larry do again?"

"For Christ's sake don't forget that. He's a copper. He's at some East End Police Station"

"O yes. Must be some psychological reason why I forgot that."

"I doesn't matter why, just don't bloody do it."

"Anything to do with police is bad news to me. I've met some right bastards in my time."

"Never mind that now. Concentrate on making sure Van thinks we're having a good time. She never seemed to warm to me. "

"Oh, you poor boy. How could any woman be so foolish?"

"Stop taking the piss. Just remember if it ever it does get a bit hairy say you had so much to drink last night you're not quite with it this morning. Also remember to send your love to her dad Fred."

"What about Lucy's Uncle Lenny?"

"I don't know if Van has much to do with him. But mention him anyway. He's a right bastard .Done serious time for GBH."

"Christ, now you tell me. He's going to love you drowning his niece."

"He's just a thicko. He's kept busy by his hoodlum bosses. Now get on that phone. Just say all's well and the weather's lovely. Say we're in a rush, we're going on a day trip and the coach is just leaving. Tell them you'll ring them again later. We've got to mingle. The more you're seen by other guests the better."

Serena hesitated before replying "Alright, I'm off to the bedroom. The reception should be worse in there."

"You're one smart lady. Make sure you use Lucy's mobile."

"Make up your bloody mind. If I'm so smart how come you think I would be that stupid?"

"Sorry darling, just checking. One mistake could ruin everything. We must make sure that phone goes overboard with you."

She gave him a two fingered salute as she answered "Aye, aye, Sir"

He poured himself another coffee and thought about the previous boating accident. It had happened less than a mile up the coast. As far as he knew there had been no subsequent accidents. At least none that the British Press had reported. He'd searched the web sites and found nothing. His fear was that if some non-British tourists had perished similarly there might be some sort of coastguard watch on the area.

The key to the success of his scheme was sex and alcohol. They had stayed late at the bar last night and would do so for all the nights that would precede "Luce's" tragedy. It was important they established their reputation as hard drinkers. Then no one would be surprised when he was rescued that he'd been well tanked up.

Serena's return dragged Byron back to the present.

"The line was bloody awful, thank God. Dot thinks I've got a cold. She says my voice is all husky. She doesn't send you her love. Even when I said how nice you were being she wasn't overjoyed. Her last words were, 'Keep an eye on that bastard.'"

"That's our Dot. She's never trusted me. What about Van?"

"She was out. I left her a text."

"Good. Let's go"

"Hold your horses. You've got the car booked?"

"No"

"Why don't you go on and book it at the desk while I become your lumpy Lucy in a sun dress. I want to get out and find somewhere to stash my coming home clothes as soon as possible"

"Don't worry. There are lots of rocky bays where they can be well hidden."

"But what if some beach bum finds them? There are always some skint buggers sleeping on beaches."

"If we hide them among the rocks it's less likely anyone will be sleeping there. Anyway you'll have more than enough cash in your money belt to buy yourself a new wardrobe if that did happen. You're definitely heading for Ibiza?"

"You bet. I've got friends there who'll tell the cops whatever I want them to tell them."

"Good. I don't want to give them any grounds for thinking I'd wanted to get rid of Lucy. This was a second honeymoon. Luce and I were making a fresh start."

"But Lucy didn't know about me did she?"

"She knew there was somebody. She'd threatened divorce hadn't she? She's bound to have told her mother and her mates. But, unless the police ask me directly about a mistress I'll keep my mouth shut."

"If they do, like the good little girl I am, I will go along voluntarily when I come back from Ibiza."

"Not before we have reunion shag. It might be months until I see you."

Byron went and booked the car. When "Lucy" joined him at the bar they spent some time drinking with other guests and being especially nice to each other before they left.

The next few days went smoothly. On the second they hired a dingy from the resort where the accident happened and were glad not to be warned to keep away from any particular part of the coast. They explored a couple of nearby bays but found nothing that seemed safe enough to stash Serena's "going home" clothes. They decided to explore the bays from the road tomorrow. They were here for ten days. They could take their time to find the best spot.

CHAPTER 14

After his faux pas with Myra, Paul avoided having anything to do with her for the next few days. He concentrated on refusing appeals against Council's Tax assessments. He paid particular attention to forms bearing Asian names. He was convinced that these people exploited every possible loophole that could be found. They were very adroit with figures. Bound to be; they were the people who invented the decimal system weren't they? In his own mind he still thought of them as "Wiley Oriental Gentlemen." He might be banned from saying it but no one could stop him thinking it. No one could censor Paul Montgomery Thelwell's mind. No Siree.

If he could find nothing wrong with Asian applicants' appeals he put them in his "four week file." It did them no harm to have to wait. The other thing he always did was check the electoral rolls for their addresses. If he found what he thought might be multiple occupancy he sent a memo to the health and safety department. If he found a different name listed he sent the details to his home computer. He used it to tell the Income Tax Authorities about the difference of occupancy just in case the original owner was letting out the property and not declaring the income from it. Over the years he reckoned he'd saved Her Majesty's government thousands of pounds without seeking any reward or acknowledgement because he sent all such communications anonymously.

He began eating his sandwiches for lunch surreptitiously some half an hour before his usual leaving time. Today there was a one of the monthly series of classical lunchtime concerts put on by the Local Arts Council. He had been encouraged by his mother to enjoy the popular classics. Every week they'd listened together to "*Friday Night is Music Night*" and on Sunday's Alan Keith's "*100 Best Tunes.*" After her death he continued listening, not only in memory of her but because it helped him feel superior to the common herd. He went to local concerts and occasionally up London to the Albert and Festival Halls. Every year he liked to find a different location where he could listen to a pre-Christmas performance of "The Messiah."

But his main reason for attending these local midday concerts was that he knew Mr. Oakman, the chief accountant would be there. Paul always tried to speak knowledgably to him about the performance having first made sure he'd studied what his *Oxford Dictionary of Music* had to say about it. This month the main item was a selection of Schubert songs, music a bit too highbrow for Paul's taste. He wasn't certain how to pronounce "Lieder" so he resolved to avoid the word. He had heard both soloists before and knew how highly they were regarded so he reckoned he'd be on safe ground discussing them.

Paul liked to get to the concert hall early so he could wait in the gallery and see where Oakman was sitting. H spotted him coming in just before the concert began. He hurried downstairs and took a seat a few rows back so that he would be in Oakman's line of vision when he rose to leave. The tenor and soprano gave their usual accomplished performances and he warmly joined in the applause. When the concert ended after four encores, Paul timed his rising a few seconds behind Oakman's. Gratifyingly, he was given a nod of acknowledgement and was waiting to step into the aisle beside him when Oakman turned away and hurried towards a side entrance. Paul hesitated, unsure whether to go after him or not. He decided that it would be best to ambush him out front. He pushed his way through the crowd, repeating "Awfully sorry, I'm late" as a hasty apology. Outside he lingered on the pavement close to the entrance's stone pillars. He had almost given up hope when Oakman appeared. Paul stood well back and almost let him pass before sidling up to him.

"Excellent concert don't you think, Sir?"

Oakman give a brief shudder, which puzzled Paul for it was quite a warm day.

"Ah, yes Thewell. Very good."

"The soloists were good, don't you think?"

"Very."

"Did you know Sir that the tenor, Patrick McCarthy was the man in 1974 who stepped out of the audience in the Albert Hall to take over the lead in Carmina Burana ? I believe Andre Previn was the conductor."

"I don't think there is a music lover in Eastern England and beyond who doesn't know that, Thewell. The poor man must be sick of people talking about it."

"Oh...yes, indeed Sir."

"If you'll excuse me I'm not going directly back to the office. Good to have met you." Oakman crossed the road almost before Paul had time to splutter "Goodbye." Immediately afterwards he cursed himself for not adding "Sir."

When he got back to work he found he couldn't concentrate. The next midday concert was Sarasate's *Carmen Fantasy*. It took all his willpower to stop himself looking it up on the internet. The council had recently told its employees that they would be subject to disciplinary action if they were found using the internet for private purposes in working hours. He resolved to make a thorough study of the piece at home, even buy the CD if necessary. He couldn't avoid feeling that he had not succeeded in making the best of impressions on Mr. Oakman today.

The other thing that disturbed his concentration was thinking that with every day that passed Fuller was escaping Justice. Tomorrow it would be a week since he'd seen the murder. He'd walked past *Sunset* again last night and it was obvious the police hadn't been near the place. The house looked deserted and the space outside the house where he was sure Fuller's car had been parked was empty just as it had been on previous nights. Meldrum Avenue houses had no garages; residents had to park their cars in the road.

Byron Fuller was now probably hundreds of miles away. He could have shoved his wife's body in the boot of his car and buried it in some forest or weighed it down with chains and rocks and thrown it into an abandoned quarry. Or at sea. Why not? He could easily own or hire a seagoing yacht. Why hadn't he thought of that before? There were four or five marinas within a twenty mile radius of Lamdon. In the summer when there wasn't a cricket match for him to umpire he liked to take Kaiser down to the sea and let him have a good swim. There was always somebody working on one of the boats. What would be more natural than him saying "A friend of mine from Lamdon, Byron Fuller has a boat somewhere down here. You don't happen to know which one it is?" If he did find out that Mr. Murderer Fuller had set sail this very week then the police would have to take heed. It was ridiculous nothing was being done. They were quick enough to come around and harass upright elderly citizens who were brave enough to reprimand young vandals. He'd had three letters published on that very subject in newspapers in the past two years.

The thought worried him. What if he became known as the one who exposed the police incompetence that had let Fuller escape? Might not the police start to harass him? They wouldn't like being outsmarted by an amateur.

Perhaps he ought to forget all about the police and concentrate on capturing Fuller himself. If he did that; he could sign up some lucrative book contract that would enable him to retire early. Then he'd have enough funds and admiring fellow criminologists not to worry about the police.

On the other hand he believed strongly in Law and order. Perhaps there were investigations going on that he knew nothing about. The police might be going to spring a trap on Fuller when he least expected it. Paul decided he'd give them a little more time. If only he could think of a way to gee them up.

CHAPTER 15

Wednesday mid-morning Byron lazily stirred his coffee and lifted his face to the sun. It was by far the hottest morning of their holiday. "This is the life," he said to himself. Perhaps Serena was right; they should retire to the sun when everything was settled. Or at least buy a villa abroad they could go to whenever they wanted.

They had come to this little town because it was where they would hire their boat. He looked around the square. Nobody was in a hurry. All the other patrons of the café were taking it easy just like.... Christ! That blonde at the corner table in the shade: she was giving him the eye. She most certainly was. He sneaked a look at his watch. It as only a quarter to eleven! Nobody could be on the game that early! He had picked up such a woman some years ago when Lucy had stayed in their hotel complaining of sunstroke. This one was a right looker and there was plenty to see; especially on the top deck. He decided she must be German. The island was very popular with Germans. He turned sideways, out of her eye line. Serena might come back any minute. He couldn't get involved. He jumped as he heard a metal chair scrape back. She was getting up, coming over to him. What could he say? She was...

"Allo Byron. Fancy seeing you here. Where's Lucy?"

He wanted to get up and rush away but fear pinned him to the chair. He tried to smile at her while racking his brains to work out who she was. She sat down opposite him, displaying an abundant cleavage as she did so.

"You don't recognize me do you? I'm Helga. Lucy's friend from Weight Watchers. We gave each other lifts to the meetings. I only live two roads away from you; I've been in your house lots of times for coffee."

His humour came to his rescue, "And cream cakes I bet."

Helga laughed. A throaty laugh that despite his panic he couldn't help being stirred by its sexiness. "Well, a chocolate biscuit maybe. Any rate, where's Lucy? Shopping?"

"Got it in one."

"Has she been gone long?"

He needed as much time as possible. He must get rid of her. "No, less than five minutes. She gone down there (He pointed in the opposite direction to which Serena had gone.) You'll easily catch her. Lucy doesn't hurry when she's on clothes patrol does she?"

"No. I don't know how I missed you. I've been sitting here at least twenty minutes."

The truth made it easy to answer that. "Oh Lucy never came here. We just spotted this place from across the road. I said I'd wait here while she donated a few more Euros to the needy boutique owners of this island"

Helga smiled and began to grope in the large carpet bag beside her. "I'll phone her. She hasn't changed her number since last year, has she?"

How Byron managed not to panic he never knew. Afterwards he attributed his calmness to his long years of lying and deceit.

"I don't know" he said slowly as if he was trying to think of her number. "You know how it is, you put someone's number in your mobile's memory and you never have to remember it again."

"I'll try the number I've..." he didn't let her finish.

"No, you can't. Lucy hasn't got her mobile with her".

He could tell instantly from the look on her face she didn't believe him. While she was trying to think of what to say, his moment of inspiration came. "Look Helga. You know how often Lucy's on the phone. Well, I'm afraid I got a bit fed up with it. Sometimes it seemed to me she did nothing else but talk for hours on it. Any rate before we came away we had a big quarrel about it." He grinned and tried to look sheepish, "Maybe I was just jealous but anyway, the thing is we both agreed that on this holiday we'd not use our phones until after 6 o'clock. They're in our hotel room now."

Helga said slowly "You mean like not having a drink until the sun's over the yardarm. That's what you say, isn't it.?"

He gave her his most effusive smile. "Exactly, Helga. What excellent English you speak."

Helga started to say something but hesitated and slipped her mobile back into the big carpet bag. Looking up she said "Maybe

I can find her." But she made no effort to move away. "Where are you staying? Peter and I are at the *Knossos Palace.* He's off playing golf with one of the other guests. I'm supposed to pick them up soon. But we've nothing on for tonight. We could meet up."

Byron tried desperately to think logically. There was no way he could stop her arranging a meeting, If he lied about their hotel she would be sure to find out and when she read about Lucy's drowning she might be highly suspicious. But to tell them the truth would be fatal. Serena would never deceive Helga. He thought he'd risk a half truth

"Ah...at the moment we're at the Lagomandra; but we might move. We're not very happy with the place"

"The Lagomandra? I've not seen that. Where's that?"

"We're not staying here. We're in the capital, right on the seafront. We've just come down here for the boutiques and (once more he hesitated before deciding that the truth would be best) "And we've been doing a bit of sailing. The conditions are ideal around here."

"Lucy sailing?"

"She's enjoying it. She likes seeing the fish in the clear waters off shore. And of course (He smiled suggestively at her) you can get an all over tan in your own boat where others can't see you."

Helga put her hand up to her mouth "Really! I must mention that to Peter." She gave that throaty laugh again.

He had to get rid of her. Serena could come back any minute. It was inconceivable that Helga would not notice how much she was made up to look like Lucy. Everything would be ruined. He rose from his chair and thrust a few Euros down on the table.

"Lucy will be mad if she misses you. As I said she's only just gone. Let's see if we can find her." He moved away from the table giving her no choice but to follow him.

"I'll check the shops on the right and you do the ones on the left. We'll come back into the street every five minutes and find each other. That way we won't get too far apart."

"I'm useless at directions Byron. I never remember which way to turn when I come out of a shop. Wouldn't it be better if we stayed together?"

"No" he said firmly; "Too much chance of missing Luce like that. We'll not get very far apart in five minutes, you'll see" Before she could reply he manoeuvred her directly over to a boutique and with a murmured "Five minuets remember" strode off to the far side of the street and into the nearest shop.

From inside he watched her hesitantly enter the boutique. As soon as the door closed behind her he was out and on his way back to the square. He searched it for a good vantage point. He couldn't be sure Serena would come back the way she'd gone. He couldn't go back to the cafe. He noticed that diagonally opposite the cafe where he'd been sitting was whitewashed church with two large grey pillars in front of its open doorway. When he walked over to it he found the doorway offered welcome shade and there was a notice board he could pretend to read. There was also a good view of the end of the street where he'd taken Helga. If she returned he could slip inside. Every moment he stood there was agony. What would Serena say if Helga accosted her? They would have to kill the fat German bitch if they met. There was no choice.

CHAPTER 16

Thursday morning Paul decided not to go to work. He phoned and left a message saying he had such a blinding migraine that he was going to his doctors emergency surgery. People at work knew he suffered from migraines so he was confident that they would accept his excuse. It was over three years since he last had a day off and that was only because he had a raging toothache. He hated being out of the office. He was sure that plots were hatched against him when he was absent.

There was a small blue car in the parking space outside *Sunset* but when he walked past it had a card saying HEALTH VISITOR on the dashboard. So he was relaxed when he knocked on the door of the house above *Sunset*. He'd got the name of the occupier, a Miss Betty Harrison from the electoral roll. After three loud knocks he gave up, deciding she must be at work or out shopping

He hummed "Land of Hope and Glory" to himself as he walked up the path to Fuller's house. All would be well as long as he kept his nerve. He just had to show his identification and say "We are just enquiring if you have made any substantial alterations to your property since the last Survey, Mr. Fuller." His answer was bound to be "No" for such an immoral man would be bound to lie to him if he had. All he had to do then was thank him and leave. Taking care not to stand too close to the door he reached out and pressed the bell. As soon as he heard its echoing ring he knew the house was empty. He stayed and pressed it twice more just in case Fuller was in the back garden but the sound was the same. He felt much braver now and envisioned how well he would have dealt with the man if he'd come to the door.

He also drew a blank at the next house where a Henry and Primrose Fawcette lived. He stood on the pavement pretending to check his forms while surreptitiously studying the houses opposite. There was nobody in their gardens and none of the net curtains twitched so he walked along to the alleyway and around to the back of the houses. As he expected few showed any sign of life in them. These properties being so expensive both husband and wife had to go to work to be able to afford them. When he came to the twelfth gate he remembered how easy it had been to open that fateful night. Would it still be as easy with Fuller absent? He checked around and satisfied he wasn't being watched he lifted the latch and pushed. Much to his disappointment it moved immediately. If Fuller hadn't secured the gate it then it wasn't likely he'd buried his wife's body in the garden. Unless…unless…as he knew from crime novels, murders always made one mistake. It would be best to take a good look when there was no one at home. Confidently he pushed the gate wide open.

"Leave that gate alone. If you don't leave immediately I'll call the police."

CHAPTER 17

Serena was coming into the square and heading for the cafe and she was alone. Maybe there was a god after all.

He had to use all his self control to stop himself rushing over and seizing her by the arm. He walked around the square so that he came alongside her. She sensed his presence and turned to speak. He uttered a curt "No" and strode on ahead.. After a minute he slowed so that she was just a step behind him. "Serena" he said quietly without turning around "Can you hear me?"

"Yes, what's up?"

"There's somebody here who knows Luce. Firstly, do not answer your mobile. Repeat, do not, Next get into this arcade and take that wig and all Lucy's jewellery off. I'll wait here."

Without a word or a glance Serena walked past him into the arcade. What a treasure! He rejoiced she was not one of these women who must ask a dozen questions before doing as she was told.

When she came out he stepped in front of her and mouthed "Follow me, not too close." He headed for the harbour and soon they were passing fishermen mending nets. There was little chance of Helga coming down here.

He led the way into a small bar and ordered two beers. There were no tourists here. Only a few fishermen drinking and smoking. When they were seated he kept his voice down as he told her about Helga.

"Jesus Christ!" she whispered "What are we going to do?"

"Drown you this afternoon" he answered.

Serena was silent for a while. She took a good swig of her beer before she answered "I suppose we've no choice. She could come to our hotel tonight. Even if we moved out it would look suspicious."

Byron nodded, "It's only a day or so earlier than we'd planned anyway."

They finished their drinks and made their way back separately to the car. When they drove off the narrow streets were so congested that it was possible to move only at a snail's pace.

Pedestrians could easily see into the cars. Serena sat in the front with her face turned to him while he crouched over the steering wheel wearing her sunhat. It took almost fifteen minutes to get clear of the town.

Back in the capital they parked two streets away from their hotel. He stayed in the car while Serena walked to it and went straight in to the toilets to put her Lucy disguise back on before getting their room key. In the room she packed a rucksack with her "going home" clothes plus a couple of towels from the bathroom. The last things she picked up before leaving the room were the local tidal charts that Byron had bought and the holdall with his sailing clothes. On the way out she went to reception and put all Lucy's jewellery in the hotel safe. She took the opportunity to tell the receptionist how excited she was at going sailing. The police were bound to come and ask questions about Lucy's state of mind before her "accident."

When she got back to the car she found Byron had been shopping. He saw her looking quizzically at the amount of food and said with a smile, "It would never do to let poor Luce pass away hungry."

When she stopped laughing she noticed the champagne and picked it up. "By Christ, Veuve Clicquot Yellow Label, this is a bit over the top Bry. It's a funeral not a wedding reception we're having."

"That's for us darling. It's going to be a long time before we have another drink together. Our last drink is going to be a good one."

She was glad she was studying the label as he spoke. The words "our last drink" jarred her mind. She hoped it was just a slip of the tongue. He wasn't going to double cross her, was he? Really drown her and have all the loot for himself? He'd have a surprise coming if he tried anything funny. She was no man's fool. She was prepared. She'd make sure he drunk most of the bottle.

"I'm not having too much of this" she said, "Not when I've got to swim ashore. If I end up seeing two coastlines, I might pick the wrong one and swim out into the wild blue yonder"

"No chance of that darling. You've got hollow legs. I've never known a woman who can hold her drink as well as you."

64

That was true. She was rarely drunk. Not just because years behind the bar had given her a high tolerance of alcohol. She was careful not to drink to excess in male company. She knew how to make drinks last. No punter had ever got her drunk unless she'd wanted to be.

They set off to find somewhere to hide the rucksack. The two beaches they'd looked at previously had had been too crowded for them to be safe hiding places. Their map showed one more bay which was the furthest one from the town but nearer to the capsize location. When they got there and saw the wide sandy access road, Serena thought it too would be crowded but they decided to give it a try anyway. They had only gone some hundred yards along when Byron slowed the car and turned down a narrow track on the right. There was a dilapidated building at the end; Serena could just make out a sun bleached sign that said APOLLOS TAVERNA hanging lopsidedly on a wall. Every window and door was boarded up at the front but when they went around the back they found a corrugated iron sheet had been pulled away from one of the windows and they were able to clamber inside. As their eyes got accustomed to the gloom they could see they must be in the kitchen. There were two large stoves along the nearest wall. Byron went over and pulled open the door of the nearest stove. "This'll do "he said and pushed the rucksack wrapped in the plastic bin liner they'd brought from England inside.

"Hadn't we best check this place isn't being used first?" asked Serena.

Byron nodded and they made their way into a large room which had probably been the restaurant. There was a circle of bricks in the middle of the floor that contained a few bits of charred wood and ashes. Byron searched around in them.

"There's not been a fire in here for a while. I think we're safe enough."

"I hope you're right Bry. These bottles and lager cans, don't they show this place is being used? "

"You mean, has been used. Look how dirty the bottle's are. Can you see one that looks as if it's been dumped recently?"

She walked around picking up cans and bottles, Byron was right, they were all covered with dust.

"I think this will be O.K. It will only be here three or four hours at the most. We'd be very unlucky if somebody found it in that time."

Serena nodded in agreement. Her cash and passport would be with her in a waterproof money belt. If the rucksack was stolen she'd have to buy another one and restock it. A woman without luggage would be noticeable. They didn't have much time to spare. "Yeah, "she said "Let's risk it."

Before they left Byron scattered some rubbish around the front of the oven to hide any signs of their presence. Serena though he'd drive straight out onto the main road, instead he turned down towards the beach.

"Why are we going down here?"

"Because, if you come ashore here, you'll know what this path looks like as you come out of the sea. There might be more than one path leading away from this beach. Places look so different when you're coming from the opposite direction."

She leant back in her seat. Byron thought of everything. He was as her father used to say "A man who could see around corners."

CHAPTER 18

Paul was immobilised with fear. The voice was elderly but authoritative. When he gathered his wits he realised it was coming from the garden of the first house he'd knocked at. Taking a deep breath he called out in his most reassuring voice "Miss Harrison?"

"Who's that? Who are you? How do you know my name?"

He leaned forward so that he could see her over the hedge. She was a tall thin woman with her white hair tied back in a bun. Despite the warmth of the day she was wearing a red cardigan buttoned up to her neck. She had a trowel in her right hand.

"It's a council tax check Miss Harrison. I have my full identification here with me. If I might just step further into Mr. and Mrs Fullers garden I can show it to you."

"Why do you need to come into their garden? They're away on holiday. I certainly am not going to give you permission to do any such a thing. You'll have to wait until they return from their holiday in Greece."

Her words shook Paul. She seemed so certain but he knew she couldn't be right. The shock made him stutter as he said "Of...of ...of course, Miss Harrison. Whatever you think best. Do...do you know when they'll be back?"

"Next Wednesday. You can see them then."

"Wednesday. Thank you."

He was pulling the gate closed when she suddenly asked, "Do you have to see my garden as well?"

He wasn't anxious to confront her but he thought it would be too suspicious if he refused. "Well, I don't think our checks really need to concern you Miss Harrison but if it is no trouble I'll just have a peep."

"H'mm. You're from the Council you say? What's this all about?"

"It's to do with the council tax Miss Harrison. As you know, all properties are put into different bands depending on their value. Houses in the same road may vary considerably in their banding depending on their amenities. Since the last valuation of Meldrum Avenue in 1995. (He was glad he'd checked that beforehand) some properties have been considerably enhanced with extensions and things like hot tubs and swimming pools. We've had a report that alterations have take place at the Fullers. That's why I was anxious to have a look at their garden."

"Spying on us, so that's what you're up to. Getting more like a police state every day. Well nothing been altered in my house or garden. Well...nothing except my rockery's got a lot bigger. I'm having a job getting enough plants to fill it up. Does that mean I'm going to have to pay more tax? Because..."

He interrupted her, "No. No. that won't affect your valuation I can assure you not at all."

"H'mm. I hope you're right. You'd better have a look at it anyway now that you're here. Come around. Mind you shut Mr. Fuller's gate properly as you leave."

"I most certainly will Miss Harrison."

Her gate opened noiselessly. He held his photo identification before him like a shield as he entered. She took it from him and held it close to her face before giving his a thorough examination. He studied the rockery while she did so. It was certainly a big one and had every sign of being newly planted.

"What are you looking for?"

The abruptness of her question made him jump. "Any new building work. I can see straightaway none has taken place on your property. There's no need to trouble you any further." As he took his identification badge back he was desperately trying to think of a way he could get a good look at Fuller's garden. A mass of yellow flowers on the rockery gave him an idea. "Lovely display of Alyssum, you've got there Miss Harrison. And that deep red Aubrietia is it Barker's double?"

"Yes. You like rock plants?"

"Yes. I have a rockery at home. Nothing as magnificent as this." It was true. He wasn't an enthusiastic gardener. He'd built a rockery because he thought it would be easy to manage. Many of the cricket matches he attended had Fêtes with plant stalls and he'd got into the habit of trying to find a different plant for his rockery each match. As well as adding to the colour of his garden they served to remind him of notable happenings at certain matches. When he was a player, the more runs he scored the more expensive the rock plant he's buy and now as an umpire there wasn't so much to celebrate except when he'd stood steadfastly by his decisions in spite of vociferous appeals from the unhappy team.

He pointed vaguely in the direction of an array of plants with small bluish-pink flowers at the end of the rockery closest to the Fullers. "Those plants at the far end of the rockery; I'm got some very similar but I've never been quite sure of their name."

"Where do you mean?"

Inching slowly forward as he asked "May I?" he moved to where he'd pointed. "These beautiful bluish-pink plants with tiny grey leaves."

She came and bent forward to peer at the plants, "My eyes aren't as good as they used to be Mr...ah... Thewell, wasn't it?" She didn't wait for him to answer but continued "People commonly call them Stonecrops but their proper name is Sedums. This one 'Sedum dasyphyllum' is one of my favourites. There are lots of varieties. Are yours exactly the same?"

"Yes, I'm sure they are." he said as he straightened up. He now had a good view of Fuller's garden. Disappointingly there was no sign of any recent activity. If anything it looked a bit neglected. "If only this rockery was in his garden" he thought

"You don't keep their labels then?"

"No. I don't like to have a lot of plastic labels sticking up all over my rockery. Spoils the natural look, I always think"

"Indeed, but if you keep them somewhere safe you an always refer to them if you've forgotten a name."

"I try to do that Miss Harrison but somehow they always seem to get mislaid."

She stared at him disapprovingly and muttered another "Hmm."

He started moving back towards the gate as he said "Thank you for letting me see your magnificent rockery Miss Harrison. Made my day that has." When he reached it he added "I've had a brief glance at Mr.Fuller's garden and there is no sign of any recent building. I don't think it will be necessary for us to trouble him again. Thank you."

She uttered a very definite "Goodbye" as he closed the gate.

He didn't have the heart to make himself any lunch when he got home so he put Kaiser in the car and drove to Northshore Island. The Crown and Anchor made a good ploughman's lunch and had tables outside where he could sit with Kaiser. There was always a couple of bowls of water provided for customers' pets. That was what had first attracted him to this pub. When he'd finished eating and Kaiser had had a good drink he walked along to where he knew there was a large marina. He had to climb up and over a steep grassy bank to get to it. He paused at the top and looked at the forest of masts below. It was as quiet as a graveyard; there wasn't a sign of life anywhere. He should have known. The people here were all weekend sailors. He'd have to come then. Dispirited, he turned away and took Kaiser along the seawall where he could let him off the lead. Kaiser's exuberance as he pursued the trail of long gone foxes and rabbits was some consolation. At least his pet's journey had been worthwhile.

CHAPTER 19

Dot Booth looked longingly at the telephone on the table beside her. It was hours since Lucy had rung and then it had only been a brief garbled call. It wasn't like her to be in such a hurry. It was that bugger Byron rushing her around. She knew he resented her phoning so much. Sod him. She was dying for Lucy to call; she'd some really exciting news to tell her.

Lucy's cousin, Tara was playing away with some Eyetie hairdresser and her bloke only some fifteen months into a ten stretch. Bloody disgraceful it was. Mind you what could you expect? Tara's mother Marge could never keep her knickers on. Even though Marge was her own sister she had to admit she was a tart. Not that she ever charged for it, at least not as far as Dot knew. Marge had been shagging like a rattlesnake since she was twelve. Dot was the one who had to hide the boys in her room if their parent came home unexpectedly.

Despite Tara's unfaithfulness Dot wasn't happy that that her brother Lenny would have to be the one to sort her out. She hoped he wouldn't be too heavy handed. A bit of a bull in china shop was Lenny. It was amazing that considering how all these years he'd been working for the Scopes brothers he'd only ever done an eighteen month stretch for GBH. Of course with their money they could always afford a good brief for themselves and their "boys" Lenny always laughed when he heard anyone say "Crime doesn't pay." "Try telling that to a lawyer" he'd say.

It was such a pity that her Danny wasn't still alive. He was a much gentler man. Not that he'd let anyone walk over him. Danny believed in persuasion rather than punches. Why did he have to go with a heart attack and him only 63? He'd have given Tara a good talking to.She'd have listened. She'd loved her Uncle Danny. Maybe it would be a good idea to get Lucy to phone Tara, she...

The phone rang. Dot grabbed it. "Dot Booth" she gasped.

"Hallo Ma. How are you?"

"Lucy. Where's you bin? I was getting real worried about you"

"I'm sorry Ma but they're so backwards here, you wouldn't believe it. It's hard to get a proper signal. I have tried to phone you a couple of times before but it was a dead loss. Anyway, now I've managed it, how are you?"

"Much worse than I was this morning. The old trouble's back."

"Oh....well...you take it easy...Get plenty of rest"

"Rest? With the Nobby Stiles? You're joking. It's agony just sitting here even with that rubber ring on my arse."

"I'm sorry you're in such pain Ma. Tell you what though; you wouldn't like to be sitting where I'm sitting now."

"Where?"

"On a boat, the wooden seats are bloody hard on the arse I can tell you."

"A boat? How big is it? How many's on it? How…"

. "Don't get your knickers in a twist Ma. It a lovely little white sailing boat. The same as the one we went on yesterday. Remember I told you how good it was? And we've both got lifejackets. No need…."

"Luce. It's dangerous. You had a sail yesterday, that's enough. You're a horsewoman not a bloody sailor. You didn't even like swimming lessons at school."

"Yes Ma. But that was because the girls were so rude about my size. It's smashing out here on the sea. I'm getting a real suntan in my bikini."

"Bikini? You're in a bikini? You said you'd never wear one again after what you heard that woman say at Bournemouth."

"Oh that. Nobody cares what you look like in this place. You should see some of the German women on the beach here! And Byron likes me in it. . Anyway, why should I let some skinny bitch decide what I can wear?"

"Skinny? I thought you said she was overweight herself?"

"Ah...well, maybe she was. I don't remember. ...whoops...hold on a minute ma, the boat's rocking a bit."

"Lucy! Make that bugger Byron turn back right now. He's a reckless bastard. You should never have allowed him to take you out in a little boat."

"Don't panic ma. It's O.K. It was just a wave from a passing motor boat."

"Never mind that. Get that fucking boat turned round. I've got something really important to tell you about Tara."

"Tara....ah...what's she done?"

"She's only playing away, that's all."

"Oh."

"Is that all you can say? Her old man Mick's in for a ten stretch, you know that don't you."

"Yes, of course I do. But...well, you know..."

"What? What d'you mean?"

"Well, I don't like to speak bad about the family but you know what Tara's like."

"What are you saying? That she's..."

"Speak up Ma, I can't hear you."

"I said what you are telling me about her. She's done this before?"

"It's no good Ma. The line keeps going dead. We must have come into a bit where the reception's bad."

"How come I can hear you then?"

"It's still no good Ma. I'll phone you again as soon as we come ashore. Love you, bye"

As soon as she clicked the phone off, Serena turned to Byron, "Who the fuck's Tara?"

"Tara? Tara? I'm not sure. One of Lucy's mates...or a cousin maybe."

"Maybe? A fucking lot of good that is. What..."

He held up a hand to check her. "Serena my sweet, calm down. It doesn't matter who Tara or anybody else is in that bloody family any more. You're never going to speak to them again. That was your last phone call...ever."

Serena pulled her beach bag a little closer. Under pretence of getting a tissue she moved the bundle with the knife to the top of the bag.

"Hold on we're going ashore"

She hadn't noticed while she was talking to Dot how close inland they had come. She was only just in time to grip the gunwale before she was jerked forward as the boat bit into the beach.

"Stay in the boat. This shingle's bloody sharp. You don't want any cuts on your tootsies annoying you when you have your swim."

She'd taken off all the "packing" that made her look like Lucy as soon as they'd got out of harbour. As she looked down at the wig lying in the bottom of the boat she said, "Christ, Bry. Did you see that Greek bloke's face when I stepped into the boat?"

"Yes. It did sink a few inches lower in the water when you came aboard. It was brilliant you filling your pockets with stones. I'd a job to stop myself laughing."

"I nearly though he wasn't going to let us have it. You could tell the way he looked at that bigger dingy that he was thinking we ought to have hired that."

"That's why I got underway so quickly."

She picked up the wig. "Good fucking riddance," she said as she chucked it at him.

"Really, such language! And at a funeral too!"

They laughed and he held her tight. As she felt him against her she wished the beach had been soft and sandy. She was starting to feel randy. She looked further up the beach but there was nothing but rocks and boulders. He squeezed her harder; "Soon" he whispered and released her. "Hand me the spade, please."

She took the children's spade from the beach bag and handed it to him. "There's no need for you to come ashore. I can easily do it"

"OK, big boy"

He strode off up the beach to find a spot to bury Lucy's stuff. She sat down on the only cushioned seat and let the warmth of the sun embrace her. Everything was going well. Byron really was something special. She'd seen him play many different roles in the years she'd known him. The plumy voiced toff, socialising with his hunting friends at race meetings. The calm sober financial expert, advising the old dears looking for a good return on their investments. In the clubs and casinos he was calm and self-possessed, whether winning or losing. She'd only once seen him fight and that had been short and brutal. He'd evaded most of his opponent's wild rushes and had punched him in the kidneys at every opportunity. When the man fell down he'd finished him off with kicks to the guts and head. She'd enjoyed that.

She sat up and looked for him. He'd gone a long way up the beach and was already was knee deep in the hole he was digging. No tide was ever going to disturb what he was burying there. It certainly didn't look like a beach that anybody would visit for pleasure. The cliffs were bare rock with only a few small stunted bushes growing out of them. There was no pathways down that she could see. He'd picked an ideal spot. How could he tell so much about a place just by looking at a few lines on a map?

She reached for the other beach bag and found the costume she'd brought with her for her swim ashore. It was a matronly all in one effort, far removed from her usual bikinis. She didn't want to attract any unwanted male attention as she walked back to where her rucksack was hidden. The broad shoulder straps would safely support the plastic bag containing the flip flops, the cotton wide brimmed sun hat and sunglasses during her swim. She'd not put it on until the last minute. Far better to stay in her bra and pants for now.

When Byron came back despite the sharp shingle she jumped out of the boat and helped him push it back into the water. When they were safely underway, she turned to speak to him there was an expression on his face that at first she couldn't place. Then she remembered where she'd seen it before. It was when she had a part in a pantomime version of Hansel and Gretel. It was on the face of the witch who'd just shoved Hansel into the oven.

CHAPTER 20

When Paul arrived home after his fruitless visit to Northshore Island, he found a leaflet lying in his hallway. He picked it up intending to throw it in the paper bin but as he read it he began to smirk. This was too good to waste.

SO YOU NEED TO
LOSE WEIGHT

**TRIED THE REST
NOW TRY THE BEST**

**ALL NATURAL PRODUCTS
MONEY BACK GUARANTEE**

PHONE MONIQUE NOW

01555 636377

SERIOUS PEOPLE ONLY PLEASE

Next morning he was in the office over an hour early. There were cleaners still working in the corridor directly outside as he entered. He listened until they'd moved away then took a small black rubber wedge from his brief case and put it under the door. No one could come in and disturb him now. Quickly he pulled at the top drawer of Myra Williamson's desk. It slid smoothly open. Stupid woman. He always made sure every drawer in his desk was locked before he went home. He put the leaflet he'd found on top of the folder that was there and rushed across the office to retrieve the wedge. Slipping it back in his briefcase he hurried out of the office and out of the building by the back entrance. There was a coffee shop far enough away for him not to be seen by any of his staff. On the rare occasions he went there he normally had only the standard cappuccino but this morning he felt a celebration was in order so he ordered a large one. He sat reading the *Daily Mail* until he was sure he would just get to the office on time. He knew the staff would think it odd for normally he was always got there before anyone else, but he couldn't risk that today. It gave him great satisfaction to think of the disappointment they would feel when he came through the office door. They were bound to have thought he was having another day's sick leave.

He was so full of joy at what he was about to see that he had to stop and wipe the smile off his face before he walked in. No chorus of concern welcomed him. Only Angie, one of the computer operators who was hanging up her jacket turned and said "Good morning Mr. Thewell. Feeling better?"

"A little, thank you Miss Timms."

Avoiding looking at the others he made his way to his desk and unlocked the drawers. When he was satisfied all his notepaper and pencils were in their proper place he sat down in his swivel chair, swung round, took the cover off his computer and booted it up. Looking over the top of the screen he had a good view of Myra Williamson's desk. She made no move to open her top drawer. Instead she took some papers out of her briefcase and started to read through them. He knew she often took work home, especially the latest legislation that this target obsessed New Labour Government issued like confetti. She was after his job, the cunning bitch. But she wouldn't catch him out.

He made sure he kept up to date just as much as she did. He keyed in his e-mails and tried to read them while casting surreptitious glances at her. Why the Hell didn't she open that drawer. He..., the message on the screen startled him; "Heads of department meeting this afternoon at three o'clock." What was that about? It had been sent yesterday. He'd missed it.! Damn. The only day he'd had off in years and this had happened. Still, if it was important they'd have to inform him. He scanned the list of e-mails to see if there was anything about it. There...he stopped. What...what if she'd gone in his place? He sat up straight and glared over at her.

She was staring straight at him. There was something in her right hand. It had to be the leaflet. She couldn't know it was him? He had to look back at the screen to avoid her accusing eyes.

77

Clenching his fists under the desk to help control his nervousness he said in what sounded to him an unnaturally loud voice "Ah. Miss Williamson. This meeting at three pm yesterday. Do you happen to know what it was about?"

She didn't answer straight away but continued to stare accusingly at him. He was gathering the courage to ask her if any thing was the matter when her expression changed. A smile spread slowly over her face until all her white teeth were showing "Yes Mr. Thewell. I was asked to attend in your absence. It was about slimming. (He felt an unstoppable blush rush across his face as she paused.) Slimming down the workforce. It seems the council will have overspent by more than three million pounds by the end of this financial year if they don't make economies. They are going to ask for voluntary redundancies. Would you be interested Mr.Thewell?"

"Most certainly not" he said indignantly. The cheek of the bitch!

"A letter is going to be sent to all the staff next week setting out the council's difficulties and giving details of the redundancy terms. Mr.Oakshaw promised us that they would be very generous."

"Ah; well they won't interest me. Is there anything else that happened yesterday that I should know about?"

"No Mr. Thewell. All went smoothly in your absence."

It was his turn to smile as he thought of his answer. "Of course. That's no more than what I would expect. I take care to train you all well, don't I?"

The only answer he got was a brief nod before she looked down at her desk. He was turning away when he saw her pick up a plastic folder and carefully put the leaflet in it. She looked directly back at him before putting the folder into one of her desk drawers. What was she going to do? Get it examined for fingerprints? No. That was ridiculous.

He felt so flustered that he got up, grabbed a folder out of his briefcase and hurried out of the office. He spent the next twenty minutes sitting on the toilet trying to sort out what to do. When he got back to his office he sensed an unusual air of expectation in the place. He immediately thought that a plot had been hatched against him. It wasn't long until he realised what it was.

Margaret Havens was the first. After questioning him about what he regarded as totally unnecessary details of a new form she left saying "Thank you Mr. Thewell, I'm glad this new slimmer version meets your approval."

Mike Harminston was next. He began by saying "I'm afraid I've got a rather weighty problem here Mr.Thewell" but it proved to be a matter of no importance.

Jane Shealling wanted him to be sure to check the estimates she brought him otherwise "we might lose pounds and pounds."

He glared around the office but every head was bent studiously over their desks and workstations. He felt as if he would explode if he stayed where he was so he hurried once more out of the office. He wandered around the other offices for an hour before going back to his own officed where he worked with his head down until lunch. He went back to the toilet. It was as he was washing his hands that the inspiration came to him.

He went straight out to one of the phone boxes in the railway station. After he'd thoroughly cleaned the mouthpiece with paper towels soaked in antiseptic soap he dialled 999. When he was put through to the police he whispered "I want to report a murder."

CHAPTER 21

Byron turned the prow of the boat into the wind and lowered the sail. He looked all around him and when satisfied that no one could observe them said "Throw the anchor overboard."

Serena reached down and grasped the rusty anchor and raised her arm to launch it into the sea.

"Wait. Make sure it's secure at this end. That bloke at the boat hire place didn't exactly look as if he'd descended from those who sailed with Jason and the Argonauts."

She didn't know what he was talking about but she uncoiled its rope until she reached the end. It looked as if it was tied securely enough but she gave it a hefty tug all the same. The rope held fast. She looked at Byron for his approval and when he nodded she chucked the anchor into the sea. He let the boat drift until he felt the anchor catch. Only when he was satisfied it was secure did he reef the sail to the metal boom.

"Thank God the tides in the Mediterranean are so small. We don't have to rush things."

He sat down and brought the Champagne out of its bag. Handing it to her he said "You're the bar lady, you open it."

Serena undid the fastening wires around the cork and holding it steady twisted the bottle until the cork popped gently out.

"Bravo, not a drop wasted, always good to see an expert at work."

For some reason his praise made her tense.. She wondered if he was deliberately trying to relax her, lull her into a false sense of security. When she saw what was in his hand she became even more alarmed; two Champagne flutes that sparkled in the sun. When he touched them together the purity of the note produced was clear evidence of their quality. These were no cheapo glasses; he had to have spent serious money for them. What was he up to? He couldn't be going to capsize the boat with expensive stuff like this on board.

"Byron, those are real expensive glasses, what the fuck are you playing at?"

He gave her one of his superior smiles. Holding up one of the flutes and turning it so that she could see it's purity he said, "What you have noticed my dear Watson is exactly what I want the Greek plods to notice when they investigate our tragic accident. We will have sunk with some very expensive glassware aboard."

"How the hell will they know that, those glasses will be smashed to pieces once this boat turns over?"

"Indeed but when I'm being interrogated about all that I did on the day that this tragedy occurred I will remember I that I bought them and more importantly where I did so. The shop will remember me because I insisted on buying the most expensive pair they had in stock. The assistant was horrified when I told him I was taking them out in a little boat. Caused quite a scene it did. 'Only the best is good enough for my lovely wife' I told him. I'll be suitably embarrassed when those words are repeated to me. Not typically English you know. Brokenheartedly, I shall reveal that this crystal was destined to be polished weekly and shine forth from our best display cabinet in our love nest in England as a constant reminder of our voyage of love."

Serena shook her head in admiration, "Jeezus, Bry you are one devious bugger."

"Thank you, dear heart. Criminologists are fond of saying that it is the little things that betray murderers. I'm trusting that it will be little details like this that will convince investigators that I intended us both to return safely to shore. Now that's enough chat. Let's get some bubbly down."

He handed Serena one of the flutes and carefully filled it with the Verve Cliclot before pouring one equally carefully for himself.

"I don't know why you're being so bloody careful Bry. We're not going to drink the whole bottle, are we? One more glass after this will do me and that's me lot. I've got that swim to do."

"True but I've got a few bruises to collect and this vintage will help dull the pain; best anaesthetic there is."

"Sure? Won't you need to keep all your wits about you?"

"Don't worry, I know my limits. Everything will be fine. Now let's enjoy our last supper as Mr. and Mrs Fuller."

He brought out a white cardboard box full of sticky looking cakes. Serena loved the honey sweet baklava pastries but she wasn't going to risk cramp by eating more than one of them. And as they ate he went over what he intended to do.

"In a way I'm not sure that you should know all these details. You were never here were you? The less you know the less chance of you ever saying the wrong thing."

"Don't worry; I know how to keep my mouth shut."

"I understand that darling but what you don't know you can't tell. You must try and blank everything that happens here out of your mind."

"Don't worry Bry. I've been questioned by both British and Spanish brass arsed Drug Squads and they got nothing out of me even when several kilos of hash were within an arm's length of where I was sitting."

"That's my girl. Now let's concentrate on your schedule. We thoroughly checked your rucksack for that passport you found and you're sure you can get your hair styled in Athens to look like her".

"No problem" Serena answered. She had told Byron she had "inherited" the passport three years ago from a fellow barmaid, Daisy Smithers. It was everyone saying that she and Daisy were so alike they must be sisters that made her keep it. The Spanish Bar they worked in had become too heavily involved in the drugs scene for Serena's liking and she was looking for any exit route she could find. In the autumn season Daisy as she often did, had gone off with a punter for the night. Next morning she came back highly excited. The man wanted her to come and live with him in Barcelona right away. Serena thought she was taking too big a risk and tried to talk her out of it but Daisy wouldn't listen. She was so excited and packed so quickly that she left her passport under the mattress. Serena found it and while studying the photo realised she could easily use it if she ever needed to "disappear." So she hadn't forwarded it to the address that Daisy had left. When the girl didn't write to ask for it Serena took it as a gift from the gods.

Now it was going to help her provide the perfect alibi in what Byron liked to call the perfect murder. After her swim ashore she would collect the rucksack and catch a ferry to Athens where she would get herself made up to look ever more like Daisy than she naturally did. If all went well the next day she would fly to London using Daisy's passport. There would be no evidence that Serena Jane Thoms had ever been in Greece. In a few days she would travel to Spain using her own passport and stay there until Byron phoned. He'd obtained a couple of cheap mobile phones for them to use in an emergency or to renew contact with her when he was sure it was safe.

He had a gleam in his eye by the time he finished his second glass of bubbly. Reaching out and stroking her hand he said softly "It will be Hell without you these next few weeks." They pressed fiercely against each other. His touch made her quiver as he reached behind her and undid the top of her bikini. As their lips met and his tongue entered her mouth she felt her whole body thrill with anticipation. She pushed her hand into his shorts and seized his thickening penis. He released her briefly while he took off his shorts. He reached over and pulled the thin cushions from the thwarts and spread them across the bottom of the boat. While he was doing this she took off her bikini bottom with her free hand but also pulled the bag with her purse and sheath knife within easy reach. The gentleness of his touch and movements reassured her but she told herself "Better safe than sorry." He was a good lover, occasionally a bit rough but she didn't mind that. When he pushed her back down on the cushions he started to kiss her breasts with small light kisses. He moved down her body but before he got very far she pulled him into her. She wanted to feel every inch of him inside her now. She had rarely felt so randy. For most of her sex life she had had to fake her orgasms but she knew she wouldn't need to do any acting today. She matched the intensity of his thrusts with the fierceness of her reactions. She dug her nails into his back and tried to pull all of him into her. Every second it seemed that they must plunge disastrously off this rollercoaster of passion but miraculously they continued until she was overwhelmed with waves of pleasure. She heard him scream her name as he climaxed above her. They clung sensuously together, their bodies wrapping each other in a blanket of warmth and tenderness.

Afterwards as they lay blissfully exhausted Serena tried to work out why this time had been better than anything she had ever experienced. Perhaps it was her anticipation that he might murder her? Or was it a subconscious fear that this could be the last time, perhaps for ever, if Byron was found guilty of Lucy's murder?

She concentrated fiercely on every thought and feeling; burning them into the CD of her mind. This was a record she was determined to play repeatedly for the rest of her life.

The warmth of the sun eventually forced them to move. Byron reached out for the Champagne bottle and shook it. "There's still a good drop left." Serena let him fill her glass to the brim. Moments like those she had just experience deserved to be celebrated. Byron suddenly said "You ought to be bathed in bubbly every night after a performance like that." He spoke with such sincerity that Serena found herself blushing. What the hell was happening to her?

Her thoughts were interrupted by Byron standing up to look around him. "There's a couple of boats seaward but they're going at such a lick that I don't think they'll be around for long. Let's see if we can get this tub a bit further inshore so that you won't have so far to swim." When he got the boat underway again he told Serena to take the tiller while he studied the charts and the coastline. After about fifteen minutes he turned the boat once again into the wind and anchored up. "I think this will be as good as we will get" he said holding the chart out to her. All she could see was a series of wavy lines. "Don't make any sense to me, Bry. Where are we?"

He turned the map and showed how the coastline opposite matched the map "Look, we're here in this bay. It's only a few hundred yards ashore but these lines show the beach is very steep. You can see it's just a mass of rocks and there doesn't seem any easy path up to the main road. However, if you swim directly towards those three big rocks in a row until you're about the length of a football pitch away and then turn left and swim around to this next bay it has a sandy sloping beach that will make it easy for you to land. That's the one where we hid the rucksack. It's a popular beach so there's no reason why anybody should notice you." He pointed to a thin red line, "This is a path you want. It's at the far end of the beach from where you'll come ashore but walking's easier than swimming. After you get the rucksack you'll have about 2 miles to walk into town unless there's a bus. It would be all right to catch that but I don't think it would be wise to accept any lifts from motorists; do you?" She agreed. At the very least there was bound to be questions from anyone who picked her up. The less she was noticed the less she would be remembered.

After Byron got dressed he turned away from her and knelt down in the boat saying "After the pleasure, the pain. Now I'll find our how good Verve Cliquot is as an anaesthetic." He told her to squat down and keep a firm hold on the side of the boat. Then he got her to hold the end of the boom. "Now bang it into my back of my head as hard as you can,"

"Really hard? You're sure?"

"Yes, it's got be a severe enough blow to make my claim that I was knocked temporarily unconscious feasible. My recollections of what happened will returned to me bit by bit as I recover from this terrible trauma. We will have pulled up the anchor and just be getting under way again after our bout of drunken passion. I will be kneeling up attending to the sail so dear landlubber Lucy will have to take the tiller. She will foolishly let the boat turn side on to the wind so that the boom swings across and hits me in the back of the head almost knocking me over the side. I'll be all confused and bewildered. The next thing I will remember is Lucy landing on top of me. Unfortunately, her lunging to help me puts her weight plus mine all on one side of the boat and causes it to capsize. I am swept under the boat and come up on the far side of the upturned boat away from Lucy. The terrible tragedy will be that we took our lifejackets off to make passionate love. Sex is such a monster isn't it? No one will be able to deny that a non swimmer like Lucy could easily drown. It will be just like the last capsize here where the woman's body was never found. The three who were rescued were clinging to the capsized boat and I will likewise be the fortunate one who manages to get hold of the boat again. Lucky bastard aren't I? Now hit me with that fucking boom and let's get this over with."

"One last kiss."

They held each other fiercely and kissed passionately.

"Now do it."

She took a couple of deep breaths and swung the boom into the back of his head.

"Again. Harder."

She closed her eyes and swung the boom once more at his scull. The impact jarred it out of her hand. When she opened her eyes there was blood seeping from the back of his head. .

"Byron!"

He turned to her. He was trying to smile but he couldn't disguise the pain in his eyes. "Well done, girl. I'll manage, don't worry. On your way."

CHAPTER 22

Paul could not stop himself from dancing a little jig as he opened his front door. He'd really cooked Fuller's goose this time. It was all so simple. Why hadn't he phoned the police from a public call box before? It was seeing the antiseptic soap in the toilets that had given him the idea of sterilising the handset. If only he'd thought of that on the night of the murder. He had plenty of antiseptic materials at home. But then he might not have found a phone box that was working. It was all for the best now. He'd been clever, just telling them what he'd seen and the location of the house and when Fuller would be back. Telling them he was a gentleman of the road who was round the back of the houses in Meldrum Avenue seeking somewhere to shelter for the night was a master stroke. Said he was traumatized by the murder because of what he'd seen while serving in Bosnia. That's why it had taken him so long to report it.

But, it wasn't just what he'd said; it was what he'd left out that showed the superior quality of his mind. He'd not mentioned the spacesuit. That was too surreal. All he'd said after that was "This is not a hoax." They weren't going to catch him by keeping him talking. He was too clever for that.

Perhaps by the time the police had arrested and charged this Byron Fuller he'd have found a way to make sure he got the credit due to him. He should be rewarded for doing his duty as a citizen.

After dinner he sat down to read the book he'd found at the car boot sale last Sunday. It was Agatha Christie's *Cards on the Table.* He'd been collecting her work for years. Only 14 more to go and he'd have every one of her 52 detective novels. That would be a real accomplishment

He looked proudly over to his specially built bookshelves where her works were displayed. As always he looked first at Ten Little Niggers. None of those emasculated politically correct titles like *Ten Little Indians* for him. *Ten Little Niggers* was what Agatha had called it and that was good enough for him.

He had liked her work right from the first of her books he'd read as a teenager, *Murder on the Blue Train*. In later years and especially with the Hercule Poirot mysteries he'd got into the habit when he'd reached the last chapters of going through the book

87

again and making notes of all the characters he thought could be the murderer. He scrupulously wrote down his choice before reading the denouements. He was right about one in five times which he considered pretty good.

Besides her ingenious murder plots he liked her observations on life. Whenever he was asked to speak at Cricket Club dinners he always referred to his bachelor status and quoted what one of her characters said in *Five Little Pigs*, "Never get married, old boy. Wait for Hell till after this life." It always got a laugh although he knew that the women didn't like it.

What did he care! He was a man. If only he didn't have to worry about the threatened redundancies at work. After all his years of service it was disgraceful that they should even think of including him in their list of candidates. Reluctantly he put down his book. He just couldn't concentrate tonight.

He decided to go out and see if he could strike lucky with his "bird spotting." That's what he called his voyeurism in the summer. It gave him an excuse to carry a pair of binoculars. Over the years he had learned the most likely spots were he might see some action He picked up his Pocket Book of Woodland Birds, his notebook and binoculars. Kaiser had followed him around like a Siamese twin while he did so. He always knew when a walk was imminent. Paul took down his extension lead. He couldn't let him roam free on these walks. There was always the possibility he might accidentally disturb a courting couple before Paul got them in his sights. But it would be cruel to keep him on a short lead in a wood when there were so many smells for him to enjoy. The extension gave him some freedom and he could be reeled in quickly if necessary.

It was only a twenty five minute drive to the woods. He counted ten cars in the car park. Some of them would be dog walkers like him but with a bit of luck there might be a few brazen lovers amongst them. The dog walkers were a nuisance for they would stop and admire Kaiser. It was tiresome having to point out that the correct breed name for his pet was "German Shepherd" not "Alsatian." He always had to have at least a brief chat with them and praise their animals even if they were common mongrels. Being too abrupt might make them remember him if later there was any publicity about "peeping Toms" in the area.

He set off on a path that he knew led to the densest part of the woods.

For over an hour he crept among the trees, keeping Kaiser on the lead. The only person he saw was a woman with two black Labradors, but they were far enough away for him to turn off on another path and avoid them. He rested for a while in a small copse that overlooked a grassy hollow where he had many years ago seen a couple passionately embracing. But the woman had suddenly stood up and marched away leaving the man to scramble after her. She'd come right past his hideout. He remembered she was well past the first flush of youth, with a face that wouldn't have looked out of place on a Pekinese. Paul thought she ought to have been grateful for anything she was offered. The man that was hurrying after her was no oil painting either. He often wondered if they'd ever married.

He decided to go past the gravel pits and over to the part of the wood furthest from the car park. Five minutes walking brought him to a path that forked into three separate trails. He was deciding which one to take when Kaiser suddenly stood still with his ears erect. Paul crept up to him. He listened intently but all he heard was a blackbird's territorial song. Only the fact that Kaiser stayed alert kept him where he was. Then he heard a soft moan. Instantly he knew it was not a moan of pain but of sexual pleasure. Paul shivered with excitement. It had come from somewhere to his left. He was afraid to reel in the extension lead in case the noise alerted the lovers. Instead he gathered the lead in hand over hand and taking care not to tread on any loose twigs inched slowly forward. He had gone only a little way when he heard an excited voice repeating "Tim, Tim." It was so close Paul froze. He stood transfixed until he heard sounds of bodies moving, followed by a faint click. The smell of cigarette smoke drifted towards him.

He was too late. He'd missed the climax. Damn. Damn. Damn. He leant forward, ready to move quickly away if he heard any movements that indicated they were getting up. But everything was still. Paul's hopes began to rise. Perhaps this was only an interlude. They could easily begin again, especially if they were young. He tip-toed around a massive oak. The couple were lying on their sides facing each other, they... he pulled his head back so quickly that for a few seconds he was sure he must have given himself away. He felt sick with disgust. They were two men. He wanted to vomit. He hated homosexuals. He stepped back on the path. For a moment he toyed with the idea of pointing Kaiser towards the spot when they were sitting so that he could noisily follow him and disturb them. A long hard stare and a disgusted "Excuse me" would let them know what he thought of them but one of them looked rather well built so he decided against it. Nevertheless, he whistled as he marched away.

He was so upset that he took no notice of where he was going. It was only the sound of voices approaching that made him slow down. Two men came round the bend in front of him. Two men, one of them wearing a dog collar! He thought they were going to walk shamefacedly past him but the priest stopped and after a brief" Good evening "added "What a magnificent animal. May I stroke him?" Paul wanted to say "Most certainly not" but the words stuck in his throat. The priest's voice was normal, not at all like a limp-wristed homosexual's. His companion's was also reassuringly manly when he added his praises. They must just be two friends out for a stroll. He was glad he hadn't said anything rude. After a few more pleasantries they walked on. Paul walked around the bend, stopped for a second and then crept back. The track was long and straight; he had a good view of them. They were walking along holding hands! For the second time that night he felt nauseated. He was getting out of here fast. If this was a place where people like that came he might meet one on his own and be accosted. Thank God he had Kaiser with him.

Something ought to be done about these perverts. He would write to the local paper telling them how a pleasant evening's stroll had been ruined by their behaviour. It didn't publish your name and address if you requested anonymity. The only trouble with that was then no one would know he was standing up for this country's moral standards. To think that our great nation which once had an Empire on which the sun never set had come to this! People should be allowed to protest without having to hide their identity. But it would be fatal for his career if his disgust at homosexuality became known. Not a month passed at work without some memo arriving on his desk saying the council was now making changes to accommodate the lame, the halt and the blind, and insisting that the rights of blacks and Muslims and even Pagans must be respected.

He was so preoccupied with his thoughts that when he came to the end of the wood he was surprised how dark it had become. He'd expected to walk out into early twilight. There was a road on the other side of the wire fence in front of him and a passing car had its sidelights on. He followed the path alongside the fence until he came to a car park. He recognized it as the one on the opposite side of the wood to where he was parked. It would be well over a mile by road to his car; he didn't fancy going back through the wood. As he walked along he had to keep stopping and squeezing himself and Kaiser in close to the hedge when cars passed for there was no footpath. It was a relief when he came to a gateway which he remembered led to a path which skirted this edge of the wood and went diagonally across the field to the car park. It would be much quicker that way.

It still seemed a long time until he could see the outline of his car. When he got closer he noticed that now there was only one other vehicle in the car park, a pick up truck. He could see the glow of cigarettes in its cabin. Afraid of another homosexual encounter he studiously kept his eyes off it as he went to the back of his car to load Kaiser into his safety cage. "We'll soon be home old boy" he said as he stroked his pet's head before pulling down the rear door. He was walking around to the driver's door when he heard the sound of feet on gravel. Three men had got out of the pickup.

"Have a good time tonight mate?" one of them asked.

Paul was perplexed by the question. He decided to ignore it and reached out for his car door but two of the men rushed up and stood so close to it he couldn't open it.

"Are you deaf, mate? I asked you a question."

Paul began to feel afraid. They were so close he could smell the beer on their breath. If only he hadn't put Kaiser in his cage. He wondered if he could get quickly back to reopen it but as if he could read his mind the third man moved behind him so that he was surrounded. "Dear God," he prayed, "don't let this be a homosexual rape." How could he carry on living if that happened?

Speaking in his most authoritive voice he said "I've been for a walk with my dog as you can clearly see. Now if you'll be so good as to stand aside I'll be on my way."

One of the two men in front of him snickered and said to the others "Don't he talk posh?"

The man behind said "His mates must love it when he speaks to them like that."

Paul was perplexed. In a softer tone he said "Look, I've been for a long walk. My dog…"

"A long walk? More likely a long wank" interrupted the man who had so far been silent.

Paul was so amazed that his fear momentarily left him. " How dare you" he spluttered. "You can see my dog in the car."

"O Yes. And you've been walking all this time in the dark? What are you? The sort of poof who likes doing it with animals?"

"Yeah, real perverts some of them"

Before Paul could reply, the man behind him punched him in the back. The others took it as a signal to join in the attack, punching and kicking him even when he fell down. "Pervert, Pervert, Pervert" they chanted as they continued hitting him until he lost consciousness. Even then one of them bent down and stubbed his cigarette out on his face before they returned to the pick up and drove away laughing.

Paul might have lain there beside his car all night had not Kaiser's howls eventually forced the retired couple who lived opposite the car park to come and investigate. When he opened his eyes again he was lying in a hospital bed.

CHAPTER 23

Serena turned over on her back and floated to give her arms a rest and her back some respite from being baked by the sun. This was by far the hottest day she'd known here and the shore remained heartbreakingly distant. Even though she had been swimming a couple of miles every week since she knew of Byron's plan she was finding it difficult. It seemed as if she'd been trying forever to round the headland to the next bay. Surely it must appear soon. When she turned back to start swimming again, her heart lifted. She could see a few meters of sand. She resumed her swim with renewed vigour but it was still over twenty minutes before the figures on the beach were recognizable. She noticed a diving platform about a hundred metres along to her left. She decided to continue to swim inland for a bit so that when she turned and swam towards it would appear that she had swum out from the beach. There were young men and girls jumping on and off the platform. She swam to the side behind them and gasped the nearest float. When she'd got her breath back she looked at her watch. Christ! It was over an hour since she'd left Byron. Blood had still been trickling down the back of his neck when she'd turned for one last look. What if he suffered concussion or something?

Byron had felt the current pulling the dingy along for quite a while now. This would definitely be the area in which to capsize. He steered a bit closer inland. There was nothing but cliffs of bare grey rock to be seen. No chance of anyone climbing ashore here. It would be good seamanship to cling to the hull of the upturned dinghy. He could explain his failure in not helping Lucy to do likewise by saying he must have temporarily blacked out. His not seeing her could easily be accounted for by his coming up on the opposite side of the dingy. He'd have no clear recollection of what happened; poor traumatised him. His head ached and he felt a bit sick. He should have drunk less and eaten more. The current seemed to have got stronger. If he went into the water here they would never believe he had been strong enough to swim after and catch the dinghy, especially when he was going to tell them he was dazed for "he didn't know how long after it happened." His story had to be believable. He looked around him to see…those dark specks ahead; could they be what he was hoping for? Had his interpretation of the charts been right? He tightened the jib, trimmed the mainsail and put his feet under the toe straps so that he could lean out and take full advantage of the wind to cut across the current. Five minutes later he was shouting with joy. Talk about fortune favouring the brave? It didn't do badly for killers either. Sticking up a few feet out of the water like the plates on the back of some prehistoric monster was a row of jagged rocks. He eased the mainsail to cut his speed. No sense in risking the bottom been torn out of the boat by submerged rocks. He needed to make sure everything was right before his "accident "occurred. He looked again at the cliffs ashore; there was little to distinguish one from the other. He could be as vague as he liked about where they'd capsized.

He eased everything off and was gratified to see that the dinghy was heading straight for the row of rocks. His story would be that he'd spent a long time in the water and that it was only by a miracle that he'd caught sight of the white hull and blue sail wedged in them. He checked his charts; he was sure that there were no shallows here. His study reassured him. It was over 20 fathoms deep all around here. Satisfied, he threw them overboard.

He tied a litre bottle of mineral water to his lifejacket. He reckoned it would be safe to keep it on for another half hour before throwing it away. He was already 70 minutes overdue. They were bound to start searching soon. The man at the marina had seen which direction they'd sailed. The two rubber inflatables he'd seen the lifeguards using yesterday had powerful twin motors. It wouldn't take them long to reach him. At least he hoped it wouldn't because he was aching all over. The trouble with foreigners was you could never rely on them. You'd think they'd be on their toes after the previous tragedy. He'd just have to hope for the best. Still, being battered and a bit sunburnt would make his story more convincing. Nevertheless, the last thing he did before he capsized the dinghy was to tuck the beach towel he'd bought this morning under his life jacket. It would help to keep the sun off his head and shoulders until help came.

Back at the boatyard Leontas Meteerus was a happy man. If he'd had a few more customers for his boat hire business today he'd be even happier. But it was 34 degrees now. The beach was almost deserted and even the English tourists were staying close to the pools in the hotels. Only three boats were out on hire and they were all due back soon. He'd have to be careful not to let that fat Englishwoman see him laugh at her again. He was sure she'd noticed him this morning. Even his wife Lydia who was expecting a baby in two weeks wasn't as fat. The baby was why he was so happy. Lydia had miscarried at three months with their first child but this time she would have gone the full term. He was going to be a father in just 14 days, maybe less. That would shut....His phone rang....it was his father. "Leo. Your mother's gone to the hospital with Lydia. She says you're not to worry. The baby's decided it can't wait any longer that's all. She says to remind you that you came almost a month early and...."

Leontas interrupted his father, "I'm going to the hospital. I've got to be there when my son is born. But there are three boats still out. You must come down ..."

"We've already thought of that. Your cousin Aeneas is on his way down to you on his scooter. He'll be with you any minute now. Now don't worry. Your mother said to tell you not to drive like a madman up to the hospital. We don't want the baby to lose its father before it gets into the world."

"Yes. Yes. You're sure it's alright? Lydia hasn't fallen or hurt herself."

"No. Nothing like that."

"You swear papa."

"Yes, yes. I was around when you and when each one of your four brothers popped out and this is just the same. I know what I'm talking..."

Leontas interrupted him as he heard the busy bee sound of a scooter: "Papa. Aeneas is here. Goodbye."

He grabbed his car keys and went out to meet his cousin. Aeneas wasn't very bright but he'd often helped Leontas when he was busy. He knew how to stow the boats and lock up. He wouldn't be able to fill out the forms if any new customers came along but that was most unlikely in this heat.

There was a big smile on Aeneas's face as he got off his scooter. "Hallo papa. You're going to…"

"Never mind that now. There are three boats still out. Their numbers are on the board. You know what to do."

"Yes papa."

Leontas didn't bother to reply. He ran to his car and roared off.

Aeneas settled himself down in the office to watch a quiz show on the black and white television. He was amazed that people could be so clever. In the next half hour two of the boats returned and he helped the people ashore and returned their deposits. One of them gave him 10 Euros tip. Now there was only one more boat to come in. At first he kept looking for it every few minutes but after a while he gave up. People often hired the boats for a whole day, especially if they wanted to picnic on one of the smaller islands out to the west. Leo hadn't said when this last one was due. It was only just after half past three. It wasn't unusual for a boat not to come sailing back until six or seven o'clock. He didn't mind waiting. He liked being in charge here.

He phoned a couple of times to see if the baby had come but his uncle said not yet. It wasn't until just before seven o'clock when it looked as if there would soon be a thunderstorm and there was no sight of any of a blue sail on the horizon that he phoned his uncle and told him the boat still hadn't come in. After getting him to check to see if there was any paperwork in the office saying how long the boat had been hired for, his uncle said "Give it another half an hour and if it still isn't in sight, go and tell the harbourmaster. If he isn't around or you know where he'll be. …Oh and you're an uncle now" .He put the phone down before Andreas could ask if it was a boy or a girl.

The thunderstorm had broken out at sea while they were talking. Aeneas wasn't as dumb as people thought; it just took him longer than most to work things out. But he was enough of a seaman to know that any little boat caught out in a storm of this intensity was going to need help. He closed the office immediately and rode his scooter full throttle to the police station at the end of the quay. Like all the other local seamen he knew the harbourmaster's office closed at 7o'clock and it was past that now.

There used to be a notice on door telling people they'd find him in the Argonaut Bar but everyone knew the harbourmaster had recently remarried and liked to get home quickly to his young wife. Aeneas decided he wouldn't be the one to disturb the harbourmaster and went directly to the police. There he was subjected to a thorough questioning before he was taken seriously enough for the harbourmaster to be phoned and a rescue operation set in motion.

It was after 10 o'clock when the powerful beams of the searchlight on one of the inflatables shone on Byron. He had been straddling the upturned hull for over eight hours and was babbling deliriously. Only the fact that he had been able to tie himself to the dinghy's dagger board had prevented him from being swept away. He was badly dehydrated for the bottle of mineral water had slipped from his grasp many hours ago. His back and thighs were badly burnt. His hands and right leg were a mass of cuts and bruises from being battered against the rocks. The first sailor to reach him thought it would be a miracle if he survived

CHAPTER 24

In England Paul was also in pain. He was sure the hospital should be giving him stronger painkillers. He'd never been free from pain during the three days he'd been there. The burn on his face felt enormous. But far worse than the pain had been the police questioning. They'd straight away assumed that he was a homosexual. They'd paid little attention to his telling them he was bird watching even though they admitted they'd read his notebook. "Didn't have much luck that night" was all one of them had said. He'd used Kaiser as his excuse for staying so late in the forest, saying he'd run after a fox and it was dark by the time he was reunited with him. They'd not shown much belief in that either. He'd tried to describe the men who attacked him but he couldn't remember much about any of them. The police had asked him to come down to the station when he was better and make a full statement. He wasn't going to do that. Let them come to him if they wanted.

It had been bad enough dealing with the police but his father had been much worse. Paul realised only when it was too late that he should never have said to him that Kaiser had run after a fox. His father often looked after Kaiser and knew the dog was far too obedient not to come back when he was called. He'd been astounded by the old man's attitude. Earl Haig Thewell had served 25 years in the army, the last 5 as Colour Sergeant. Paul had almost choked with indignation when his father said, "I always had my doubts about you, Boy. Don't worry; I knew many a shirt lifter in the Services even though it was a dismissible offence in my time. Some of them were quite good blokes and we weren't bothered as long as they didn't make it too obvious. I got along fine with them" Then with a horrible cackle that sprayed spittle and God knows what else all over Paul's face he added "Just made sure I didn't turn my back on them."

All Paul's indignant protests were in vain. His father eventually said with obvious insincerity "O.K. Boy, whatever you say" and then started to talk about how much he was enjoying looking after Kaiser. "If you want to take a holiday after they let you out, don't worry about Kaiser. He's perfectly happy with me. Gets three walks a day, he does, although the middle one is just down to the pub. They think the world of him there. Drinks Bitter out of a bowl he does. You didn't know he liked a drop did you?"

Normally Paul would have ordered the old man not to take Kaiser anywhere near his pub but he was too obsessed with thoughts of what being labelled as a homosexual would do to his reputation to do more than say "You shouldn't allow him to do that." He couldn't believe how quickly every thing had gone wrong. It was preposterous he could be labelled as a homosexual when he hated them so much. He was sure his career as an umpire would be finished. And work! If they found out what would happen to him it would be a disaster. He'd phoned to say he was ill in hospital but had said nothing about the assault. As far as he knew nobody in the office lived in Lamdon. But then he didn't know where any of them lived. He should have taken more interest in his staff's life outside work. He'd been surprised when he realised he'd never had a long conversation with any of them in the thirty years he'd worked in the Council offices unless it was related to Council business. "But then" he thought brightening up a little "if he didn't know much about them then perhaps they didn't know much about him." He hoped to God it stayed that way.

A reporter from the weekly Lamdon Chronicle had turned up at his hospital bed but he'd told the young man he'd nothing say and if the paper printed his name he'd sue them. Then he'd rung for a nurse to get rid of him. The hospital had assured him that they never gave a patient's name to the Press but how had the man known to come to his bed?

When he was eventually allowed home he'd just taken his coat off when he heard his letterbox rattle. It was the local weekly paper being delivered. He grabbed it and hurried into the living room praying that the news of his attack wouldn't be on the front page. It wasn't. What was there was so startling he had to sit down. Under the headline HOLIDAY TRAGEDY he read, *"Local woman, Mrs. Lucy Fuller is missing presumed drowned after the dingy she was sailing in with her husband Mr. Byron Fuller off the Greek island of Letsos capsized. Full story page5."*

He started at the words in disbelief. Fuller couldn't have killed two women in one week. It was ridiculous. He fumbled his way to page 5. There was a photo of Fuller and his wife at a racecourse. He studied it carefully but he couldn't tell for sure if the woman on the page was the one he saw being strangled. A wide flower strewn hat hid most of her face. But it couldn't be her. It was impossible. He'd seen her killed. Fuller had kept pressing her down on the bed. She couldn't have come round after that. If she had she certainly wouldn't have gone off on holiday with him. Women were unbelievably stupid and irrational but surely not even the most gullible would be that daft.

He was so confused by what he'd read he momentarily forgot he'd opened the paper to see if there was anything about his attack. When he remembered; he had only to turn one more page and there it was.

LOCAL MAN ATTACKED IN DARESBURY FOREST.

A Lamdon resident has become the fourth man to be attacked in Daresbury Forest in the last six weeks. After returning to his car and putting his pet Alsatian aboard he was set upon by what is believed to be a group of three men who alighted from a nearby pick up truck. This is the fourth such attack on a man in these woods in the past six weeks. He was left unconscious beside his car and could have remained there all night if the continued howls of his faithful dog had not alerted the Bryddon family who live opposite the car park. Mr Bryddon said "We had just switched on the BBC ten o'clock news when we became aware of a dog howling. We knew that none of our neighbours let their pets out at that time of night. We assumed it might be a lost animal looking for its owner. When the howls continued we went outside and it was quite evident they were coming from the car park. My wife and I went over and we found a man lying unconscious beside his car with a dog inside it howling his head off. We'd heard of other attacks on men in past weeks and so we called the police as well as an ambulance. ... "

Paul read on with increasing anger. There was not one word to indicate that he was an innocent man walking his dog... *"Increasing complaints from Forest users of homosexual activities taking place...police would not confirm or deny that the attackers might be a homophobic gang...police patrols to be stepped up...victim wishes to remain anonymous..."* Perhaps he shouldn't have been so abrupt with the reporter. He should have taken the time to explain how Kaiser had run away after a fox. He knew all his neighbours read this rag. If that nosey bitch two doors away, Mrs. Happenton identified him it would be all over the town in no time. If she'd seen the taxi bringing him home she was probably already thinking up some excuse to visit him. This bloody bandage on his head was such a giveaway.

He'd have to avoid her at all costs. He'd not take Kaiser for a walk locally for a few weeks. Drive out somewhere. Keep his hat on even in the car. But...then...if she didn't see him on his usual walks she might come "just to see if you're all right." That's what she'd done ten years ago when he'd had the flu. He'd had a terrible job getting rid of her. His heart sank when he remembered she was often in her garden when went out with Kaiser. Always spoke to him. He'd have to go away. Take a holiday until his wounds had healed. That's what he'd do. But, his absence would give Myra more chances to undermine his position, It was all so horrible, He... A stabbing pain above is right eye interrupted his thoughts. He brushed the paper aside and went to get the painkillers the hospital had given him. He'd take double the dose they said. He could buy more at the chemist. Mr. Singh would advise him. Even if he was coloured he was a gentleman. He was better than any of the local doctors.

He pushed the newspaper aside. It was all such an unbelievable mess. He'd planned to drive over to his father's and collect Kaiser but he didn't feel like it now. He'd phone the old man and ask him to walk Kaiser round. He could pay for a taxi to take his father home again if he didn't want to walk back. He'd ignore his homosexual jibes. Show him his bird book and his notebooks. That was one of the unexpected benefits of his voyeurism. He really had become interested in identifying birds. He'd become a genuine "twitcher"; interested in getting as many different species as possible ticked off in his list. He'd got over 60 recorded so far. His father knew of his interest in birds. Why shouldn't he believe he was looking for a little owl?

Feeling slightly better he took his tea into the living room and sat down to read about Fuller's boating accident again. He read and reread it but it still didn't make sense, It must be some tart he'd picked up while on holiday. Fuller would be good at that. The Greeks might have got it all wrong. There were no direct quotes from Fuller in the piece. He was in hospital and it seemed he'd been lucky to survive. It might not be such a puzzle after all. He decided to put it all to the back of his mind for a while; he was in no fit state to think logically at the moment.

CHAPTER 25

Serena read of Byron's ordeal in the European edition of THE TIMES while she waited for her flight at Athens airport. She was upset it had taken so long to rescue him but thankful he was at least in hospital receiving treatment. She knew Byron was one tough cookie. He would pull through. She'd no doubts about that. The most satisfying thing was that the report was headlined "WIFE FEARED DROWNED." Their plan had worked. It was all being reported as an accident. If the Greek police investigation didn't turn up anything different they were going to get away with murder. That meant she and Byron would be bound together forever. They could never fall out. If they married it would certainly be a new slant on "until death do us part."

Her life had been far from uneventful since she'd waded ashore. It had been an exhausting walk to recover her rucksack and she'd had to wait ages for a local bus back to the capital. She'd missed the last ferry to Athens and had to stay overnight on the island. She thought of booking into a hotel but decided against it. A single woman staying for only one night might easily be remembered. Tired though she was she went to the strip of tourist bars where drink was cheap and brains befuddled. She danced with all the blokes who asked her and bought her drinks until she landed one who was sober enough to also want to eat. She had found out he was staying in a local hotel and had a room of his own before she agreed to come with him for a meal. She made sure he drank twice as much as she did. When they finished eating she allowed him to think that his silver tongue had persuaded her that the gates of paradise would open wide for her if she came back to his hotel room. As soon as the door closed behind them she had to endure a long bout of French kissing and English groping before she excused herself to go to the bathroom to "get ready for it." She stayed there half an hour enjoying a good soak in a luxuriously scented herbal bath. As she relaxed she thanked the advertisers who made men believe that having as many toiletries and bath oils as a woman were essential for success as a stud. When she came out he was as she expected fast asleep. She wrapped the light duvet around him, pulled the sheet up for herself and was soon asleep beside him. The alarm on her watch work her before six and she was dressed and on her way out of the room in less than 10 minutes. She toyed with relieving his wallet of one or two of its 100 euro notes but decided it wasn't worth the risk. Instead she printed in lipstick on the bathroom mirror "You were a tiger." She'd left feeling more virtuous than she had for many a long time.

Back in England she stayed in her flat a couple of days and saw several friends who was willing to swear on oath, if anyone asked, that she had been with them all this past week Next day she went to the agency for bar staff abroad that she had worked for many times before and left with a contact for work in a bar in Ibiza for the rest of the Summer Season.

In his bed in the Greek hospital Byron kept drifting in and out of consciousness for the first two days. On the morning of the third, his doctor decided he was well enough to be briefly question by the police. Two came to his bedside, a severe woman in civilian clothes and a villainous looking older uniformed man who appeared well capable of beating up anyone who didn't give him the answers he wanted. Before any of them could say a word he asked, "Where's my wife? Where is she?"

"Mr. Fuller" the woman said quietly in excellent English, "I assure you as soon as we have any definite news we will immediately inform you but..."

"She's not here? Not in this in hospital?" he interrupted; "Why? "

A nurse hurried past them and Byron allowed her to calm him down. He was determined to be seen as the deeply concerned but confused husband in this interview. As the nurse stepped away from him he heard her say something in Greek. He had picked up a little of the language during his frequent visits to the Islands and he was sure she'd said, "10 minutes, No more."

He was careful to keep eye contact with the woman as she introduced herself as detective Matsoukis and the uniformed officer as sergeant Galanopulos. She wasted no time in asking if he remembered about how he came to be in the water.

He told them his prepared story in fits and starts being careful to keep enquiring about Lucy and repeating how little he remembered after the metal boom hit him on the back of the head. The sergeant watched him like a hawk eyeing its prey while Matsoukis questioned him. Byron was glad to be able to concentrate on her; he found Galanopoulos's scrutiny unsettling. They seemed to accept every thing he said and when the nurse came back they made no effort to prolong their stay He felt tired after the interview and settled back to get some sleep. As he relaxed he examined his surroundings. He was in a spotlessly clean private room with an air conditioner humming quietly somewhere. He drifted off to sleep thinking how clever he had been buying the most expensive medical insurance available.

The next time he opened his eyes he immediately closed them again. He waited hoping it was a nightmare but the woman's voice he heard yelling "Nurse, Nurse" was worse than any nightmare. Dot was there. "Don't pretend you're asleep with me, you bastard" she snarled breathing into his face; "You killed my daughter. You'll fucking well pay for it." As footsteps hurried nearer Dot became all Florence Nightingaley, saying excitedly "He opened his eyes, nurse."

Dot coming here was the last thing he'd expected. He cursed himself for not foreseeing it. Bloody East Enders. Family was God to them. He'd know that but he'd not expected to have to face her until he got back to England. Then he'd have had the Greek authorities' acceptance that it was an accident to shut her up. Now, Christ knows what she was telling them. They wouldn't listen to her, would they? Surely they'd think she was distraught with grief. The nurse's voice interrupted his thoughts, "Mr. Fuller. You have visitor. Your mothers has come."

The idea was so ludicrous that he had difficulty preventing himself from smiling. Instead he twisted his face into a grimace of pain. As the nurse fussed around him he looked straight at the red faced woman glaring at him and haltingly gasped "I'm so sorry Dot. I'm still confused as to what happened. They won' tell me anything. What have you heard?"

She didn't speak until the nurse left the room. "Lucy hasn't been found."

The pain in her face and voice was so acute that if he hadn't hated her so much he'd have felt some sympathy for her. But all he could think of was how quickly could he get rid of her. She was big trouble. She'd tell the police anything that presented him in a bad light. She hated him. Even if he could by some miracle get her to think it was a terrible accident she'd want him punished.

"How long?" he asked, "How long have I been in here?"

"You mean how long since you pushed Luce overboard, you fucking bastard."

"Dot. I nearly died. What have they told you about Lucy? They're still searching? They've not stopped have they?"

"What the fuck do you care? You've wanted to get rid of Luce for along time."

"That's rubbish. Now tell me. What's happening?

She gave him a long hard stare before she grudgingly said, "They say they're still looking but it looks like they're doing bugger all to me. Lenny's out there on a speedboat. He's not giving up."

Byron was glad he'd looked down as she spoke otherwise she'd have seen the fear in his face. Lenny was a thug. A thug who thought he could do as he liked because of his gangster bosses. Byron had been careful to keep well out of his way during his years with Lucy. Immediately after his first meeting he'd made enquires about Lenny. Nothing he found out gave him any cause for joy. A few years ago it seems as if Lenny and his mates were clearly in the frame for race fixing but it had all fizzled out. The chief witness against them had disappeared. Byron had often had a pint with the man, a gregarious gypsy, "Snake Eyes Smith." He was called that because of the heavy gold ring in the shape of an entwined snake with two small rubies as eyes that he wore. Some said Snake Eyes "had fled back to his native Ireland." Byron had hoped if he had; it was not in a coffin.

"Lenny'll be in to see you this evening. He'll help you remember better what happened."

"He can come if he wants, nobody's more anxious than me to get all this sorted out. This is a bloody awful country. Any one who wears a uniform here thinks they are God Almighty. They can stick you in jail for years if they feel like it."

Dot made no effort to hide her delight at the idea. He seized the chance to say something that he hoped would at least give her pause for thought.

"Look Dot. I know you don't like me. But do give me credit for a bit of common sense. If I wanted to harm Lucy do you think I'd do it in a country like this?"

He couldn't tell if she'd taken in what he was saying for she stood up abruptly and as she turned to leave sneered "I'll be back, with Lenny." As he watched her waddle her way out of the ward; he could hear the swish, swish of her stockings rubbing against her thighs. It reminded him of Lucy and of how embarrassed he'd felt as she'd swished alongside him.

He spent the rest of the afternoon trying to think of ways of foiling Lenny and Dot. It would be no use telling the Staff he didn't want them as visitors. Lenny would just barge his way in. He was sure they wouldn't let him discharge himself; the police would have told the hospital not to let him leave. He'd just have to try and bluff his way through. He drew some comfort from thinking at least Lenny wouldn't be able to assault him in here.

Nevertheless, that evening he was filled with dread every time his room door opened. As each hour passed he became more convinced that Lenny and Dot were deliberately making him wait just to torture him. Even when it passed ten o'clock and the nurse assured him that no more visitors would be allowed he couldn't settle. Those two were up to something

When he awoke next morning he expected to see them at his bedside but the morning passed without any sight of them. It was two o'clock before he had visitors, the same two police as yesterday. They didn't try to offer him any false hope that Lucy might still be alive. When he suggested she might have been picked up by a passing ship which had to continue on to its destination, the man said that the news would have been radioed ashore by now. The questioning gradually became more and more intense with the sergeant taking a much greater part in the examination. Although his English was far from fluent it was evident he knew a great deal about boats: he asked Byron many questions about his sailing experience. Byron told how he had regularly hired dinghies on his Greek holidays and emphasised he'd often sailed Enterprise dinghies before. He admitted he had no knowledge of the local waters and seized the chance to protest vehemently that he had been given no warning of the presence of any dangerous currents when he hired the boat. "I shall be taking this up with my lawyer when I return home" he told them. The woman answered coolly "As you wish, Mr Fuller" but he felt sure they were discomforted by his threat. He thought it best not to pursue that idea any further. The last thing he wanted was to antagonize them. He acted suitably embarrassed when he confessed that he and Lucy had taken their lifejackets off for sex. He said he thought Lucy had panicked when the boom had hit him, adding. "When I landed on top of her the boat just heeled over." He didn't like the look the woman gave him when he said, "My wife was rather generously proportioned, you see." When they asked how much he and Lucy had drunk, he first said he couldn't remember but eventually admitted they'd emptied the bottle of Verve Cliqco

All the time they were questioning him he was dreading Dot and Lenny barging in for he knew they would start accusing him of abusing Lucy for years. Dot would say anything to get the police to suspect him. She'd probably told them a bunch of lies about him already. He tried to find some way of introducing his mother in law's hatred of him into the conversation but neither of his interrogators would let him do anything other than answer their questions. As soon as one had finished the other came in with another. Neither expressed any sympathy with his hours of exposure clinging to the dinghy on the rocks. Although when he kept apologizing for how little he could remember the woman said "We have a proverb here in Greece Mr. Fuller, 'Ignorance of one's misfortunes is clear gain." Not knowing what to make of that he mumbled a brief "Thank you."

As they were leaving he thought of asking if he could go back to his hotel now that the doctors were letting him get up for 5 minutes or so but decided against it. Here was a better place to be questioned than a police cell. He'd hang on here as long as they would let him.

Now he was alone again the dread of Dot and Lenny returned. He crept to the door to see if there was a policeman sitting outside his room but the corridor was empty. The fucking police were the same the world over, you could never find one when you needed him.

CHAPTER 26

"It is an old maxim of mine that when you have excluded the impossible, whatever remains, however improbable, must be the truth"

Paul sat in the kitchen looking at the words of Sherlock Holmes which he'd copied out into his Day Book in his best italic script many years ago. He enjoyed knowing famous quotations. He'd got the Day Book out to help take his mind off his bruises. The medication didn't seem to be working, everywhere hurt when he moved. The burn on his face was the worst, eating was a painful process. He was in the kitchen because it wasn't overlooked. His doctor hadn't hesitated to sign him off for two weeks. "You can't be too careful with a head injury" were his parting words.

The only good thing was that none of the neighbour had visited him. He read the Sherlock Holmes quotation out aloud. He liked the sound of it and the inescapable logic of the words. He thought of the times he'd used its logic to solve the mystery and murder stories he read. It hadn't always worked but perhaps it might work for him now. This was a real life mystery, the most important he'd ever faced.

He opened The MELDRUM AVENUE MURDER file he'd made. He read again Wednesday's Weekly Gazette.

"I CAN'T REMEMBER" SAYS HUSBAND.

Mr. Byron Fuller whose wife Lucy has been missing since their hired dinghy capsized ten days ago off the coast of the Greek island of Lestos has said in a statement released by the Greek police that he has no clear recollection of the accident. "All I know is the metal boom swung across and hit the back of my head and that I fell into the water. My recollections are very hazy after that. The next clear memory I have is that I was in the water, with a strong current dragging me along. I have no memory of seeing the boat or my dear wife Lucy at any time. She must have been nearby but I never saw her nor heard her call out. It was tragic that she was not a swimmer and that we had both taken our lifejackets off because we felt uncomfortable in them.

What saved me was the dinghy getting trapped in a line of rocks. The current must have dragged it there and fortunately it took me in the same direction. I only saw it because its blue sail was snagged on the rocks. Seeing that was my Salvation, because only a few minutes after I began to swim towards it the sail disappeared. I've been told since that the mast must have snapped as the sail became waterlogged. Fortunately the unturned hull stayed trapped in the rocks and when I reached it I was able after several tries to clamber on to it. I was still only partially conscious, the pain in my head was crucifying. I spent the next hours looking around and calling for Lucy. I even gathered up enough strength to slip off the hull and dive underneath in case my wife might be trapped there. But everything was gone including the lifejackets. The only thing that remained was our beach towel which was trapped beneath one of the thwarts. Rescuing that was fortuitous for I was able to use it as a protection from the searing heat of the sun by constantly soaking it and draping it over my head and shoulders. My thighs got painfully burnt. It was I believe the hottest day of the year in Lestos.

Eventually I was lapsing in and out of consciousness. I was afraid that the boat would break up on the rocks. Then I saw a rigging line floating beside the hull and managed to fish it out of the water and tie myself to the dagger board. That's the last thing I remember until I woke up in hospital. I've been told I must have been over eight hours in the water. If it were not for the terrible loss of my wife I would say I was a very lucky man."

Mr.Fuller has been released from hospital but is staying on in Lestos to help the police with their inquiries and also in the hope that his wife's body might be found. "I want to bring her back to England with me" he said "so that her family and I will be able to have a suitable memorial erected to a wonderful woman who was not only my wife but also my best friend."

To Paul, the fact that Fuller's story was so convincing only proved how well it had been planned. That's what murderers did in detective stories. Fuller had probably expected to be rescued much quicker. The fact that he wasn't had worked in his favour by making him seem more of a victim. But Paul knew he was a killer, maybe even a double killer. He had seen him strangle one woman. If it had only been a sex game and she'd recovered and gone to Greece with him she was certainly dead now. On the other hand if the woman in the boat wasn't his wife, whoever she was Fuller had killed her too. She could be a mistress he'd got tired off just as he'd got tired of his wife. He might have got a new woman

109

altogether and wanted to get rid of both the old ones at the same time. .

What made him certain it was no accident was that at the weekend *The Mail on Sunday* carried a brief report of the event and mentioned that a similar tragedy had occurred two years ago in the same area. He'd searched the Web and found a report of a dinghy with two couples aboard capsizing there. It was as the newspaper said just two summers previously. Three of the occupants had been rescued but one body had never been found. Paul was sure Fuller had read about it and that was what had given him the idea of staging a repeat "accident." He could easily have knocked the woman on the boat unconscious, tied some rocks or even the anchor to her body and thrown her overboard. Or maybe he'd just drowned her after knocking her out and let the current take her away. But how could he be sure the body wouldn't be found?

If it was another woman why did Fuller kill her? Why did she go with him to Greece anyway? Her accompanying him must have been planned in advance. If that was the case then (Paul began to tremble with excitement) then…then… why should she not have known he was going to kill his wife? She could even have been some sort of accomplice. Maybe she'd even helped him dispose of his wife's body! If that was the case then she would always be a danger to Fuller. Women were notoriously loose lipped. If she and Fuller ever quarrelled in the future or if he took another mistress and she found out about it she could always expose him. Look at the wives who reported their husbands' tax fiddles to the authorities when they were abandoned in favour of another woman.

Paul looked again at Sherlock Holmes words. What he was thinking wasn't even improbable. It was perfectly reasonable. Above all it provided a motive for Fuller drowning the woman on the boat. It all fitted perfectly. He picked up his pen and wrote down all his conclusions in brief sentences. When he'd finished he surveyed all he'd done with great satisfaction. He'd always felt like this when he'd worked out some murder mystery. Often he'd be right but gallingly, more often he'd been wrong. His conclusions had all fitted but the final chapter had revealed that someone else had committed the crime. He had learned not to be too sure too early. Best to do what he always did now when he thought he'd unmasked the murderer in a book; put his conclusions away for a few days, try to forget about them and then come to them afresh. Doing that had worked for him before. He rearranged everything neatly on the table and got up to make his lunch.

After lunch he got the car out and drove to Bellsea so that he could walk Kaiser along the sea wall. Although the sun was shining, there was a cold wind coming off the sea and he had to walk briskly to keep warm. The white horses on the waves made him think what a cold calculating bastard Fuller must be to drown someone. He had read somewhere that drowning was one of the most horrible ways to die. He had come out here to distract his mind from Fuller but he couldn't stop thinking about him. Why was he still puzzling over it? He really must be strong and leave the whole thing for a day or two. So determined was he to follow his own advice that the first thing he did when he got home was to gather up everything on the table and put it away in his desk.

That night he tried to distract his mind from Fuller with the latest Iain Rankin but even tartan thuggery failed to hold his attention. He decided that an old friend might succeed where a new one failed. From his bookshelves he selected Agatha Christie's, *The Murder of Roger Ackroyd*. What a clever writer she was. No one before had ever though of having the murderer be the one to tell the story. He'd been able to hide his guilt because he was the narrator. Yet he'd not actually lied but he'd misdirected people by what he didn't tell. That's how Poirot had got unto him. If only he could do the same with Fuller. No, he wasn't going to think about him this evening. To hell with what he'd said. Paul hesitated...what was it he'd said? He was staying on in Greece in the hope that his wife's body might be found. "His wife's body." But how could he be absolutely sure that the body of the woman pretending to be his wife would never be found? The fact that a body had never been found from the previous capsize was no guarantee that the woman he murdered would not be found. Even bodies that had been weighed down with chains and rocks had eventually floated to the surface or had been dragged up in some fishermen's nets. It would be fatal for Fuller if the woman they found wasn't his wife. It wasn't until their third day on the island that the "accident" happened. If the woman had been pretending to be Fuller's wife all that time she must have known what happened to Fuller's real wife. Surely then she should have realised what danger she was in? Once she was out of the way there'd be no one to tell what he'd done. But, the question remained; what made Fuller so confident that the woman's body would never be found? How can you make sure a body never resurfaces?

By burying it on land? Paul almost dropped his pencil as the thought sunk in. Fuller could have killed the woman and come ashore and buried her. That was one sure way of ensuring her body would never be found at sea. He was so excited he had to get up and walk around the room. But before he was out of his seat his excitement vanished like the air out of a pricked balloon. There was a fatal flaw in his answer. Burying a body on the beach was risky. Even if he took care to select a deserted beach how could Fuller be sure he wouldn't be seen from the land? There was bound to be lots of holidaymakers as well as locals around. A man on his own digging a hole big enough to hide a body must be noticed. Even if he got it dug unobserved how could he be sure he wasn't seen carrying the body from the boat to the grave? No. it was too dangerous. It was just the same problem as before only transferred from the sea to the shore. The same problem? Then…then….why not the same answer? How could anyone be absolutely certain not to be seen burying a body on the shore? The same way as one could be sure a body would never be found at sea. By there not being one. No body, no danger. Paul found he was shaking again with excitement. What if Fuller and this woman had come ashore and she had gone to some prearranged hiding place? That could be it. It was so simple. The absolutely one hundred percent cast iron way to be sure that a body would never be found was for there not to be one. No body. No risk.

That would mean that the woman was definitely an accessory to murder. Fuller must trust her implicitly not to betray him. But then, how could she when she'd co-operated with him. She was as much involved in the murder as he was except for the actual killing. They had to trust each other. They would think that as long as they each kept quiet no one else would ever know what had happened to Fuller's wife. But they were wrong. He knew.

CHAPTER 27

Two uniformed police Byron hadn't seen before came into his room just after 10 o'clock Sunday morning. After they'd introduced themselves they immediately asked, "Mr. Fuller, you know a Mr. Leonard Smith?"

Byron had to think for a moment, he wasn't used to hearing Lenny called Leonard. "He's my wife's uncle."

"Has he been here?"

"No."

"You sure?"

Byron nodded so emphatically a pain shot across the front of his skull. "No. The only visitor I've had from England is his sister, Mrs. Dot Boothe. What about my wife? Have you found her?"

It was the policemen's turn to do some headshaking. Byron did his best to look suitably mortified. When the police remained silent Byron began to feel uncomfortable. He couldn't read their faces. He wished he could look away but was afraid it might hint at guilt of his part. On the other hand he didn't want to stare them out. He eased himself a bit more upright in the bed and said hesitantly, "It's three…or is it four days now."

Again all he got was a nod. Then one of them asked, "Mrs. Booze, you say she can take out from the hotel your wife's possessions?"

Paul was instantly alert. "Certainly not. No way. Mrs. Boothe doesn't like me. She's never liked me. Didn't want me to marry Lucy." Then in a flash of inspiration he added "She's a Gorgon."

The men didn't respond. They continued looking questionly at him.

"Jesus Christ", he thought, "Greek Comprehensives must be as shitty as ours."

"So, Mr. Fuller, no one had from you permission to go into your hotel room?"

"No. No. Has Dot, …Mrs. Boothe … tried to do that"

They nodded in unison. "Mrs. Booze tell... told... the receptionist that you asked her to gather up...collect... your wife's belongings."

"That's a lie. They didn't let her, did they?"

"No. The receptionist refused. Mrs. Boothe demanded to see the manager and he also refused. Mr Smith got angry."

"He would. He's a very violent man. He's been in trouble with the police in England."

"Yes." said the policeman who had done all the talking so far. Byron was surprised when the other one suddenly added "We know."

Byron thought he seemed inordinately pleased to be saying that. Then it dawned on him that Lenny must be in trouble if the police had gone so far as to get this information on him. "What's he done?"

"Mr.Smith tried to go behind the desk and take the keys to your room. Mr. Karamasis the manager go to stop him. Mr. Smith pushed him away very strongly."

"He hit his head on the desk" the other policeman added.

Byron was about to ask if Lenny had got hold of the keys when he thought it would be better to express some sympathy with the manager first. "That's terrible" he said," I hope that the manager wasn't hurt."

"His head hurt bad. He's in hospital, here."

"What about Lenny? Mr. Smith? I hope you've arrested him."

"Mr. Smith ran off. He not gets far. All the ways out from the island are being watched."

Again the other policeman broke in. "We want to know if he comes here. You understand?"

"I most certainly do. He'll get no help from me." While he was speaking Byron was thinking what Lenny would do to him if he got into this hospital room. "You've got police guarding me here, haven't you?"

"Yes. Many. We catch him don't worry. You say in court that you did not give him any permissions to go to your room? You do that?"

Byron hoped fervently he'd never have to do any such thing but that didn't stop him saying confidently "Yes. Of course."

The police didn't thank him or say anything other than "Good Bye" as they rose to leave. They were almost at the door when Byron yelled "Wait. Mr. Smith's got a motor boat. Dot told me he was using one to look for my wife."

One of the policemen hurried back to him while the other took up a radio from his belt and began speaking into it.

"Where did he get motorboat?"

"I don't know; must have hired it from one of the firms at the docks or somewhere."

"You know anything about this boat. How big? It's colour?"

"No. Nothing. All she said was he'd hired a motorboat. Sorry."

They hurried away, one of them still talking into his radio.

Byron let himself sink back unto his pillows. No wonder Dot hadn't been back to see him. Perhaps she was in the nick. She might have tried to prevent the hotel staff from nabbing Lenny. If she was, it would be great if they kept her there until he left the island. But that would be too much to hope for. The gods had smiled on him once; that was enough He knew if Dot came in that door she'd want him to swear he'd given her and Lenny permission to take Lucy's things. If he didn't Lenny or his mates would do him over when he got back home. There was no way he could avoid them forever. They were all bastards. Even if he got Lenny off they'd probably still do him over because Lucy was dead. They'd not accept it being an accident as any excuse. When one of their tribe was killed somebody had to pay. Why hadn't he thought of that? Jesus! What a mess. He'd have to write a letter or something and give it to a solicitor he could trust. Tell him to pass it on to the police if anything happened to him

If only Serena was here. She was a dragon. She'd know how to sort out Dot and Lenny. Since the Greek police hadn't mentioned her he assumed she'd got safe away.

He was discharged from hospital two days later. When he'd told the police he was staying on Letsos for a least another week in the hope that his wife's body might be recovered they'd told him he must inform them first before leaving the island. He was back in his hotel by mid-day.

CHAPTER 28

Serena felt the woman's resentment even though she was sitting three tables back from the bar. The woman was a muscular blonde, too heavy to be Scandinavian. She was probably Russian, certainly East European. There were lots of them with money to waste in Ibiza these days. She couldn't work out why the woman was so antagonistic, she was sure she'd never seen her before. But drink affected people in different ways and this blonde had been knocking back bottles of Blue Ice for the last hour. She had come into the bar alone and had stayed that way, refusing all offers from optimistic men to buy her a drink. Both Yvonne and Tilly had served her and commented on her brusqueness. Yvonne had said "I wouldn't want to be whoever she's waiting for." Serena couldn't rid her mind of the thought it was her woman had in her sights. But why?

In the three weeks she'd been on the island Serena had kept a very low profile. Last night had been her night off and she'd spent most of it at an Internet café trying to find news of the Greek investigation into the drowning but all she found was "investigations were proceeding." There was no mention of whether Byron was still in Greece or back in England. She was tempted to contact him on the cheap mobile he'd bought for emergencies. She took it everywhere with her, secured to a silver chain attached to her belt and slept with it at her bedside.

She'd not missed a single shift at work no matter how much she'd drunk the night before. She'd short-changed only the most inebriated of customers and had never taken more than twenty euros a night from the till. There had been no complaints from Alexandro or his brother Juan who ran the place. She got on well with the two other English girls here, Yvonne and Tilly. She was sure that they were fleecing the punters for a lot more than she was. Tilly had as good as told her not to be shy putting a few extra euros on the bills, especially after midnight. "They're often too drunk to remember to tip you so you're just helping them out." she'd said.

The next hour was exceptionally busy and Serena had time only to catch occasional glimpses of the blonde. The cheerful Geordie lad that she'd just served with six pints of lager had given her a 100 euro note and she'd taken it to Juan. It was bar policy that all notes above 50 euros went straight into his back pocket and not the till. When she got back to her pump position she saw to her dismay the woman standing in front of her. Putting on her best barmaid's smile she asked "Yes madam?"

"A Harldy Wallbangers............. pleeze."

She'd never heard the cocktail called that before but she was in no mood to be an educationalist.

"Certainly"

She mixed the vodka and orange juice carefully and stood well clear of the optics so that the blonde could see she wasn't being given short measure. She poured the Galliano generously into the highball glasses and offered it to the woman. The blonde put a pearl studded purse on the counter. Very deliberately she took a 100 euro note from it and offered it to Serena. The falseness of her smile should have alerted her but she was so anxious to get rid of the woman that she was totally unprepared for her wrist being seized as she reached out to take the note. She was savagely pulled forward, her hair grabbed by the woman's hands and her face banged down on the bar. Despite the agony Serena had the self control and the experience gained from years of barroom brawls not to pull back. Putting both hands on the bar she levered herself forward and kicking her legs out behind her she launched herself over the bar. Her momentum forced the woman backwards and temporarily eased the agony in her skull. As they collapsed on the floor Serena forced her head into the woman's face and bit it. The resulting screams were partially smothered by Serena's head as she bit again and again while kicking out with her knees and legs. But the woman's body was so thick and muscular that the kicks were hurting Serena more than the woman. Bunching her fists she clubbed the sides of her opponents head and neck. The woman's pull on her hair reached a crucifying intensity as she pulled Serena's head away from her face. Serena let her head be forced back to give her a few seconds relief. The increased gap between their bodies gave her the chance to elbow the woman in the throat. The resulting choking gasps made her think her opponent was collapsing but instead she managed to knee Serena in the groin. The sickening waves of pain almost overwhelmed her. She twisted sideways and forced herself between the woman's legs to prevent her from doing it again. Using her rage to block out the pain she managed to grab the blonde's ears and lifted her head high before banging it down on the wooden floor, once, twice, three times. She was going to beat this bitch to pulp. Only the fact that she was then seized from behind by two pairs of arms and dragged off the woman stopped her but she still managed one satisfying stamp on the woman's left breast as she was pulled away. "Enough, enough" a voice she recognized as Juan's was yelling.

In pulling her up and away he'd twisted her around and she saw herself in the long mirror behind the bar. Blood was dripping from her nose and mouth but she'd no time to think about it. Juan pushed her behind the bar and out into the passageway where the toilets were. Instead of shoving her into one of them as she expected he hustled her down to the bottom of the passage to a door marked PRIVATE. He opened it and thrust her inside. Before she could say a word he pressed a Yale key in her right hand and said "Go upstairs,open the door on the left at the top. Make sure you close it behind you." Without another word he hurried away.

She had to sit down on the stairs to regain her strength before she could move. She had never been up these stairs but she knew where they led. The brothers also owned the gift shop next to the bar and this was the way to the flat above it. She sat in a daze, determined not to be sick. Why in God's name had the woman attacked her? She was certain she'd never seen her before. Was there anything more sinister behind the attack? Someone settling an old score? She'd made a few enemies on the island over the years but she could think of nothing connected to the blonde. The ambivalent taste of blood trickling over her lips made her move. The pain in her groin made her waddle wide legged up the stairs. She'd kicked many a man in the balls in past rucks, now she had some idea what it felt like. No bloody wonder it was such a showstopper.

When she got into the flat she went immediately for the bathroom. In the mirror her face was looked like a badly bruised russet apple. Her hair stuck up like a scarecrow's. Her nose started to bleed heavily. She tore off a length of toilet paper, soaked it in cold water and held it against her nose. When the bleeding stopped she carefully moved her nose from side to side, there was no sound of anything grating, so it probably wasn't broken. That was a blessing. She'd always been enough of a realist to know she'd never win a beauty contest but she'd no wish to improve on Nature's neglect.

Here body ached as if she'd been kicked all over. She noticed the medicine cabinet and if she'd had the energy would have cheered when she saw the packet of Neurofen. She swallowed three with a handful of water and made her way into the living room. There was a small settee but she wanted to stretch out so she lay down on the carpet. Starting from her big toe she began to relax every part of her body using Yoga techniques she'd learned years ago. She tried to completely empty her mind but there were too many unanswered questions swirling through her brain for her to succeed. It was exhaustion rather than Yoga that tipped her into sleep.

CHAPTER 29

Byron stood in the open doorway of his hotel room watching Dot yanking out the drawers of the dressing table. She'd rushed past him as he'd opened the door, all dewy eyed and whining "I just want to see where she last slept." He could run over and stop her but that would get him into an undignified fight. He couldn't hit her. She would charge him with assault. Perhaps that what she wanted, it would only be his word against hers.

He'd been too surprised to prevent her rushing into the room. He supposed it must have been the drugs they'd given him in hospital had made him lethargic but he should have been alert enough to stop her. "Dot" he said in his most authoritative voice "Stop that or I'll call the police."

She turned towards him, her face red with exertion and hatred. "Where are they Fuller?"

"What?"

"Don't act the innocent with me, you bastard. You know bloody well what I mean. Lucy's charm bracelets."

He shook his head. "You've no chance of getting them Dot."

"But they're ours. Danny and I was buying them charms for Lucy ever since she was a baby. We paid for them. So stop pissing about and hand them over."

What could he tell her that would get her off his back? He'd try the truth for a start. "You can't have them because Lucy didn't bring them."

"You fucking liar. She'd never go anywhere without her bracelet with the gold horses."

He nodded his head in agreement "If you'd let me finish you've have heard me say 'Lucy didn't bring them all. Just the horses' one. I didn't want her to even bring that. This place is full of pickpockets and thieves. You've seen all the posters at the airport and café's telling you not to wear your valuables in public haven't you?"

She stood staring at him trying to convince herself that he couldn't be telling the truth. Lenny had told her not to wear her Rolex outdoors here. "Right, well "she said "I'll have that for starters."

He put on the most sorrowful expression he could muster and looking her straight in the eyes said in a sorrowful voice, "Dot, I'd give anything in the world for you to lay your hands on it this minute. If it was here then Lucy would be here too. She was wearing it on the boat."

"What the fuck do you take me for Fuller? I wasn't born yesterday."

"I'm not trying to fool you. Lucy was wearing it on the boat."

"You fucking liar. That blow in the head has made you so stupid you can't even remember your own lies of a minute ago. You just told me Lucy didn't wear it because of all the pickpockets and thieves here. C'mon, give."

"Dot, you know what Lucy was like. As you say she wouldn't go anywhere without that bracelet. I managed to persuade her not to wear it when we went shopping and eating out but when we were going sailing she argued she'd only be walking a few yards from the car to the boat and there wasn't much chance of anything being stolen in that time."

Dot suddenly snarled "If Lenny was here, he'd soon get the truth out of you."

"It would make no difference whether he was here or not. Lucy's…"

She interrupted him, "Don't give me that. Lenny's made blokes with more bottle than you'll ever have talk. You're going to regret the day you were born when he gets his hands on you."

"Whatever you say, Dot. But if he was here the police would soon have him in jail."

"You think so? Well they'd have to catch him first and they haven't managed that yet."

"This is a small island. He can't hide forever."

"That's what you think. Lenny's well on his way back to England by now." She stood up. "I'm not going to waste my breath any longer with you, Fuller. But if you value your miserable hide you'd better have all Lucy's jewellery ready to give him when he rings your bell."

"Don't kid yourself Dot. Greece has an extradition treaty with England. You know what that means?"

"I don't give a tuppenny fuck what it means. Lenny's got friends who'll look after him when he gets back home. He'll never see Greece again but by Christ he'll see you."

As she marched past him she lashed out at his face with her nails but he'd been expecting her to do something like that and had moved out of the doorway so he had room to jump back. As she stood in the corridor glowering; he knew she was considering rushing him. It would be so embarrassing running away from a woman but that would be the wisest thing to do. Not wanting to challenge her, he avoided her eyes and looked expectantly over her shoulder as if someone was coming. She stayed her ground for what seemed a very long time. Then with a final "Bastard" turned and walked towards the lifts. He was back in his room with the door locked before she'd taken two steps.

CHAPTER 30

Serena was awakened by someone stroking her arms. Opening her eyes she saw the tearstained face of Tilly. When she tried to ease herself up Tilly put her arms around and mumbled "I'm so sorry Renna,"

"What? What for?"

"It's my fault. I'm sorry, really sorry."

"What? How come?"

Between sobs, Tilly said something like "It...it... should have... been....me ...that that woman attacked."

"Why didn't she then? You were there. She could see you. Why pick on me ?"

Tilly wiped away a thin trickle of blood coming down Serna's chin with a paper tissue before she answered "You were off last night. So I was serving behind the bar instead, wasn't I?"

"Well? What off it? Did you rob her or something?"

"No. Nothing like that. Well not exactly"

"Go on."

"Didn't you hear what blonde bitch called out when she grabbed you?"

Serena shook her head.

"Uri. She was yelling 'You attack my Uri'."

"Uri? I don't know any fucking Uri."

Nervously squeezing Serena's right hand as she spoke, Tilly began. "You know how sometimes punters make us an offer we can't refuse?"

"Yes?"

"Yeah, well last night this guy comes in near closing. Six footer, real looker he was, blonde, blue eyes. Real Viking type. He tells me he's called Uri and he's Russian. Well, after a few drinks he offers me 300 Euros to…"

She stopped as Juan came in. "Reena, got your bag? You need to go."

Serena intended to say "Thanks for asking how I am" but the words that came out were "My bag's under the counter, next to the dishwasher."

"I get it." He said and hurried out.

"Don't forget my jacket"

Serena turned to Tilly but she put her hand up to stop Serena speaking, "I'll be quick. This bloke turned out to be a real pervert. I should have known a looker like him didn't need to pay for it. Any girl…"

"Just say what the fuck happened?"

"Well it was all right at first. He put the money on the dresser and we got down to business. Then he produces some silk scarves from Christ know where and started to tie me up. He was so strong I knew it would be useless to resist. It was all laughing and casual like. Then it got heavy. Put one of the silk scarves round my neck and started squeezing. "

"Jesus, how'd you get out of that?"

"What he didn't know we've got a video camera rigged up. Gives us a bit of extra income in the winter if we find out where a punter lives and…"

"Who's we?"

"Me and Mick, my boyfriend. He always watches. Likes to take care of me he does. When he sees what's happening he creeps

125

in and beats the shit out of this Uri with a baseball bat. Then stripes him a few times in the face so's he'll never forget."

"What's this got to do with me?"

"Tilly reached out and touched Serena's hair with the tips of her fingers: "Not you. Your ginger nut, that's what."

"But your not...Oh"

Tilly nodded; "Yeah I was yesterday wasn't I? Real ginger. You had a go at me about it, didn't you?" (Tilly was nicknamed "The Chameleon" because she changed her hair colour so often.) Now it was raven black. "Thought it best like to change it today in case there was any trouble like. Never thought about you being..."

Juan came in with Serena's bag and leather jacket and knelt down beside them. "You take. No come back. We give you money in bag. It's late now. The police have gone. We say you only temps, on approval two days. Tell police we don't know you much."

"What about the bitch who attacked me?"

"She flat out. You fuck her up bad. Took to hospital."

Tilly interrupted "She was breathing, Honest Reena. I watched her. Nothing to worry about."

Juan snorted "Police come back tomorrow looking for you. You must vamoose. Not come back."

He helped Serena up and with Tilly assisting got her into her jacket. He pressed the bag into her hands and hustled her down the stairs. At the bottom he said "We let you out back way. Tilly and me check first. You wait here. "

When they came back he said "All clear" and eased Serena out into the alley before Tilly could finish saying her goodbyes. Serena leaned back against the door, undecided which way to go. Each end of the alley led to a busy well lit street. There were still lots of people about. She and Tilly and Yvonne usually left the bar together and saw each other home. Serena lived the furthest away in a quieter part of the resort.

Serena realised she couldn't call a taxi because the police were bound to check them tomorrow. Perhaps if she picked one up when she was a few streets away and got out before she got home that would be O.K. She'd almost got to the top of the alley when two figures came around the corner; Tilly and Yvonne.

She squealed when they embraced her, but she didn't mind the hurt. This was what sisterhood was all about. "Sorry, sorry" they chorused. They walked all the way home with her. She wanted them to come in to her flat but they both said their boyfriends would be getting worried about them being so late. As they parted Tilly thrust something into her hand. Looking down she saw it was a roll of euro notes.

"No. No. Tilly I can't take your money."

"It's not mine, it's Juan's. I nicked it from his back pocket when he was bending over you. It's only the severance pay he forgot to give you." She turned and ran away. Serena tried to say "thanks "but she was so chocked with emotion that she was speechless.

She noticed the bar opposite still hadn't closed. She decided to go in and get a double vodka on ice. The barmen, Danny was from the same area of Belfast as her father and she often chatted with him. She'd hardly got the words out of her mouth when he said "And what corner were you in Reene? The blue or the red?"

She shook her head. "It's a long story. I'll tell you in the morning if you keep your trap shut now and let me drink in peace."

"Ah sure, don't you know it's the night that's made for talking, so it is"

"Christ, Danny, can't you talk like a normal human being?"

"I'm not a normal human being. I'm a genius in waiting. When my great European novel is published you'll be proud you once knew me. Any rate, what have you done, murdered somebody?"

Serena hoped her laugh wasn't too hysterical as she answered "Not yet, but the night's still young. Have the cops been around here?"

Danny shook his head "Not a breath of them darling. And if they do come I never saw you. Want another?"

"No thanks, I'm almost out on my feet."

"We're closing now. Want me to come over and read you the latest chapter of my novel before you nod off?"

"You guarantee that'll put me to sleep?"

"Cheeky bitch. Just for that I'll withdraw my offer."

She leaned over and patted his hand, "You're breaking my heart, Danny Boy. Buena's notches."

"Buenas notches with knobs on to you darlin"

Despite Danny's assurances Serena was still apprehensive as she climbed the stairs to her flat. But there was no one waiting to arrest her. She thought she'd be too wound up to get to sleep quickly but she was wrong.

Next morning she thought about packing her bags and leaving the island immediately. But Byron had often told her "Never do the obvious." When she counted the money Tilly had given her it was 2500 Euros. Juan was bound to come looking for her with all that money missing. Luckily she never told any boss her exact address. She always made one up that was close enough to the truth for her to be able to say she'd just made a slight mistake if she was found out.

She'd have to move well away. The decent hotels wouldn't normally let a single girl have a room; certainly not one with a face like the one that had stared back at her from the mirror this

128

morning. Her rent was paid until the end of the month, so she wouldn't be missed immediately. She decided to go to a luxury Beauty Spa she'd only once before been able to afford to visit. She'd have the full works and follow Tilly's example and change her hair colour. That and some designer gear would at least make her more presentable. With a new leather suitcase stuffed with newspapers and magazines she might be able to bluff her way into somewhere more salubrious at the other end of the island.

CHAPTER 31

Byron was happy as he walked out of Stanstead airport. Even having to pay for 18 days car parking didn't dampen his mood. He was home. Having to promise to return Greece for an inquest didn't bother him. He was sure they'd never have let him leave if they had any suspicious about the "accident."

Only when he opened the front door of his house did his mood change. Everywhere felt cold and depressing even though he'd phoned ahead and got Mrs. Patton, the cleaning lady to switch all the utilities on yesterday. He put the feeling down to tiredness but he avoided the bedroom where he'd strangled Lucy. He took his suitcase into the front bedroom instead and unpacked. When he'd finished he stood for a while looking out of the window.

He'd stood here in the dark after he'd strangled Lucy. That little fat bloke crouching down by the front gate had given him a shock. How relieved he'd been when he saw the Alsatian. Only a solid citizen cleaning up after his dog. He remembered saying quietly to himself "Good for you mate."

He decided to get the back bedroom redecorated immediately. He was sure he hadn't left any traces of his crime but better safe than sorry. He'd pick whichever firm could do it soonest. He undressed, ran a hot bath and lay soaking in it until the skin on his hands started to wrinkle. He poured himself a full tumbler of Glenlivit and lay down on the single bed in the guest bedroom...

Now he was home he had to decide what to do about Lenny. There were no reports of the Greeks catching him. He could turn up in England anytime. He might even be back already. Even if he couldn't get back quickly he could easily get a couple of his goon friends here to do his dirty work for him. He'd never been to *Sunset* but Dot would give him or them the address. No matter what alarms and locks he put in the house he could never be sure that Lenny wouldn't catch him outside. The odds were too great against him, unless...unless he moved. The more he though about it the more obvious a solution it seemed. He could move both from house and business. Everything to do with his business was leased, even the office furniture. Even Lucy's car was leased as was his own. She was down on the books as an employee. He could change the name of his firm when he moved. As for the house, it wasn't even mortgaged. He got a pal to buy it cheaply for him when one of his clients died and left it to two distant cousins in Australia. They hadn't queried his valuation; all they wanted was their hands on the cash as soon as possible. He'd intended to sell it straight away but as soon as Lucy had seen it she'd insisted on living in it. Now he was free to sell it as he wished. It had at least trebled in value since he'd bought it. What the hell had been the matter with him? All that time spent worrying about Lenny when the solution had been obvious.

. Moving house would be a natural thing for a grieving husband to do. Too many memories of his dear departed wife for him to cope with, He'd get on to the Estate Agents tomorrow. There was no need to have the bedroom redecorated. New owners were sure to do it anyway. Maybe moving south of the river would be a good idea. The girls in the office might be a problem; they were a good bunch and well worth what he paid them. He'd have to keep their travel arrangements in mind when picking a new location.

Dawn, his office manager was the one he'd have to be most careful about. She knew more about his scams than he liked to admit. She was one smart cookie. It had taken her less than six months to work out what he was up to. Fortunately she proved to be as crooked as he was and a substantial yearly cash bonus kept her happy. He'd tried to get her into bed but she'd told him she was a lesbian. He'd thought she only said that to keep men like him at bay until another woman began to regularly pick her up from work. Such a waste. Whatever happened he would ask her to come with him. He'd ask them all. It would make it easier to get rid of any who decided not to come. With a bit of luck the new location would not be too inaccessible from where they lived. It would save a lot of retraining if he could hold on to them but if they had to go, so be it. He wasn't risking his neck for them.

His Salesmen only came in once a week to collect their commission and hand in the paperwork. That could all be done by post or computer if he decided to keep them. Why not a new name: He dismissed the thought as quickly as it had come. It would look very suspicious if the Greek police got the local plods to investigate him. He could change his name later. No rush now.

He lay back and thought of all the places he could move to until he drifted off into sleep.

Next morning after breakfast he got out the details of everything that he'd leased and as he'd thought he was only required to give four working weeks notice of termination on everything except his office. Its lease didn't expire for another five months. That wasn't too bad. It might take him that time to find a new place anyway. He'd start searching today. But, first get the house sold. He rang three estate agents and arranged for them to come and value it. They all assured him that houses in his road sold quickly.

He checked the time. It was only five to ten. Too early to make the one call he'd been longing to make. If Serena was doing bar work she'd told him she often slept until midday. He'd wait a couple more hours. What a reunion they'd have.

He made himself another coffee and cancelled the lease on his own and Lucy's cars. He changed his BMW for a silver Mercedes C Class Kompressor, a car he'd long admired. As he thought, arranging to lease a more expensive car made the company not insist on his having to pay the full terms on the two he had now. He was delighted when they told him he could pick it up the day after tomorrow. He was one happy man as he set off for the office. He'd take the four girls out for a pub lunch as a thank you for the way they'd held the fort while he was away. No need to tell them about moving until he had to.

The lunch went well. He thought he'd played the part of a grieving husband "bravely bearing up" sufficiently well to not turn the occasion into a dirge. Even Dawn had been sympathetic; he must be doing well if he'd convinced her. The time he'd spent in the office beforehand had been reassuring. Things were ticking over well. Dawn agreed that one new Salesman's figures looked a bit too good to be true. He wouldn't be the first crafty bugger he'd employed who'd thought that he could turn in a big list of supposed customers and swan off with his commission before they turned out to be false. The small print instant dismissal clause without any monies due that he had written into all his employees contracts had served him well over the years and would do so now. Nobody put one over on him.

He stayed in the pub after the others had left drinking a final brandy. It was just past two o'clock. The first of the estate agents was due in half an hour. He'd better be on his way. But first, he took the so far unused mobile out of his briefcase to text Serena. "Come home. All well. Notify time and place."

He drove home carefully; he couldn't afford to add any more points to his licence. Bloody speed cameras. Sneaky underhand tax collectors for a nanny state. Set up to penalise hard-working businessmen who couldn't afford to hang about. He got home safely and was in the kitchen making a strong coffee when the doorbell rang. He looked at his watch, only twenty past two. This estate agent must be keen. All the better for him if he was, a quick sale was just what he needed. Not that he'd appear too anxious, he wanted the top price for this place. He walked with measure steps to the door and opened it with just the hint of a smile.

"Well, you're …" his words of welcome died on his lips as soon as he saw the woman and man before him. Estate Agents they were not.

The woman spoke first, "Mr. Byron Fuller?

"Yes."

"I'm D.I. Morrison and this is D.C.Bullerton. I wonder could we just have a brief word." She stepped forward as she spoke.

He wasn't falling for that trick. He stood resolutely where he was "How brief?" he asked "I'm expecting a business acquaintance any moment."

She didn't back away. "This will only take a few moments, Sir. But as it is in respect of your missing wife it would be best to discuss it indoors, don't you think?"

She was a clear eyed middle aged woman with an air of authority about her. More like a headmistress than a policewoman. A garish silk scarf around her neck contrasted strongly with her dark business suit and hinted at an extrovert personality that made Byron instantly wary. The man had the soft well cared features of many of his hunting acquaintances. He had that languid air of innocence about him that Byron had often found to his cost hid a sharp business brain. Byron thought he was probably a university bod on a fast track path through the ranks. He intended to say "As long as it's brief "but remembered just in time he was supposed to be a heartbroken husband: "My wife ? Have you found her?" he asked with all the excitement he could fake.

"If we could just come inside Sir" the woman replied, moving forward and smiling while scrutinising his face. He opened the door wide for them; he was going to have to be very careful with this one. As he closed the door he added an encore to his "grieving husband" role. "You've got news of Lucy? Have the Greeks found her?" He stood still as he spoke; he wasn't going to let them settle down to grill him in his own house. He felt he would be more in control if he kept them standing in his hallway.

"I'm afraid Sir we have had no information from the Greek authorities other than the circumstances of your accident."

"Oh? Why are you here then if you have no news of my wife?"

"Nothing in addition to what I'm sure the Greek authorities have already informed you. The reason for this visit is to tell you that we have received some serious allegations about your treatment of your wife before you went on holiday."

"Dot. My mother in law. She hates...."

D.C.Bullerton interrupted him, "The informants are almost certainly male sir. They..."

"They? What do you mean 'they'? Who are they? "

The woman nodded at Bullerton so he continued "Both of these persons Sir are claiming to in the vicinity of your house late in the evening of Friday 30th. June. That was the night before you went on holiday, wasn't it?"

"Yes. What of it?"

"Well, one of them has given a rather vivid description of a struggle between yourself and a woman in the back bedroom of this house around about 11pm on that night. He says the woman was being strangled."

"Nonsense. In our back bedroom? How could anyone possibly know a thing like that?"

"He claims to have been around the back of your house, seeking shelter. Apparently he is an itinerant, who…"

"A tramp? You've come here on the word of a tramp? This is ridiculous. Is this all you've got to do? I cannot…"

The woman interrupted "We are not just relying on one person's word sir. Someone else who was walking their dog in this road at about the same time claims to have heard screams coming from this house. We are not saying that we accept that these accusations are correct. It's just that we are wondering why any such person or persons should make them especially in view of your subsequent tragedy in Greece."

While she was speaking Byron's mind was racing. That bloke with the Alsatian. Was that why he'd been crouching down at the gate? Of course Lucy had screamed but only briefly and certainly not loudly. More like a high pitched gurgle as far as he remembered. He'd soon shut her up. The sound couldn't possible have travelled as far as the front of the house. The bloke had to be lying. Why? Why? He looked respectable but that didn't mean he was. All the time he'd lived here he'd never heard anything about tramps seeking shelter in the back alleyway. What if it had been that dog walker in the garden? What …His thoughts were interrupted by the doorbell.

The police gave no sign of moving. He'd have to get them out of the way. He didn't want them knowing he was selling the house so soon. "Excuse me. That must be the business acquaintance I'm expecting. If you'll just go through to the lounge, I won't be a minute. I'm intrigued by what you've told me." He turned away from them before they could reply. He didn't open the door until they'd entered the lounge.

It was the Estate Agent. Byron told him he had some unexpected guests but they would soon be gone. Could he come back in half an hour?

"Certainly Mr. Fuller. See you then."

All the while he was talking Byron was thinking about what the police had said. Some nosey bastard had seen something that was for sure. He was going to have to weigh every word carefully if he was to get out of this. From experience he had knew it was always best to tell as much of the truth as possible. Lies were more believable if they contained a grain of truth. He composed his tale as he walked down to the lounge.

The detectives were standing apart, one at each end of the fireplace. He put on the shyest smile he could muster as he said "Do sit down please. My friend will call back later." He hoped they'd both sit together on the settee but they chose an armchair each. He had to sit on the settee. Although he took care to look at both their faces he decided to concentrate on the woman. It would help him better get over the impression of embarrassment the wanted to convey.

"Look, my friend's call has given me a chance to think about what you've just told me I've no idea where you could have got your information from unless it was some pervert like a Peeping Tom. That's the only sort of person who could possibly have seen into the back bedroom. Any rate, be that as it may, I think I can explain what this person may have thought he saw." He paused and looked down at the floor "It's not easy telling you this" another pause "it's just, well, Lucy and I were rather excited about our holiday. It was to be a rather special one. Like many other couples we'd had our up and downs in the past year but this holiday was to be a fresh start for us. We were so looking forward to it. So much so we decided to start it a day early by going out to our favourite restaurant, 'The Pink Gooseberry' in Tillingsbury. Ever been there?"

Morrison shook her head but he thought Bullerton nodded.

"Wonderful food, superb wine list. Anton the chef trained with Marco White you know." He paused but when he got no response continued "We had a marvellous meal there and when we got home I'm afraid we were a bit ....well...frisky. Lucy loved her food, a good meal always acted as a bit of an aphrodisiac with her. Anyway, we sometimes liked to play about a bit melodramatically when we (He paused again to reinforce the impression of shyness) when we felt like that."

He stopped and looked down at the carpet; he was determined to make them respond. Eventually Morrison said "Bondage, with all the trimmings?"

"Something like that...You know this is very difficult ....well...my wife's death, you know I still can't believe it. These memories....are painful."

The woman said "We understand Mr. Fuller. You don't have to continue if you don't feel up to it. Perhaps you could give us a statement later." But she gave no sign of moving.

"No. No. It's alright. We had a very active sex life Lucy and I. It's shocking to think someone could have been spying on us. I'd no idea we could be seen from the back. How much would anyone be able to see from there anyway?" When there was no response from either of his listeners he added, "Would one of you like to go in the garden while I and the other one of you accompany me up into the back bedroom. Then perhaps we can get some idea of what an onlooker could have seen?"

Much to his disappointment they agreed. He led the woman up into the back bedroom and they stood in the window waving down at DC Bullerton. He waved at them to move back into the room and then from one side of it to the other. He was unprepared for the woman saying "Perhaps Mr.Fuller you'd like to join my colleague in the garden and see for yourself how much it is possible to see from there?" He realised immediately she was making the suggestion so she could look around the room while he went down to the garden but couldn't see how he could refuse her.

"Yes, I think I'd like to see for myself" he answered.

When he joined Bullerton in the garden she had switched the bedroom light on and he was amazed how much they could see of

137

her as she moved around the room. Noticing they were both six footers set him wondering how much a much smaller man would be able to see, he almost made the mistake of crouching down. Only at the last minute did he have the wit to check himself.

Back inside he stayed in the hallway so that they wouldn't get back into the lounge and took the initiative by commenting "I think any Peeping Tom could only have seen part of what was happening. He could easily have misinterpreted our playacting as something violent. But it wasn't really, I assure you. We were up and on our way early next morning without any aches or bruises. Mrs. Harrison saw us go. I left a key with her. Lucy said goodbye to her. Yes, I'm sure she did."

"So you've not received any threats, any attempts at blackmail?"

Byron shook his head. Morrison looked at Bullerton but he remained silent. She took a step towards the door as she said "Well, thank you for your co operation Mr. Fuller. I hope it hasn't been too painful for you. I'm sure you will understand why we had to make these enquiries, especially if there was any possibility that someone was trying to blackmail you."

"Of course. But I assure you all I've had since I returned home are messages of sympathy and condolence. Lucy was very well liked."

"I'm sure she was Mr. Fuller. But if you do receive any threats along the lines of what we've told you will let us know immediately, won't you?" said Bullerton.

"Certainly" Byron replied as he ushered them out.

In the police car before he started the engine D. I. Morrison turned to her companion and asked "Well Bully. What do you make of that?" When he didn't answer immediately she added, "All that sado-masochistic stuff got you going has it? Your imagination working overtime?"

He turned to her smiling "With respect ma'am; for a vicar's daughter you've got a very filthy mind. But the view into the bedroom was quite extensive. Whatever went on in there would certainly have been seen from the garden."

"What about the garden Bully? No freshly dug earth? No suspiciously bare patch among the parsnips."

"Nothing that I could see. What about the bedroom ?"

"Normal, I'm afraid. Didn't look if it had been specially Hoovered or anything. No heel marks in the carpet either. "

"Damn. It's so much easier on the telly."

"And so much better paid. So you think he's in the clear, do you?"

He paused before replying, "It's all very plausible but…well…I didn't want to say anything that would tend to prejudice your mind before the interview but I do know him. Or rather I should say my family knows off him."

"Jesus, Bully, is there anybody in the county that yours family doesn't know?"

"I don't suppose there is. I'm afraid there are rather a lot of us and we've been around for rather a long time. I'm sure Caroline, the eldest of my three sisters knew Fuller rather well once."

"Knew. As in the Biblical sense?"

"Probably. Carrie was rather keen to" know" as many blokes as she could before she got married. Never tried to hide it."

"Really? You think she could tell us more about our Mr. Fuller do you?"

"I'll e-mail and ask her, discretely of course. She's married to a millionaire rancher in Texas now."

"Bloody hell! I knew it was a mistake for me to stay a virgin until I met the right man. All I got was the deputy headmaster of a crap comprehensive."

"Life's very unjust ma'am. But to get back to Fuller. He has got a bit of a reputation as a wide boy in certain circles."

"You mean that blood-thirsty lot on horseback you call relations. Any hint of violence?"

"Not as far as I've heard. More dodgy insurance and share dealings and things like that."

Morrison nodded, "Yes, he's the type. Why do you think he was so keen to tell us his wife had spoken to the next door neighbour before they went on holiday?"

"I noticed that. But it does prove his wife was alive next morning doesn't it."

"Yes but there's something not quite right about this whole thing. Do you think that is why the Greeks asked us to have a look at him?"

"I'm sure of it. We certainly would never have gone anywhere near Fuller on the basis of those letters."

"What a pompous twit that letter writer is. Do you think the letter writer also made the phone call?

"It's more than likely. You know that the computer analysis indicate the speech patterns of the caller match those of the letter writer. It's marvellous how everything is cross referenced nowadays. I'm trying to keep up date with computers. I'd like to get into Police intelligence."

"You would? Well keep trying. My father says miracles still happen today; people just don't notice them. Dig out all you can on Fuller. Something's not quite right about this affair."

CHAPTER 32

Paul found it difficult to get to sleep. He was so excited about his theory of what had happened in Greece. If only there was some way to make sure. The world ought to know how clever he'd been. He let himself imagine the praise that would be heaped upon him when Fuller and his mistress were jailed. He could see the headlines *"A LOCAL HERCULE POIROT. Murder Mystery Reader Solves Real Crime."* He'd be modest of course....

His dreams of glory were cut short when he suddenly realised if Fuller ever found out about him, his life would be in danger. When Fuller got home the police would tell him that someone was saying he's strangled his wife in the back bedroom. Once he knew he'd been seen, Fuller would come looking for him; he was that type of man. The thought of being stalked by a killer was frightening. He tried to reassure himself that there was no possible way Fuller could find him. If the police didn't know who he was, how could Fuller ever know? Nevertheless he would exercise extreme care from now on. Not go past Fuller's house so often and make sure to vary the times he did so. After all, everything depended on how successful the police were in proving Fuller's guilt. Their forensic team might find proof that a murder had been committed in that bedroom. There was no need to rush things.

His more immediate problem was returning to work. His two weeks were up on Monday and God know what plots had been hatched against him while he had been away. His head wounds weren't so visible now but the burn on his cheek still looked nasty. He couldn't pass it off as a shaving cut or a bruise. What was he to say when people asked him about it? Not that any of his colleagues were in the habit of enquiring about his health, he'd never been one to encourage small talk. But what if Mr. Oakshaw asked him? What...Paul stopped and shook his head. What was the matter with him? He could cover the burn with a plaster! Say he'd been hit in the face with a cricket ball and had injured his head when he fell. There had been so little rain these past weeks the ground was rock hard so there would be no reason why that couldn't have happened. They knew, or at least Mr. Oakshaw knew he was a cricket umpire. He'd not covered the burn because the hospital said it would heal quicker if exposed to air and light. But what did it matter how quickly it healed? As long as nobody ever found out he'd been assaulted by homophobic thugs. That was all that mattered.

He decided that the only thing that it was necessary for him to do was write out in meticulous detail what he had "Accidentally" seen at Meldrum Avenue. He would give it to his solicitor with instructions it was to be immediately handed to the police if he disappeared or died under mysterious circumstances. He would do it first thing after he returned from taking Kaiser for a walk in the morning. Thinking about Kaiser he decided he'd book him in for a trim and groom tomorrow. He regularly combed and brushed his coat but it was getting a bit too long for this warm weather. Millicent, the groomer was always so complimentary about Kaiser and the excellent condition in which he was kept. With these pleasant thoughts in his mind he eventually drifted off into sleep.

The next few days went well for Paul. Kaiser had his grooming and compliments from Millicent. After four rewrites Paul produced an account of what he'd seen Fuller do that he was sure would convict him of murder when it was read.. He didn't let himself to dwell upon under what circumstances it ever would be used. He left it with the solicitors who had his will. On Saturday Paul umpired an important top of the league cricket match. No one disputed his decisions and his father behaved himself despite his frequent visits to the sponsor's beer tent.

On Monday he entered his office fairly confident that he'd got his story about his "cricket ball injuries "well rehearsed. The staff seemed genuinely pleased to see him but Myra made him wince inwardly when she said loudly after commiserating with him, "You should go careful Mr. Thewell. Head injuries can be so dangerous." Everybody in the office must have heard her. He knew what she was up to, trying to suggest that he might be brain damaged. Deliberately putting the thought in the others minds. In a voice whose volume he made sure would equal hers he said "I appreciate your concern Miss Williamson but Mr. Wells, my personal surgeon has assured me that there is no permanent damage. I was just kept in hospital as a precaution." He wondered why everyone looked up at him as he spoke. He was tempted to stare them out but thought better of it and turned away to his desk. He must get rid of that woman. His career would never be safe while she was here.

It was much trickier with Mr. Oakshaw when he met him in the corridor. When Paul told him about his facial injury being caused by a cricket ball he immediately asked in which match it had happened. Paul realised he couldn't lie; the director was a keen cricket follower and would wonder why such an incident hadn't been reported in the Sporting Press. "Oh, it happened at a knockabout down at the club" he answered "All my own fault, wasn't paying attention. " Mr. Oakshaw seemed to accept this without any reservation but Paul's relief quickly diminished when he added "Well do take care Thewell. Nasty things blows to the head. If you do get any dizzy spells, don't hesitate to take another few day's rest. You've got a very able deputy in Miss Williamson." Paul had to force himself to nod and say, "I'm glad you think so Mr.Oakshaw. I've always taken the time to thoroughly train my deputies. Miss Williamson has made excellent progress, rather slowly I must admit but she gets there in the end."

Mr. Oakshaw nodded and said with a smile "Perhaps that's the best way Fuller. The tortoise always beats the hare Eh?"

"Very true Sir. Very true. Must go. Lot's to catch up on." He hurried away before he was forced to listen to any more compliments about that black bitch.

His mind was in such turmoil as he hurried to the lifts that he didn't even break stride when he heard the low wolf-whistle. It was only while waiting for the lift that he became conscious that he had been the only one moving around. That whistle couldn't have been for him? No, of course not. He was telling himself not to be so stupid when the lift came. As he stepped inside he heard the whistle again. He swivelled around but there was no obvious culprit in sight. It was an open plan office and all the heads were bent over their desks. He stood as near the doors of the lift as possible watching to see if anyone looked up as the doors were closing. No one did. He resolved not to allow himself to take such a whistle seriously, just some brainless clerk's idea of a joke. It didn't mean anything. It couldn't.

Back in the safety of his own office he began to clear his IN tray but he couldn't concentrate on his work. All he could think of was Myra Williamson. He risked a quick glance at her. She was typing at her computer keyboard with her usual calm assurance. He was going to have to think long and hard to find a way of discrediting her. But he'd do it. He was a true born Englishman. He wasn't going to be outwitted by some first generation immigrant from Jamaica. Most likely one of her brothers was a Yardie gangster or drug dealer. He'd see what he could find on his computer at home.

He lifted another file from his IN tray and made himself work through it. By lunch time he had managed to get into some sort of working rhythm and was starting to feel better. The office was all working smoothly. He wasn't being interrupted by staff asking his advice. In fact he couldn't remember when anyone had last asked him for help. Why was no one asking his advice nowadays? He looked across at Myra's desk just in time to see Gaynor turning away from it. He was sure she was saying "Thanks." Was everyone now coming to her instead of him? He'd soon put a stop to that. He set up his computer and typed a memo. TO ALL STAFF. ANY AND ALL QUERIES ABOUT WORK RELEATED MATTERS ARE TO BE BROUGHT FIRSTLY TO MY ATTENTION. He decided to send it immediately so that they would receive it before they left for lunch. That would give them something to chew over!

He watched their heads bob up and look across at him as the e-mail arrived. He stared back at them, daring them to come and query his edict but none came, not even Myra. One by one they left the office for lunch as usual. When they had all gone except Gaynor and Maureen who took a later lunch than the others so that the office was never unmanned. He took out his own sandwiches and flask and continued to work through his lunch hour.

The rest of the day was uneventful. There were no mistakes in any of the letters he was given to check and sign and where it was necessary to refer to recent legislation all the references were correctly applied. His only disappointment was that no one had come to him with queries. He'd not been able to discern any of the staff coming to Myra either despite keeping a close watch on her.

It was as he left the building on the way to the staff car park that he was wolf whistled again. He'd just passed a group of young men talking on the steps when he heard it. He forced himself to keep on walking. Whistled at three times in one day.

He was just settling into the driving seat of his car when the realisation struck him. Men whistling at a man? Why? Because they though he was a homosexual? It couldn't be the reason. It couldn't. If it was the consequences were too horrible to contemplate.

CHAPTER 33

Byron read the text message on his mobile again.

G8 TO HEAR FROM U. CANNOT COME UNTIL FRI. ARRIVE S'TEAD 9 PM. LUV U.

Why wasn't she coming straightaway? She must have been able to get a flight before Friday. He needed her here now. The police visit had shaken him. They had seemed to accept his story about what had happened in the bedroom but he knew better than to trust them. He decided he wouldn't tell Serena about being seen strangling Lucy. It might make her think he was not as clever as she'd thought. Once confidence in anyone's judgement was weakened it could never be fully restored. It was sheer bad luck of course that that some pervert had seen him killing Lucy. Bad luck was like leprosy, nobody wanted to be anywhere near it. But how could he avoid telling her? He needed her help to find and silence this lowlife.

All he had to go on was his memory of a plump little bloke in a tweed hat and a rather splendid looking Alsatian. He gone over and over that night in his mind and it seemed to him beyond the bounds of possibility that two passers by could have seen or heard anything suspicious. When Serena was here he'd think of some pretext to get her to scream in the back bedroom while he stood at the front gate. If he couldn't hear her (and he was sure he wouldn't) then the dog walker was a liar. Why would he lie? Because he was the Peeping Tom. There was no other explanation. He couldn't live far away if he walked his dog around here. He might work in a local shop or bank. He could even be a teacher in one of the schools. Probably married to a frigid wife.

How the Hell could he find him? If he had talked more with the neighbours he might have been able to ask them if they knew who the bloke with the Alsatian was. Make out he was interested in getting a dog from the same breeder. Lucy had been the one who'd had most to do with neighbours. Even then she'd spent so much time down at the stables she didn't really mix a lot with them. It was just good fortune that Lucy had found out about Betty Harrison and the rockery. But Betty's eyesight was too poor to have seen who was passing her front gate and he remembered her telling him she was always in bed by 10 o'clock. The couple in the house opposite; they were often up late. He might have been able to ask them if only he knew their names.

If only…Byron suddenly stopped. Why on earth was he getting himself so worked up? He could prove his wife went on holiday with him. Lucy had drowned, that couldn't be disputed. So it was impossible for her to have been killed here. So why should the police ever believe this pervert? His bedroom romp story was perfectly reasonable. All that evidence he'd accumulated to prove Lucy had been in Greece was beyond refute. But why had the police even bothered to come to him with this "blackmail" story? Maybe it was the Greeks who'd asked them to check him out. They were a devious lot. But without witnesses what could they do? So why waste time worrying about this pervert? If the police did nothing and the bloke did try to blackmail him then he and Serena would deal with it. His immediate concern was avoiding Lenny.

All three of the Estate Agents had valued the house between r £380,000 and £392,000and had assured him it would sell quickly. He'd toyed with the idea of selling it himself on the internet and saving their fees but decided the agents were safer. If things didn't progress as quickly as expected he still needn't stay here. He could rent a property until the house sold. He'd lots of contacts among Mortgage Brokers. He wasn't going to remain here like a sitting duck for Lenny to trap at his leisure.

He spent the days until Serena's arrival turning Lucy's jewellery and gold into cash and looking for new premises for his Insurance and Investment business. He had always taken great care not to live too near to his business and he hoped to hell that Lucy hadn't told Dot any of the names he traded under. Gold prices were at their highest for several years so he was well pleased with what he was getting for Lucy's things. Once he'd shown the company the Greek police report they let him open the deposit box that he and Lucy shared. The other two were in her name alone and he'd have to wait until she was legally declared dead but he'd been prepared for that. He found 15 Gold ingots, a platinum necklace and ten half sovereigns. He dismantled Lucy's three bracelets and sold the charms in twos and threes mostly in Hatton Garden. Other jewellery including her rings and watches he sold to individual jewellers throughout the county. In all he received over £25,000 for Lucy's treasures. He spread the money throughout various accounts he owned or managed, intending to transfer it all in smaller amounts into his two personal accounts later. He'd had two extra bank accounts in false names for many years which he used for tax evasion and his "fail safe" refuge for his money if he ever needed to declare himself bankrupt. He was never going to suffer his father's fate.

On Friday waiting at the Arrivals he almost missed Serena, so great was the change in her appearance. Only her rather mannish walk identified her. All traces of her reddish hair had disappeared and in place of her tight curls were long strings of blonde plaits. She wore an ankle length ethnic skirt and a blue blouse instead of her usual shirt and jeans. There was a well groomed softer look about her instead of the athletic blokish image she usually conveyed. But there was no change in the ardour of her embrace.

"Christ Bry, am I glad to see you."

"You're glad? I'm bloody ecstatic."

They went for a drink but the bars were so crowded they decided to go straight to his car instead. On the way he was surprised when she told him tonight was the earliest flight she had been able to book.

"Bit flash for a grieving widower" she said when she saw his new Mercedes. He knew then even if he kept quiet about the pervert he'd have to tell her about Lenny.

In the car the passion of their kisses and embraces were so intense that if the car park hadn't been so well lit they'd have had sex straightaway in the back. Byron broke all the speed limits on the way home. There was a FOR SALE notice at the front gate now but Serena said nothing about it. Indoors, they left a trail of discarded clothes along the hall and up the stairs. Byron entered her before they reached the top step. Never had he felt such a stallion. His mind was flooded with images of the couplings he'd seen at stud farms, For Serena with her legs wrapped around his back it was their final lovemaking on the boat all over again.

When they eventually dragged each other into bed Byron nipped downstairs to fetch the Champagne from the fridge. They had only a few sips before they were having sex again. It was savage triumphal sex rather than lovemaking. Everything they had risked together was celebrated in these couplings.

Afterwards they lay silent in each others arms. Byron 's mind kept replaying every second of the sex they'd just had; Serena found herself thinking if she died at this moment everything in her life would have been worthwhile. Nothing in the future could ever be better than this. Soon they drifted into an exhausted sleep.

Byron awoke alone in bed but the sound of the shower immediately reassured him. He lay back on the pillows savouring the pleasure he would get from seeing Serena naked. When she came into the room she had a big bath towel wrapped around her. When she saw he was awake she slowly and provocatively unwound it and let it fall to the floor. His anticipated pleasure faltered when he saw the bruises on her sides and thighs.

"Jesus Christ, I wasn't that rough, was I?"

"No Bry. These come via. a Russian fruitcake."

"What? Why? I mean…what happened?

She poured more Champagne and in between sips told him how she'd been assaulted in mistake for Tilly.

"I hope you beat the shit out of her." he said angrily.

Proudly she told him, "I did and then some. The papers said they had to keep her in hospital overnight."

"Terrific. You must have had to scarper fast. How did you keep out of the hands of the cops?"

He laughed and hugged her when she told him how Tilly had nicked the roll of notes from Juan and the hair and beauty treatments she'd had while she hid from the police.

"Good for you. It suits you. You look a right little cracker now."

"Whereas before?" She let the question hang in the air.

"You want an honest answer?"

"You, give someone an honest answer? That'll be the day."

"Sweetheart, whatever you choose to look like is O.K. by me. But I'll tell you this. You're my mate. You always will be."

"O Mr. Fuller you say the sweetest things "she replied in such a girlish voice that he spilled some Champagne laughing. When both glasses were empty and they relaxed back on the pillows Byron's mind battled between a desire for sex or food. Hunger won.

"Want to eat now?"

"Sure Bry. I'm starving."

At the table he told her about the long delay in being rescued and all that had happened in hospital afterwards. She didn't say anything when he mentioned the threat from Lenny. He kept quiet about the police visit and what the Peeping Tom had seen. It was when he was telling her of the steps he was taking to avoid Lenny finding him, that she shocked him by saying casually, "Why are you bothering with all this hiding? Get yourself a shooter and blow him away if he shows up."

"What here? In this house?"

"Yeah. If he arrives on your doorstep, act casual. Tell him you've got all Lucy's stuff ready for him. Invite him in and shoot him. Not in the back mind. Make sure he's facing you."

He gazed at her in astonishment. "Just like that?"

"Of course. If you give bastards like Lenny even a gnat's prick of a chance he'll do for you. I can get you a shooter from one of the pubs I used to work in. I'm sure most of the dealers I knew are still in business. You know to aim at the body not the head don't you. It's a much bigger target. I'll back you up. I'll say I was upstairs and crept down just in time to see him draw a gun on you. He most likely will have one on him. After you've shot him take his gun and put in his hand and fire it. I'll say I saw it all. We'll swear you had to act in self defence."

He shook his head not so much as to contradict her but in absolute astonishment at her ruthlessness. "I'm afraid Lenny never carries a gun. I remember Luce telling me he was proud of being a knife man."

Serena considered this. "There's got to be some way we can stiff him."

"No No. That's not on. It would only add to our troubles instead of solving them."

"How so?"

"You've heard of the Scopes brothers."

"I'll say. An old villain I know told me they make the Krays seem like social workers."

"That's putting it mildly. They're ruthless. Lenny's worked for them for years. If I killed him they'd have a contract out on me before his body hit the floor."

It was Serena's turn to shake her head. "This is serious shit. They're the last people on earth you'd want as enemies. I've known some really hard men turn a paler shade of White if they think they've crossed the Scopes. The word is they've got someone very high up in the Met in their pockets. Nobody dare testify against them. We're going to have to think hard about this". She paused then added, "I still think you ought to get a shooter."

"Actually I do already have a gun or rather a pair of guns. Inherited them from the old man. A lovely pair of Purdy's." Seeing her bewilderment he added "Shotguns. Purdy is a famous maker."

"You know how to use them?"

"Brought up with them. My old man loved his pheasant shooting. I've always enjoyed it. I go whenever I can. I'm quite a reasonable shot actually."

"Oh actually" she mimicked. "You've got a proper licence and everything?"

"Yes. I've always taken care to renew it."

"Well, you could at least use one of them to scare Lenny off if he does turn up."

"Maybe. I'm not sure it would be a very good idea though. If it did work it would only be the once. It wouldn't solve anything long term."

Serena poured herself another coffee and sat quietly. She stared down at the tablecloth as if seeking the answer there. Suddenly she raised her head and said "Got it. Nutters. Druggies. Know any Bry.?"

"Not really. Some of my acquaintances are into heavy cocaine use that's all."

She shook her head "What we want is some crack addict. Someone so far out of their skull that they wouldn't be afraid of dropping Lenny if you gave them enough money. Ten grand used to do it but I've heard it's cheaper now there are so many guns around."

"But what sort of shot is some drug crazed hoodlum going to be?"

"They don't have to be any good. They use automatics; some even have AK47's. "Point and Pray" is their slogan. All they need is to get close enough."

Byron wondered if it would work. He knew of more than one incident from his horse racing world of people who had "disappeared."

"Snake eyes Smith" he heard himself saying.

"What? Who the hell's that? "

"Ah, well. Snake Eyes Smith was a gypsy acquaintance of mine from the racetracks. I mention his name because the word is someone disposed of him in the same way as you're suggesting we arrange for Lenny. Some say the Scopes brothers were involved. Mind you his body's never been found. It's possible he scarpered back to Ireland."

"H'mm. What you just said about the body disappearing would be a good idea. But it would cost a lot extra if you wanted to make sure there was no trace of Lenny afterwards."

"I suppose so." He was silent for a while then added "What you're saying has possibilities but only as a last resort. And there's one big drawback."

"What's that?"

"Blackmail. Even if all went well and Lenny was blown to Hell, what's to prevent the hit man coming back and blackmailing me?"

"He won't know about you. I'd arrange it all. Trust me Bry, I've got plenty of contacts."

He couldn't stop himself getting up and coming around the table to embrace her. He professed not to believe in Luck but at this moment he was convinced that some benevolent force had led him to this treasure. "You are one sodding special woman" he whispered as he lifted her up.

Arms around each other they made their way back up to the bedroom.

CHAPTER 34

Paul sat in his car in the Council Car Park until he saw two staff who worked on the same floor as him leaving their cars. He got out and hurried in behind them. No way was he going through that building all on his own. He was sure no one would dare wolf whistle at him in the presence of witnesses. He'd tried in vain to dismiss the whistling as meant for someone else. The more he thought about it the more he was sure it wasn't all just a coincidence. Someone was taunting him as a homosexual. He felt sick at the thought. Nobody could despise homosexuals more than he did. What made everything worse was that he knew he couldn't complain. Not because the Council wouldn't support him. It most certainly would. The Council was awash with anti-discrimination rules and regulations. The staff notice boards were littered with leaflets for Gay Pride groups and telephone help lines like Stonewall. But he couldn't let himself be tainted with anything to do with homosexuality. He would have to ignore the perpetrator even if he caught him red lipped. He allowed himself a brief smile at the cleverness of the thought.

He reached his office unwhistled. He was later than usual but no one seemed to take any notice. Relieved he settled down to work. For the first hour all went well; then the queries began. Among other matters it was his department that dealt with the public's complaints on Council Tax matters. If it was straightforward or was clearly subject to the current Council regulations; the staff were allowed to answer the letters directly and just bring them to him to check and sign. More serious complaints were dealt with by Myra and himself.

He had always concentrated on what he liked to call inter-council matters, problems between different departments or queries from other councils. He thought that was the kind of work that befitted his status. But this morning they were plaguing him with minor matters that should have been perfectly clear from the Council guidelines they all had in their folders. He got less than half his usual work done that morning. What annoyed him even more was that Myra seemed as busy as ever despite the fact that he was doing some of her work. If only he could catch her idling he might be able to get her transferred to another department.

He was exhausted when he got in his car to drive home that night. Not only had the queries got more and more frivolous but he'd had to sit poised waiting for Bill Thompson and Fred Stables getting up to leave. He knew they shared a car so he would have their company on the way down to the car park. Myra was still working when he left, something he'd always tried to avoid. For years he'd been the last one to leave the office.

His mind was so preoccupied by his plight that he didn't notice the speeding Land Rover at the roundabout just before the flyover. Its blaring horn was the only thing that alerted him to give way. When he swerved to the left, he got another couple of angry blasts from the cars on the inside lanes. Only the fact he was driving an automatic prevented the engine stalling. He was used being hooted at as he drove for he scrupulously obeyed every speed restriction he saw on his journeys. But now, all he wanted was to get home. He followed the flow of the traffic no matter how often he infringed the Highway Code.

He was so upset when he got home he couldn't think of eating. To calm himself he brushed and combed Kaiser with slow steady strokes. He thinned his coat with the special comb he'd had for his pet ever since he was a puppy, then trimmed it with the expensive stainless steel scissors he'd bought for his pet's ninth birthday. They were actually hairdressing scissors but he told himself only the best was good enough for a pedigree like Kaiser. Only when Kaiser lifted its face to his to nuzzle him did a ray of peace enter his soul. He found himself reflecting on the vagrancies of life. To think if it hadn't been for that common lout accosting him around the back of the council flats he'd never have had such a loyal companion.

He still couldn't face cooking or eating so he put Kaiser on his lead and went out into the evening sunshine. He'd no clear ideas where he was going; he just strode along basking in the reflected glory of the admiring glances Kaiser received form passers by.

It was only when he realised he was about to turn into Meldrum Avenue that he checked his stride. He'd been avoiding coming here in case he met Fuller. Now he was so near he decided he'd risk a brief peep into the Avenue. There was still an empty space outside the house. Nevertheless he crossed to the opposite side to *Sunset*. He'd only gone a few yards when he saw the FOR SALE sign at its gate. He had to force himself to walk on and stare straight ahead as he passed.

His mind was in turmoil. What was he to do? What could he do? The man was fleeing and the police were doing damm all to prevent it. No wonder the crime figures were rising. He'd warned them three times! Yet nothing was being done. Fuller wouldn't be allowed to sell his house and move if they had him as a suspect. The expression used in the detective stories was "in the frame" wasn't it? It looked as if the useless bloody police still had the hood covering the camera lens instead of having Fuller "in the frame." It would seem that catching this murderer was going to be all down to him.

When he got home he decided he couldn't think properly on an empty stomach. Such a momentous task required a properly nourished body. "A healthy mind in a healthy body," wasn't that what the ancients preached? He forced himself to settle down and cook a meal. He tried a new recipe he'd got from *The Daily Mail* for Chicken Chasseur; then gulped it down so quickly that he knew he'd get indigestion. He spent the rest of the night thinking how he could expose Fuller. He went through his notebooks where he had listed the steps Hercule Poriot had taken in each book to unmask the killer but nothing seemed to fit the present situation. He was still without any clear plan of action when he got to bed just after midnight. He didn't sleep well; twice he had to get up for a glass of Andrews Liver Salts, his long time indigestion remedy.

Next day, at work his IN tray was so full he worked through the coffee break morning and afternoon. He'd not had time to make sandwiches so had to risk a lunch time journey through the outer office to buy some. He walked briskly with his head down, avoiding any possibility of eye contact and was relieved to get out and back without being whistled. He ate at his desk; it was a relief not to be interrupted by queries. Nevertheless the pile of folders in his IN tray seemed to be going down very slowly. Throughout the afternoon the queries recommenced. He tried keeping his answer brief and to the point, several times he referred enquirers back to their staff manuals and pointed out where they could easily have found the answer without bothering him. All of them seemed to be particularly stupid today. He became more and more abrupt with his answers.

There was less than half an hour to the end of the working day when the explosion occurred. He was trying to frame a coherent answer to a problem he'd not encountered before when he looked up to see Gaynor at his desk.

"Mr. Thewell, I know you've told me before but I keep forgetting. That word Principle? Is the end p-a-l or p-l-e when I'm referring to a Council regulation that someone's asking about? You know; our rules thingy."

His immediate reaction was to tell her to go away and formulate a proper question in English but he wanted rid of her. "It's p-l-e Miss Brown, p-l-e. Do try to remember. For a person it is p-a-l. Your principal at School was your best PAL." He turned back to the file in front of him but what he was going to write had vanished. He clenched his hands to try and keep control of the anger rising inside him. Looking up, his annoyance increased when he saw Gaynor still there. She was shaking her head.

"You keep saying that Mr. Thewell but it's not true. That's what confuses me."

"What? What confuses you?"

"She wasn't. She was a right old cow. Only interested in the A stream girls."

"Who?"

"The principal of my school, St.Brigit's."

It was the laughter from the nearby desks that tipped his anger past boiling point. He yelled at her, "You idiotic girl. Go away. Get out of my sight. Don't waste my time with your stupidity."

She turned quickly away but not before he saw tears welling up in her eyes. He felt no sympathy for her. It was beyond his comprehension why the Council employed morons like Gaynor. She was hardly fit to be behind the counter in Woolworths.

As he carried on with is work he gradually became aware of how silent the room had become. It must be they didn't like the way he'd spoken to Gaynor. So what? He was tempted to lift his head and glare at them. No noise meant no work as far as he was concerned. But he had to finish this report. He'd deal with them tomorrow.

He was so preoccupied with his work he didn't hear Thompson and Staples leaving. Now he would have to run the whistler's gauntlet alone. But before he could dwell on that he noticed the clock. It was only a minute past five; they must all have been sitting waiting at their desks ready to leave. He would speak to them about this tomorrow; they were supposed to work until five and then get ready to leave. Standards were dropping everywhere. Maybe he should write to the Daily Mail about it.

As he was getting into his car a wolf whistle startled him so much he banged his head on the door frame. The pain made his eyes sting. He forced himself not to look around. He would not respond to their baiting. He had to grip the steering firmly to help take his mind off the pain in his head. It was over five minutes before he felt well enough to drive away. As he did so he consoled himself with the thought that all great men had had to suffer the ridicule of ignorant fools.

CHAPTER 35

Detective Constable C, S. Bullerton had been called "Bully" for as long as he could remember even though it had always been a monumentally inappropriate nick-name. The reason he had never tried to dissuade anyone from using the menacing epithet was because it prevented people from asking what the "C.S", stood for. He dreaded being exposed as "Clarence Sassoon." His muscular six foot two inch well proportioned body carried no hint of menace because of his open frank face. He turned out regularly for the local police Rugby team for he enjoyed the camaraderie and the (not always sporting) competition of his peers.

His relaxed manner made people feel at ease talking to him. Criminals often thought his cornflower blue eyes were the windows of an innocent, easily deceived soul. That was very far from the case. He was a careful rather than a quick thinker and was becoming well known in the force for the thoroughness of his investigations. Just now he was concentrating on finding out all that he could about Byron Wesley Fuller. His enquiries among his friends and relations had produced a list of answers that made him want to investigate this man much further. Many of the women described him as "charming" "an attentive partner." Some of the bolder ones (Including his sister Caroline described Fuller as "Good in bed but not one to marry." Hunting chaps said he was a good horseman and a good judge of horseflesh. He was known as a regular and well informed gambler. There was no record of him ever welshing on his debts. Sporting opponents while admiring his athleticism tended to qualify their assessment with words like "ruthless" and "shows no mercy." It was people who worked in the City who were most wary about him. "Don't let him know your granny has premium bonds" was how one of Bully's university friends who was now a stockbroker had described him.

Bully had decided to widen his enquires to Fuller's dead wife's relatives which was why he was now sitting in Dot's ornately furnished bungalow. She had been initially hostile when he'd shown her his warrant card but changed completely as soon as she knew it was Fuller he was investigating. He'd hardly sunk down into the big green velour armchair before she said, "I'll tell you now to save you asking. He's a murderer and a thief. He drowned my Lucy to get his filthy hands on her money." The vehemence of her words told him he would be wasting his time contradicting her.

"I hear what you say Mrs.Boothe but the problem is how can we prove it?"

"I don't need no proof. I know. A mother always knows...and call me Dot. Everybody does"

He nodded sympathetically as he answered "I'm sure you do, Dot. But unfortunately as you also know we need evidence to convict him. Evidence that will stand up in a court of Law."

"But you've got something haven't you? You must have, otherwise you wouldn't be here."

He hated to disappoint her but it would be cruel to raise any false hopes. So he told her the truth. "I'm afraid, Dot, we're nothing specific at the moment. We're just compiling a report at the request of the Greek authorities."

"Fat lot of use those greasy buggers were. They did nothing but persecute me and my brother." She paused then added "You know it's terrible not being able to bury my Lucy."

"Yes Dot." He said quietly. "That's one of the worst things about tragedies like Lucy's. It makes it difficult to mourn properly doesn't it?" He stopped, not sure of what to say next.

Dot's eyes were glistening as she answered, "Yes, it does, but I won't give up hope. She could turn up at any time you know. I've been looking into it. There's a lot of information on the Internet about bodies dumped in the sea and lakes. They often turn up even when they've been weighed down with chains and rocks. Storms and earthquakes can free them to return to the surface." She told him of two recent cases where bodies resurfacing had lead to murder convictions.

Bully looked at Dot increasing admiration. He could see that from the way her clothes hung loosely on her how much she was being physically affected by her grief. But her voice was strong and vigorous when she talked about Fuller. She was almost evangelical about the time to come when he would be exposed as a murderer. He was careful to maintain eye contact with her so that she could see he was paying attention. When she'd exhausted herself he started to ask her about Lucy's marriage and if there had ever been any violence or ill treatment on Fuller's part.

160

"It was all lovey dovey at the beginning but after the first couple of years that was it. He'd got what he wanted. He tortured her mentally you know. Always casting aspersions on her size. Her father was big boned just like me. It was only natural Lucy would be a bit plump. She didn't have the height you see. Only five foot two she was. She almost starved herself to death for that bastard. He never appreciated what she put her self through."

As tactfully as he could he returned to his questions about physical violence but she reluctantly had to admit she had no evidence of that, "He took all his energy out on tarts. Told Lucy he was entertaining them as clients. How she put I with it I'll never know. She was always making excuses for him. Never wanted her dad to know what a bastard she'd married."

Bully went to speak but she continued: "He's a crook you know. He's into all sorts of insurance fiddles. Calls himself a consultant but he's got no exams or nothing. My Lucy said he dips into his clients savings. You could get him for that couldn't you?"

"Yes. But again we need proof." It was clear Dot was a woman eager for vengeance but nothing she said gave him any reason to think that Fuller was a murderer. The man's account of what had happened on that boat was perfectly plausible. He might be a scoundrel but that was far removed from being a murderer. What her words did was eliminate any possibility of Lucy being killed in her own back bedroom for she spoke of having several telephone conversations with her from Greece.

"When Lucy spoke to you, did she say anything that would indicate she felt anxious on this holiday? Did you get any impression at all that she might be in any danger." he asked.

Dot shook her head "No I can't say that she did. She sounded happy enough. But she should never have been on that boat. She'd never learned to swim. She phoned me you know while she was on that effing boat. I told her to get him to turn back but she wouldn't have it." She paused before adding sorrowfully "I must have been the last person she spoke to before Fuller drowned her."

"And she never gave you any reason to think she was in danger?"

"No. Mind you I 'm sure she'd been drinking. Her voice was a bit funny at times. I sometimes thought she was drinking a lot more than usual. It would have suited Fuller to get her drunk so that he could do away with her." Again she hesitated before saying "I keep trying to convince myself that's what happened. It's not much but I think that at least if she was drunk she'd not know what was happening. Maybe she passed out before he dumped her overboard. He might even have spiked her drink. She'd not suffer so much then, would she?"

He was glad to agree with her. He knew that drowning it was one of the worst ways to die so it would indeed be a blessing if Lucy had been unconscious. Wanting to get Dot as quickly as he could away from the subject he asked "So there was nothing Lucy said to you that was much different from other times she was on holiday with him?"

"Nothing that I noticed. There was one thing though. She never talked as long as she did on other holidays. We was always getting cut off. Van said the same thing."

"Van?"

"Vanessa, Lucy's mate. She and Lucy was mates right from infant school. Lucy talked to her every day. Van always looked after her animals while she was on holiday. You ought to have a word with her."

"Yes, I'd like to. I take it you've got her address?"

"Yes. But she's often out. I'll phone and see where she is." Instead of picking up the telephone from the little table beside her she produced from somewhere in her armchair a mobile phone.

"Van. It's Dot. How are you?...me too. Look, what you doing today? I mean in the next hour or so. At home, you've seen to Paddy already? He misses Lucy terribly doesn't he? Yes. Yes. You'll be in then? What's it about? I've got a copper here. He's asking about Fuller? No. Not so far. Yes, I hope so too. Look he'd like to come and see you."

She lowered the phone and nodded to Bully "That O.K with you? She's only lives three miles from here."

He'd been wondering how tactfully he could leave this intense little woman. "Yes" he said" If there's nothing more you'd like to tell me, I'll go round there now."

"You hear that Van? Yeah, he' a big bloke. I'd tell you the size of his feet but I don't want to frighten you."

162

Whatever Van replied made Dot shriek with laughter. "Dream on girl" she said as she put the phone down. Bully felt himself blushing as she smiled at him. "She's a girl she is, our Van. You'd never think to look at her she's got four kids. Ian the oldest, he's a copper. I don't suppose you'll know him. He's up in the East End."

"No. That's too exotic a territory for a country boy like me. I can just about manage down here among the turnips and mangleworzels."

She gave him a shrewd look before saying, "I don't know. I reckon you're not as green as you're cabbage looking."

Bully blushed again and started to ease himself out of the depths of the armchair. "If there's anything else you think of after I leave you can always phone me at the station or on my mobile." He handed her a card with the numbers on it.

She thanked him and gave him very clear and explicit directions how to get to Van.

When he got to the door he turned to say "goodbye" but there was something about her stance that made him hesitate; "You're sure there's nothing else you'd like to tell me. Even what appears to be a very minor matter can turn out very important in our investigations."

She answered him slowly, "Well, you know I'd give anything to find my Lucy? Well, I went to this medium. Famous she is. Been on the Telly." She stopped and looked down at the carpet again.

"I hope she was some comfort" he said quietly.

She looked up and shook her head, "She couldn't get in touch with Lucy, didn't try to fool me that she could. I'd deliberately not told her much. Afterwards when I said Lucy had died abroad at sea, do you know what she said, "I'm surprised. I know I couldn't get through to her but I got the feeling that Lucy's not that far away. What do you make of that?"

Ignoring his own agnosticism he replied "Perhaps she means her spirit's here with you now."

"That's what I thought but when I asked her she said she had more a sense of Lucy's physical presence."

He shook his head. "She can't be right, can she?"

"No. But she wouldn't take any money off me although I offered her quite a wack."

"Did she suggest you come back and see her again?"

"No, but she promised she'd let me know if Lucy got in touch."

Bully instantly thought Dot might be being set up for a "sting." The medium could easily use the time to find out more from the papers about Lucy's demise. "If she does, make sure you she's not telling you things that she could have learned from news reports. Mediums can use the Internet too."

Dot nodded "Don't worry. I've still got all my marbles "

"I'm sure you have Dot. Now take care. If this medium does get in touch, would you mind letting me know what she's got to say."

"I will, Mr. Bullerton. I promise."

He followed Dot's directions and easily found Van's ranch style bungalow. She was a tall talkative blonde but after a few minutes conversation he realised she was far from being an air head. She was articulate and specific in her comments. Her observations about Fuller matched those of Dot's. She admitted she'd never liked Fuller but that Lucy had never said he'd hit her. She confirmed she had spoken several time to her on the phone from Greece and like Dot remarked that the calls had been "unusually brief."

Although he'd learned little from his visit he consoled himself by thinking she'd make an excellent prosecution witness if ever a criminal case was brought against Fuller.

CHAPTER 36

Gaynor didn't come into work the next day. Paul sensed an air of hostility in the office but refused to let it bother him. He was in a better mood today. He'd risked coming into the building unaccompanied and no one had whistled at him. Nor had there been any whistles as he'd walked through the large outer office on the way to see the Mr. Abramonson who dealt with the Council's legal matters. Perhaps his tormentors were getting tired of the joke. As the day progressed and not one of the staff came to him with a query, he congratulated himself that he'd been so firm with the stupid girl. He'd asserted his authority. From now on he'd get no more frivolous enquires and if any of the staff were refusing to come to him because they were unhappy about Gaynor then they'd have to take the consequences for any mistakes they made. Working in silence suited him and he was able to substantially reduce his backlog of work. On his way home he called into Tesco's and treated himself to their two of their Finest Fare Gammon steaks. He liked to eat like a gourmet at least once a week and Kaiser always approved of his selections.

He spent the evening trying to work out what to do about Fuller. He found many tracing agencies and private detectives on the Internet but they were all very expensive. He decided that he'd only use them if Fuller disappeared completely from his view. He had at work access to electoral rolls and the last National Census. That should help keep Fuller in his sights.

Knowing Fuller's whereabouts was one thing but knowing what to do about him was another. Then there was his accomplice. Who was she and how could he trap her? Of course he could save himself all this trouble by writing to the police again and setting out in meticulous detail how Fuller had managed to get people to believe his wife had died in a boating accident in Greece. But they'd taken no notice of his letters and phone call so far, so how could he be sure they'd do anything with what he told them now. If they did and Fuller and the woman were caught and convicted then the police would get all the glory yet he would have done all the detecting. This was his one big chance to make a name for himself: to show all those who mocked him how mistaken they were. If the police didn't have the brains to work out what had happened, so much the worse for them. He would do what Hercule

Poirot did. Not only did he solve their cases for them, he made sure his "little grey cells" got the proper recognition and praise for what he'd achieved.

The next day was Friday and once more he'd had an untroubled walk to this office and Gaynor remained absent. Paul hoped she'd asked for a transfer. If she had he'd insist that her replacement was a person of higher intelligence.

It was a miserably wet weekend; both cricket matches where he was to umpire were cancelled. He spent his time reading a book on true crimes in the hope of finding something that would help him trap Fuller but got no inspiration from it. What he did get was strong reinforcement of his belief in police incompetence. He was particularly horrified by the Donald Neilson case. They had only been yards from the manhole where his victim had been incarcerated when they'd called off the search and even when the local police had wanted to search the park again next day they had been overruled by senior Scotland Yard detectives. Paul was all the more certain that it would be up to him alone to expose Fuller.

On Monday morning he was disappointed when Gaynor came in to the office. As usual she was only a few seconds away from being late. He'd have to speak to her about that. No one came to him with any queries and he was able to work uninterrupted. He was enjoying dealing with a particularly complex involving several different addresses when his computer alerted him to an internal e-mail. It was from Margery McHaddan, a woman he particularly disliked. In his view even since she came to the council four years ago all she had done was use her position in Staff Welfare to spew out loads of totally unnecessary information and regulations about equal opportunities, gender awareness and other sexual perversions. She wanted him to come to her office at 2pm for "an important matter concerning your department." He knew it was pointless refusing, so he clicked the acknowledgement button to signify he'd be there.

When he knocked on her door at exactly 2 o'clock to emphasise his reputation for punctuality; he got an immediate "Enter." As he advanced towards her desk the way the light reflected off her steel rimmed glasses and her long angular Highland face made him think of the Nazi leader Himmler. After a brief exchanged of formalities she told him directly why she wanted him here.

166

"I'm sorry to say Mr.Thewell that the reason for this meeting is that there has been a very serious complaint of harassment made against you by one of your office staff."

He was so shocked that he didn't hear the rest of her words. He took a deep breath to control the anger arising inside him before replying; "That's ridiculous, I demand to know who it is that is making such an unwarranted allegation?"

She leaned forward and said in what seemed to him excessively measured tones, "There is no need for you to demand anything, Mr. Thewell. You have every right to be informed of the name of the complainant, it is Miss Gaynor Green."

"Huh! Her! I might have guessed. Well, Mizz McHadden, let me inform you that in the time she has been in my department I have found Miss Green to be a young lady of somewhat limited intellectual ability."

He didn't like the way she looked at him as she answered "Is that so Mr. Thewell? You know how long has Miss Green been in your department."

He wanted to tell her that it was her job to know that but he kept his tongue in check, "Three years?"

"Three years eight months Mr. Thewell. I have her assessment records here before me. I cannot see any complaint that you have ever made about her or the standard of her work in all that time."

"I'm a very tolerant man Mizz McHaddan; I've been willing to make allowances for her youth and inexperience. But lately her performance has been far from satisfactory."

"In what way, Mr Thewell? Can you give me a particular example?"

All he could think to say "Well, she keeps coming up to my desk with queries to which I have already given her the answer." McFadden looked as if she was going to say something but he decided to size the initiative and go on the attack. "I do not know Miss McHaddon if you are aware of the importance of my department's work? It..."

"The work of all Council departments is important, Mr. Thewell."

He noticed the stress on "Mr." Maybe he was rattling her. "Indeed...but I am speaking of financial importance. I...we... my department's work saves this Council tens of thousands of pounds each year in preventing avoidance of proper Council Tax demands. I repeat tens...maybe hundreds of thousands."

"That is very praiseworthy but that is the reason for your existence is it not?"

"Are you trying to say we do no more than what is expected of us? Because if you are; you are very much mistaken. What we achieve is far in excess of mere competence I can assure you."

"As I've said that is very praiseworthy but could we return to Miss Green please. Apart from the example you have given have you any other complaints about Miss Green?"

"Isn't what I've told you enough? I'm a very busy man. As I've tried to explain to you my department's work is of great financial benefit to this Council."

"Mr.Thewell, I appreciate that you are a very conscientious and as you say very busy head of your department. May I ask then why you ordered all your staff to come to you with all their queries? "

He could not believe the cheek of her question. "Mizz McHaddon, I hope you are not trying to tell me how to run my department?"

"Not at all, Mr. Thewell. I am merely enquiring why when there was a long-established practice of minor queries being dealt with by your deputy or other senior staff, you wished to burden yourself with this additional work?"

His reply was out of his mouth before he had time to think. "I'm afraid that I have not been satisfied with my Deputy, Miss Williamson's work for some time."

"Indeed." She paused and looked down at her desk. When she looked up again she said, "If you wish to complain about Miss Williamson's work you know the procedures we have set up to enable these matters to be resolved?" She didn't let him reply but continued "Actually, I am following these guidelines now in your case. Why I have asked you here for is to get your response for a very serious complaint of bullying and public humiliation made against you by Miss Green."

"Utter rubbish. Miss McHaddan, I've already told you I am a very busy man. If Miss Green is unhappy in my department then I suggest the best thing is for her to be transferred to another department." He rose to go.

"Please wait Mr. Thewell. I'm afraid things are far from that simple. I'm sorry to have to tell you there is also a great deal of disquiet among all your staff about the way you exercise your authority. And I do mean all. Miss Green has supplied me with several testimonies from members of your department verifying her account of your treatment of her. I have personally spoken to each of them and every one is willing to testify at the enquiry that will have to take place that her account is truthful." She stared straight at him as she added "The word 'dictatorial 'is the one that most frequently occurs in their testimonies"

He sank back down in the seat shocked. He couldn't think of what to say.

She too remained silent for what seemed to him a very long time. When she spoke he was astounded to notice that her voice was softer and there was a look of unmistakeable concern on her face. "Mr. Thewell. As you know we are very much an anti-discriminatory Council and we have in place strong and sympathetic support groups for all our staff. I understand you were recently the victim of a brutal homophobic attack and I would urge you to take full advantage of the support that our gender equality groups can offer. If you feel that a further few weeks recuperation would be…"

He stood up his face reddening with anger. "How dare you" he shouted. "How dare you suggest that I am (he struggled to find the words for Miss McHadden made no secret of her lesbianism) that I am in any way associated with practices that I find ab…ab…abhorrent…I will not listen any further to your ridiculous insinuations. I…"

He was afraid to say any more. He turned and rushed out of her office. He went straight to the staff toilets and locked himself in a cubical. An avalanche of emotions shook his body, anger, confusion, hatred and above all fear. His whole career was at risk. His staff had betrayed him. After years of setting them such a good example of a proper management they had chosen to take the side of a moronic girl against him. It was probably one of them that had spread the news of the car park attack throughout the Council. How could he ever work with them again? His career was in ruins. Unless…unless he could get a transfer to another department. Without loss of salary or status, of course. He tried to think of where he could go but every office he thought of was as far as he knew fully staffed. Redundancies…the Council were talking about redundancies? If he asked for a transfer might it not make him a candidate for redundancy? He couldn't risk that. It would be better to go to another Council.That could be the answer. The London boroughs were always having trouble keeping their staff. He wouldn't enjoy the travelling but anything would be better than working where he wasn't appreciated. Unappreciated and labelled a homosexual. How dare that woman include him in her rabble of perverts! He'd soon put her straight on that as soon as he'd time to think of a way to do it. That's what he needed now. Time.

He got up slowly and listened to make sure there was no one else in the wash room. All around him seemed quiet but he still opened the cubical door cautiously and was ready to close it quickly if anyone entered. When he was satisfied he was alone he made his way over to the wash basins. The face that stared back at him from the mirrors didn't seem much different from normal; a bit redder than usual that was all. He gave his hands and face a thorough wash and practiced breathing slowly. Looking at his watch he was surprised it was only a quarter to three. Over two hours to spend in the company of Quislings. Well…he could do it. He'd show them. Squaring his shoulders he marched out of the toilet swinging his arms the way his soldier father had taught him as a child.

Despite his evangelical upbringing he wasn't an especially religious man but before he entered his office he did literally "Thank God it's Friday."

CHAPTER 37

Byron was irritated. Yesterday one of his *Secrets from the Stables,* a horse called "Debs Delight" had won a race at odds of 40 to 1 and he hadn't had a penny on it. Not that he ever backed his long shots, but he was annoyed nevertheless. His annoyance increase when he phoned Dawn at the office and she couldn't wait to tell him that everyone there had backed it. "With two Debbies here we just had to have something on it." What was it about women that made them so irrationally lucky? It reminded him of Lucy at the races. She normally risked only £20 on a race but there had been times when she'd put all her winnings on some whim and had come home with more money in her handbag than he had in his wallet.

He knew it was useless asking Dawn how much they'd won; she was far too astute to tell him. All the girls got a profit sharing bonus (decided by him). They knew he'd try to get away with giving them less if he knew what they'd won.

He went to tell Dawn to increase his newspaper advertising highlighting his success with "Deb's Delight" but she'd already done it. Her words made him think again about the wisdom of moving his business elsewhere. He couldn't risk losing someone like her. The others were no slackers either. It had taken him years to build up such a top-notch team. Maybe it would be best to leave them where they were until Lenny actually threatened him. He'd had no news of the thug since he came home. Perhaps the bastard had drowned at sea.

Apart from missing out on a 40 to 1 tip things were going well at the moment. He'd had an offer for the house that was only two thousand less than the advertised price. If nothing better came along in the next two weeks he'd take it. He'd seen several likely properties but none were near enough to a motorway to suit him. Whatever he found he'd decided he play things by the book and tell the police and the Greeks his new address. He'd do nothing to arouse their suspicions.

He'd make a big profit on the house. Serena said he should use the money to buy a property abroad, preferably somewhere without an extradition treaty with Britain. He knew that made good sense but he felt that it might be time to have a really substantial wager on the horses. He'd an over 70% winning ratio in the last three weeks. The trouble was they'd all been very short priced winners. His highest successful wager had been £2500 on an even money favourite. He'd known it would win. Why hadn't he had the courage to make his bet £25,000? He'd had bigger wagers than that in the past. The trouble was most had failed for one unforeseen reason or another. Some, like those that had fallen had been sheer bad luck.

That's why he had plundered Mrs.Theatley's money so rapidly. He had access to over a quarter of a million pounds belonging to this ex-civil servant. Suddenly she had turned from a healthy hill walking 78 year old to a frail bed bound invalid. All because she had caught pneumonia after falling and breaking her femur. Her nephew had told him she could die anytime. The tone of the man's voice told him it was a wish rather than an observation. He had been in danger of suddenly having to account for a missing £30,000 from her estate. That had been an additional factor in getting rid of Lucy.

Now, with the Sale of the house practically assured he felt financially safe. But he was bored. Everything seemed a bit too tame. Hadn't he taken the greatest risk of all? Murder; and got away with it. There was no denying that in these past weeks he had a sense of certainty about his gambles that he'd never had before. Or was he kidding himself? Could he afford to take such risks again? But then wasn't taking risks what his life was all about? No matter what form or breeding or the ability of a horse to run well under certain conditions like either soft or hard ground or its success rate at a particular race track all was still a risk. He was a risk taker. Maybe it was time to make some really big bets that would set him up for life? Him…and Serena. Maybe she was the real reason why he felt so confident now. What a woman. What a winner she was. What a team they were.

Thinking about her took his mind of betting. His more immediate problem was deciding when Serena should move in with him. They talked about it every time they met. He was anxious to have her with him but at the same time he agreed with her on the need to be cautious. She'd said "It's supposed to be all over between us ain't it? If the law finds out about me, they'll think I was your motive for getting rid of Lucy. I think we should wait at least the Greeks drop everything. Wherever you decide to live I can always get somewhere nearby." At present she was in a flat about six miles away and working as a Gym instructor. The pay was crap but it covered her expenses and she could choose her own hours. So they'd plenty of chances to meet.

He'd known he have to wait seven years before Lucy could be declared legally dead. Being prepared for it didn't make it any easier to endure. There must a hell of a lot of money in her two safe deposit boxes. She'd been such a squirrel. Last Sunday Serena had found an envelope with £300 in fivers hidden in a flour container in the kitchen. They'd looked in every other container and drawer but found nothing else of value. It was getting late when they finished and they decided that pleasure was preferable to treasure and went to bed

CHAPTER 38

When Paul returned to work on Monday he had a memo telling him Gaynor had been transferred "temporarily" to General Accounts. "Temporarily" disturbed him. What did that mean? He thought of e-mailing staffing to ask exactly what they meant but he decided to "Let sleeping bitches lie." He had more important things to do. He'd determined that come the last half-hour of the day he'd call all his staff together and give them a good lecture on their responsibilities. Leaving it so late would ensure there'd be little time for debate. He'd been rehearsing some of the phrases he'd use as he drove into work. "Duty, Respect and Responsibility" featured prominently in all of them. He'd speak in measured Churchillian tones. He'd show them who was boss.

The atmosphere in the office was noticeably sour but the thought of the lecture he was going to deliver sustained him through the morning and early afternoon. He'd just checked his watch and seen that it was only an hour to go before his big oration when the message flashed up on his computer screen, "Please report to Mr. Oakman Immediately." He tidied his desk and left the room. His meetings with his boss were rarely lengthy but he didn't want to take any chances of being detained and having to rush his speech to his staff. "Perhaps" he thought as he hurried along the corridor "I'm going to get an apology for McHaddan's behaviour."

After he'd been welcomed and settled in a chair Mr Oakman picked up one of the papers he was shuffling before him and said "I see you are one of our longest serving employees, Thewell."

"Yes. Mr. Oakman. This is my 28th[th] year here."

"Indeed, a year longer than myself. And you were nine years with Lamdon Council before that."

"Yes, I went there straight from leaving school"

"Very good." He paused and looking at him in what Paul took to be a very approving manner, added "We've seen some changes in that time, haven't we?"

Paul agreed. He was tempted to add "not all of them for the good" but decided against it.

"Well, as I'm sure you're well aware we here at Cleedon, like all other Local Government Authorities up and down the country are under great pressure from the Government to make considerable economies in our finances."

Paul seized the chance for a bit of self promotion. "Oh, yes indeed Mr. Oakman. That is why I make sure that my department is most efficient at getting the highest possible returns from all our council tax payers."

Oakman nodded, "That's very commendable." He paused before continuing, "But I'm afraid that after a very thorough review it has been decided that amalgamation of a number of departments will contribute greatly to our efficiency and your department is one of those chosen for amalgamation."

He paused again and looked down at the papers on his desk, Paul's heart leaped. Promotion!   Oakman had got him here to offer him the management of this new department!

"You understand, Thewell that such an amalgamation will mean the disappearance of a number of senior posts and I am sorry to inform you that yours is one of them."

Paul blushed "But this new department, I will have a responsible position in it, will I not?"

The answer didn't come as quickly as Paul would have liked. He sensed something ominous when he heard Oakman say, "This amalgamation will necessitate all employees having to re-apply for their jobs, but as there will be fewer positions available I'm afraid that we will have to offer redundancies to a number of our staff."

"Of course Mr Oakman"

"The one bit of good news for you, Thewell, is that because one department head's position is vanishing we are able to offer you greatly enhanced redundancy terms."

Paul could not believe what he was hearing. All he could do was whisper "Me?"

"Yes Thewell. That is the purpose of this meeting."

Paul waited for him to continue but all the man did was to look expectantly at him. Suddenly he heard himself saying loudly, "But I don't want to be redundant. I understood that any redundancies in this Council would be voluntary? I've most certainly not volunteered. I want to be considered for any of the new senior management posts that will be created. I think in view of my long and loyal service I'm entitled to expect that, am I not?"

The directness of the answer startled him. "You are entitled but I must tell you Thewell, and believe me, I am saying this as a kindness to you, there is not the slightest possibility of you being successful."

All Paul could do was croak "Why?"

Oakman let out an audible sigh. "I had hoped to avoid mentioning this." He paused before continuing "There are a number of reasons why you would not be considered suitable to continue in a managerial position in this council. If you force my hand I will read them out to you from the list of written complaints I have here in front of me. They come from both senior and junior staff in both your own and other departments. An inquiry is already in progress about your managerial style. If it proceeds you will be given every opportunity to answer these allegations but I must tell you that from what I read and noticed over the years you would have very little chance of refuting them. Wait…" he held up his hand to stop Paul interrupting. "You are an educated man Thewell, so I trust you will understand when I say that I find your position rather analogous to that of Captain Blight of the Bounty."

Paul felt stupid nodding but he couldn't stop himself.

Oakman continued "The thing is Thewell, if this enquiry found against you, you could find yourself dismissed from our employment. Then there would be no obligation on our part to offer you anything other than the bare minimum redundancy in monetary terms. However, if you were to leave under this "voluntary redundancy" package, you would be the recipient of a very generous financial settlement. For example your pension would be enhanced to the equivalent of 45 years service."

"Forty-five?" Paul heard himself parroting. He felt as if he was witnessing this conversation from another part of the room

"Yes, and the other benefits are not insubstantial believe me. It is the loss of a position that makes this possible." Oakman's voice became softer and more confidential "I'm sure you'll agree Thewell that the world has changed a great deal from what it was when we began our council work. I know from my own experience how difficult it is for us older staff to get used to the less formal working conditions of the present day. I realise what I have told you has been a bit of a shock. It is only natural that you will want time to think about it. I will ask Mizz McHaddon's department to set out your redundancy terms in full. I suggest you take a few days to think about them and come and see me, say, this time Friday afternoon."

Paul nodded and watched himself leave the room.

When he got to near his own department he was shaking so much he had to stand still and clench his fists until he regained his composure sufficiently to open the office door. He made his way blindly to his desk and picked up the first piece of paper his hand touch and sat stating at it.

"Redundant. After over 30 years in Local government." The words seared his mind. He...

"Mr. Thewell." He looked up to see Myra hovering over him. "These letters" she pointed to his IN tray, "they need your signature now if they're to go in today's post."

He dismissed her with a nod and reached out and lifted the papers. Forcing himself to read the words in front of him gradually brought him to some semblance of normalcy. He remembered that when he began his Council work as a 16 year old it had been his job to go around all the departments collecting the outgoing post. He'd worked so hard to improve himself. Years of study at night school. All for what? To be cast aside like yesterday's newspaper. Him...a man in the prime of his life.

Looking at the office clock he saw there was still forty minutes until 5 o'clock. Damn it. Damn them all. He scribbled his name at the end of each letter and switching off his computer he picked up his briefcase and walked out of the office without a word. He'd left his desk unlocked but what did it matter? Nothing in that place was of any importance to him any more.

The next thing he was conscious of was Kaiser greeting him as he opened is front door. He had no recollection of driving home. He let the dog put its front paws on his shoulder and lick his face instead of commanding it to "sit" as he usually did. He knew his face was already wet with tears. Gently he eased Kaiser down, groped his way to the kitchen and found a large biscuit treat for his pet.

He collapsed into one of the kitchen chairs and half heartedly tried to stop the tears. He'd always considered it most unmanly to cry but now it seemed that all the standards he had lived by were not worth a penny. The world had gone mad. Discipline and self-control were obsolete. Was it any wonder there was no respect for authority any more? He wanted to shout out but he told himself he'd more self control than that. Besides he didn't want to upset Kaiser. He decided to walk off his grief. After a brief wash he told the dog to fetch his lead. Kaiser went immediately and came back wagging his tail and laid the lead at Paul's feet.

He determined this would be no aimless meander. He had a clear destination in mind. Meldrum Avenue. Fuller wasn't going to get away with murder. If he was forced to leave the Council's employment then at least he'd have time to pursue the man. He was relieved to see that the FOR SALE sign was still there. Outside the house was a brand new Mercedes Kompressor, its steering wheel secured with a large bright yellow anti-theft bar. Paul walked some way past before looking back and memorising the car's number plate. On his way home he stopped at a Patel's newsagents and bought a small hard backed notebook in which he wrote the registration down.

The brisk walk partially restored his appetite. He got out a rump steak from the freezer along with some frozen peas and chips. He'd nothing to celebrate but he deserved a treat after the shock he'd had today.

. He remembered his father used to say, "Never defend a weak position. Fall back and counter attack." He didn't see anyway he could counter attack. Unless, unless he took up a completely new position. He could set himself up as an independent accountant, specialising in Income Tax Returns. Even quite clever people often had an aversion to filling in forms. He could even help people appeal against their Council Tax assessments! He smiled at the thought. Yes. Why not? He could make life hell for those who had betrayed him.

CHAPTER 39

Byron was alone in bed and unable to sleep. He wished Serena was beside him. It would be almost 48 hours until he saw her. They'd agreed it was best to take things slowly, not draw any unnecessary attention to themselves but he wasn't fining it easy. There had been three prospective buyers for the house so far but no definite offers. He'd phone the Estate Agents in the morning and tell them to get their fingers out. He'd found a suitable property to let close to the M11, only 40 minutes drive from the office. He didn't want to lose it.

At least that was one thing settled. He'd decided to keep the office where it was. All his business affairs were now backed up on computer by a specialist firm. Now that his records were safe he wasn't worried if Lenny tried an arson attack on the office. He'd surely not do a thing like that in the daytime so Dawn and the girls should be O.K. There was no need to warn them. Anyway they were all young enough to move quickly if Lenny went mad. If the thug did attack the office either day or night he'd not lose financially for he'd doubled the insurance on the business.

He was going to the race meeting at Beverly tomorrow. Most punters would be concentrating on Saturday's big race but the two horses he strongly fancied were in high grade races on the first day. He planned to have a really substantial bet on the second if the first one won. He drifted off to sleep thinking of all the pleasant things he could do with his winnings.

After a substantial breakfast he turned on his computer to check the weather and the conditions underfoot at the racecourse. He was heartened to learn they were ideal for the horses he'd selected. He decided he'd phone in a few extra bets on them with his off-course bookmakers on his way to the meeting. He picked up the satchel in which he kept all his racing form books and notes and checked its contents. He...the phone rang. He answered (as he always did) without identifying himself.

"Hallo"

"Hallo, you murdering bastard."

"Dot. Keeping well?"

"Better than ever, especially since the Law came to see me. Wanted to know all about you."

"Oh. I'm sure you told them how much I'm missing Lucy and…"

"Don't you dare speak my daughter's name. You're not fit to have it pass your lips. I told them alright, all about you robbing old ladies of their savings and all your other fiddles. They're on to you Mr. Bastard Byron"

He was tempted to put the phone down but he wanted to know what she'd said to the police. He'd never remembered mentioning any of his clients' names to Lucy. There was no possible way she could have found out who they were, was there? "I'm afraid your behind the times Dot. I've already had a long chat with the police and they are perfectly satisfied with the answers I gave them."

"That's what you think. The one who came to see me wasn't. He went on to see Van you know. She said he promised he was going to look into your scams."

He decided it was all talk on her part. If she knew any names she'd have mentioned them by now. "Whatever you say, Dot. But I've got to go now. I…"

"No point in running away. These things take time, especially when it's money. They'll get you, I know they will. Oh and the Greeks aren't finished with you either."

"Always glad to hear from you Dot. Bye."

As he put the receiver down he thought he heard her shriek "Lenny's back." For a moment he stood irresolute, not knowing what to do next. He decided there was nothing he could do except be extra vigilant. Today was not the day to be distracted by Lenny.

The traffic was very heavy all the way up the A1 and he had to concentrate every mile of the way. He prided himself on his driving and enjoyed using the powerful engine to weave past the plebs and the commercials. It certainly helped to keep his mind off Dot and Lenny. .

Once at the racecourse, he forgot all about them. This was where he really came alive. He made his way through the smartly dressed men and women up to the Grandstand restaurant and had a light lunch. He believed his mind was more alert when his stomach wasn't overloaded. It was the same with drink; he always had a pint of bitter with his meal and another to nurse as he mingled with the other punters in the bar. He stood greeting old acquaintances and making his usual non-committal camouflaged remarks about his betting intentions to his fellow professionals until the horses for the first race were making their way into the parade ring. He wasn't betting on these first two races but he enjoyed casting a critical eye over the thoroughbreds in the parade ring. There was always the possibility of learning something for future use. He was jotting down his observations about a horse called "Highland Reel" when a familiar voice said "Fancy that one, do you Old Boy?"

He turned to greet a small elderly white haired man whose tweeds, bow legs, ruddy face and monocle made him look for all the world like an ex -cavalry officer who was now the squire of some country estate. But Byron knew he lived in a flat in Mayfair and that his military bearing came not from the Army but from years of service in the RAF which was why everyone knew him as "Aviation Anderson." or "AA"

"Maybe in the future AA."

"Good thinking. A good reconnaissance is always pays. Like to see how these two year olds acquit themselves before putting any cash on them. I suppose like me you're waiting for the big race?"

Byron nodded and added "Yes. I assume 'Trumpeter' will be a strong favourite but there are three or four others who also seem to have serious claims, don't you think?" He said this because 'Trumpeter' was the first of the two horses he was having a substantial bet on and he hoped that if a serious punter like AA knew anything detrimental to the horse's chances he might let him know. AA owed him a few favours. Byron had sometimes taken him home when he'd been too drunk to drive after a meeting. He had done this not out of any altruistic motives but because AA liked to boast about the "good chaps" he knew at some of the major stables and he'd occasionally let slip information that Byron had been able to use to his advantage.

AA answered as circumspectly as a judge's mistress, "That's the glory and the curse of this game isn't it Fuller? Still it wouldn't be worth the effort if everything always went according odds would there?"

"And the bookies we love so much would be sweeping the streets."

"If only. Perhaps those who say that the best bet is not to bet at all are on to something eh?"

"Spoilsports. Anyway we'd soon find other ways to waste our money."

"Ah, but with wine and women we at least get something for it."

"Like a hangover or the clap."

"A young man like you shouldn't be so cynical."

"Not so young now. Fancy another" said Byron nodding towards AA's almost empty glass.

"Not just now thanks. I want to have a good look at one of this lot. Her dam added considerably to my war chest in her day."

"I won't insult you by asking which one" Byron answering hoping AA would be flattered into telling him.

"Wise fellow. Don't like to refuse a friend but in this game we've all got to make our own mistakes eh?"

"Too true. I think I'll just nip up to the bar for a quick one before the off. See you later."

"You're sure to. I'll hold you to your offer when we meet."

"My pleasure"

Byron hurried away up to the Grandstand bar but not for a drink. There was a good view of the parade ring from there and he thought he might be able to see which horse AA was particularly interested in. Betting was a long term business and every scrap of knowledge was valuable. But although he watched the old man closely he couldn't see that him paying particular attention to any one horse. He decided he'd look up the pedigree of the runners when he got home and see which of them had the most successful dam.

When the horses were going into their starting stalls people crowded over to the windows to watch the race and he was able to find a seat at a corner table. He sat down and studied the other runners in Trumpeter's race. There were three obvious dangers to his choice; "Wonderful Will, Brighteyes and Neverest." He knew if Lucy was here she'd be backing "Brighteyes" because she liked the song. She'd do her usual £10 to win and £5 each way bet. Brighteys odds of 5 to I made that not a bad each way gamble. She hadn't been altogether a fool when it came to horses, hadn't Lucy.

He considered his strategy for today. In total he'd got £12,000 invested in Trumpeter who was quoted in the papers as clear favourite for his race at 5/4. He'd been backing it over the past weeks at odds from 4/1 down to its present price. In all he reckoned that if the odds didn't slip below 5/4   he'd win over £28,000. He had £3,000 in cash with him, should he risk a bit more on the horse? It really did seem to have an outstanding chance. He decided to wait until he'd seen it in the parade ring.

The favourite was beaten in each of the first two races. That didn't worry him because there were so many unknowns in these preliminary events. When Trumpeter's race was called he was leaning on the parade ring rails as the horses were lead in. Trumpeter looked magnificent and walked calmly around completely unfazed by the excited behaviour of a horse named Brighton Peer. Brighteyes was the only grey in the field of nine, another reason why Lucy would have chosen it. After five minutes of close scrutiny he hurried over to the bookmakers pitches. Trumpeter was holding his price of 5/4. He fingered the notes in his pocket, what should he do? He walked briskly up and down trying to decide.

He'd also got £5,000 invested in a horse called Calculator, (half of it each way) in the next race at ante-post odds of   8/1. He intended to invest some of his winnings from Trumpeter on Calculator. At least that way if it did lose it would be some of the bookies money down the drain and not just his. Yet...Yet...his eyes scanned the boards, there was only about 5 minutes to go now.

What was this? Harry O, the biggest local bookie was changing Trumpeter's odds to... 6/4. Byron turned to the next bookmaker, he'd followed suit. 6/4... That was another £250 quid for each £1000. Punters were rushing to take advantage of the increased odds. He fingered the notes in his pocket. Now a bookie was offering 13/8 on Trumpeter…If…Suddenly he froze. He'd seen this happen before and almost always the favourite had lost. Frantically he rushed up to Harry O "£500 each way on Brighteyes. 5/1 Yes?" The man hesitated, for a moment Byron though he was going to refuse but he took the bet. Byron grabbed the ticket and rushed to the next pitch. Brighteyes was still 5/1. "£500 each way Brighteyes, 5/1? "he gasped. The man shook his head ""I'll take £250." Byron didn't argue. The horses were going in the stalls. At the next pitch they were shortening Brighteyes' odds to… 4/1… No… 7/2. Byron saw the empty Tote window out of the corner of his eye. He dashed over "£500 win and £500 place Brighteyes." The woman didn't even look up as she punched out his bet. Immediately, the bell went for the start of the race.

Byron felt sick. Clenching his fists to keep control of himself he elbowed his way up the wide steps to where he had a good sight of the course and took out his binoculars. His heart sank as Trumpeter was slow away out of the stalls but as it began to steadily overhaul the field he let himself begin to hope that perhaps all was not lost after all. By half way Trumpeter was one of three horses just about a length and a half behind Neverest. Three lengths in front of them all was Brighton Peer. That didn't worry him as he knew it was only in the race as pacemaker for its stable mate Wonderful Will who needed a fast run race as his strength lay in stamina rather than finishing speed. Sure enough with only two furlongs remaining Brighton Peer was quickly overtaken by Wonderful Will who opened up a three length gap on his pursuers. Byron cursed his impetuosity at backing Brighteyes as Wonderful Will had been his second form choice when he'd made his selections at home. There was a great roar from the crowd as Trumpeter and Brighteyes began to close on Wonderful Will. In the last furlong they were both less than half a length behind. The noise of the crowd increased as Brighteyes came up on the rails alongside Wonderful Will. Trumpeter was holding its position half a length behind them but that was all. About a hundred yards from the finish as Brighteyes seemed as if it would squeeze past Wonderful Will. Byron began to yell him home; all might not be lost after all. But his joy was short lived for as the two horses passed the finishing post it was clear even to the naked eye that Wonderful Will had won by a head. That was the result announced. Trumpeter only just held on to be third from the fast finishing Brewers Whoop.

CHAPTER 40

Paul had half decided he would take the retirement package offered; provided that it matched the figures he had worked out over the weekend. He knew that once a man was past 50 there was very little chance of every getting another job but he would insist on a good reference as one of the conditions for accepting it. A man of exceptional ability like himself was always likely to be snapped up by a discerning employer.

When he entered his office he was shocked to find Gaynor at her desk. He was tempted to go up and ask what she was doing here. Was she here to apologize for her appalling behaviour? Had the Council decided her complaints were groundless? But as he was about to do so, another thought crossed his mind: had the Council already decided he was on his way out? Was she back because she thought she wouldn't have to work with him much longer? Watching her out of the corner of his eye he had a terrible feeling from the insolent way she was behaving that it might be the latter. He didn't have to wait long to find out. A message arrived on his computer screen requesting him to see the hated McHaddan at 11 am.

He was deliberately 10 minutes late; offering her a brusque apology about pressure of "very important work"

"I understand Mr.Thewell. We are all under a great deal of pressure nowadays are we not?"

He didn't know how to respond so he just nodded. She didn't waste any more time in generalities but started immediately to itemise the redundancy package the council was offering him. It was almost exactly what he had worked out at home. A £50,000 lump sum and an earnings related pension, enhanced as if he'd retired at fifty five. She raised no objection to his request for a reference and said there would be no barrier to him working for another council in a similar position. Then she amazed him when she looked him straight in the eyes and said "Of course you'd be wise to also take advantage of all this good weather we're having now."

When their import of what she'd just said began to sink in he asked peremptorily,"What exactly do you mean Mizz McHaddan?"

"It's really quite straightforward Mr.Thewell. As I've informed you we plan to start amalgamating departments in six weeks, so your redundancy would have to be fully operational by then at the latest. You have 21 days holiday entitlement due to you, so you would be absent for half of those weeks. We think it would be rather confusing for whoever is selected to have charge of your office for those weeks to have to revert to other duties for the three weeks you would have returned. In view of your long years of service to the council and considering the callous physical assault you recently suffered (she held up a hand to prevent him interrupting) we feel that you quite rightly qualify for a period of extended sick leave. Therefore we are prepared to let you vacate your position a week today."

Paul's anger welled up inside him "You want to get rid of me that quickly?"

"Not at all. We just feel it would be in your interests... and ours for you to leave then?"

"And if I refuse?"

She looked down at her desk and carefully arranged some papers on it. When she looked up and spoke every word was cuttingly precise. "I hope you realise Mr. Thewell, that there is still this outstanding matter of serious complaints about your harassment of your staff..."

"Lies, all lies."

"If they are then I'm sure our investigation will uncover them. But if on the other hand these complaints were to be proved justified I'm afraid I have to tell you they could seriously jeopardise the terms of the generous redundancy package we are offering you."

He wanted to shout "Blackmail" but thought better of it.

Taking advantage of his silence she continued in a slightly gentler tone, "Mr. Thewell, I understand how much your work must mean to you after almost 30 years here. But if you are here for any part of the remaining six weeks we would have to hold our inquiry. It would be grossly unfair to the complainants not to have this matter resolved quickly."

He went to speak but again she checked him. "Also as you have requested a reference I feel duty bound to let you know that

186

whatever the outcome of such an inquiry the fact that one was held at all would have to be included in the reference we would write you. We could face serious legal action in the future if certain circumstances arouse with any new employer of yours and it was revealed that we omitted to mention that an inquiry had to be held into your management style. You do understand?"

He nodded. He understood only too bloody well.

"I'm sure all of this must be quite a shock to you. If you would like some time to think it over by all means do so. Would it be agreeable to you to let me have your answer in writing by noon on Wednesday at the latest?"

"No it would not. I have no desire to stay where I am so evidently not wanted. I will type out my resignation immediately I return to my office. Satisfied?"

She slowly nodded and rose from her seat, "Whatever you wish Mr.Thewell."

He looked at her with all the contempt he could muster, stood up very slowly and marched out of her office with his head held high.

CHAPTER 41

Byron felt sick. He had to hold onto the iron support frame in front of him to prevent himself collapsing. £12,000 down the drain. With his place money only returning a little over what he'd staked on Brighteyes he'd have only a few hundred pounds compensation. Even if the horse had won he'd still have been almost three grand down. No real consolation but a dammed sight better than losing all twelve. His despair was magnified by knowing that Trumpeter had been nobbled. That was a dead cert. The horse was normally one of the fastest finishers in its class. AA's words came back to him; "The best bet is not to bet at all…" Had the little man been trying to warn him? Even at the time it had struck him as a peculiar thing for an inveterate gambler to say. He'd have …a plumy voice came over the public announcement system "Ladies and Gentlemen, there is a Stewards inquiry on the last race. I repeat, a Stewards inquiry on the result of the Hardmore Stakes. Do not dispense with your betting slips."

Byron felt for the slips in his trouser pocket even though he knew they were there. He always kept them until he got home. He moved to where he could see the big screen showing a replay of the race finish. Sure enough it looked as if Wonderful Will had moved slightly over to the left; blocking Brighteye's run on the rails. Would it be enough for the judges to reverse the placings? As Byron waited for their decision his anger at AA increased. The bastard must have known Trumpeter wouldn't win. That wasn't the same as knowing who would win but he might have got longer odds on the second and third favourites if he'd had more time. Maybe those who had nobbled Trumpeter had inside knowledge on Wonderful Will's form? Why not? As sure as Christ was crucified such things happened. He'd find AA and beat the...The public address gong checked him.

"Ladies and gentlemen. Here is the result of the Stewards inquiry into the Macmorris Stakes. Wonderful Will has been found guilty of interfering..." The rest of his words were drowned by the crowd's cheers. There was a very high proportion of high pitched female screams among them. Bright Eyes winning odds were shown as 7/2. He'd been lucky getting 5/1. He felt a lot better in himself now. Maybe it was going to be his lucky day after all. Maybe he should put a few thousand of what he'd rescued on Calculator? Maybe...he shook his head. How many times must he tell himself he didn't believe in luck? Yet he'd experienced both winning and losing streaks. Calculator had won for him last time out and he'd only been given a couple of pounds more to carry in this race. His sire had won carrying much greater weight over this distance. He went down to the parade ring again using every scrap of equine knowledge he'd accumulated over the years scrutinized every movement the horse made. Nothing he saw gave him any cause for concern. He decided he'd risk another £2000 on the horse. He collected his winnings and immediately began putting bets of £50 and £100 on Calculator. He put half the money on to win and half to place and spread it around all the bookies and the Tote. He got most of his money on at 6/1 before the horse's price began to shorten. Calculator's odds were high because the favourite in the race was the son of a Derby winner and had won its only other race easily. Too easily in Byron's opinion. He doubted its ability to fight out a tough finish whereas Calculator had shown real guts in battling out its last win. Other punters must have shared his opinion because it was backed down to 9/2 just before the off. The race was over the classic distance of 1mile 4 furlongs with a big field of fourteen horses but Calculator never gave him a moment's worry. It was always in the first four and drew ahead in the last furlong to win easily by a length.

Checking in the small notebook where he kept a record of all his bets he reckoned he'd won about £29,000. Subtracting the £3000 he was down on Trumpeter he was 26 grand in pocket. Thank Christ he hadn't doubled up the two horses in combined bets. That was for mugs in his eyes. Betting with the bookies money was the best way to be sure of a profit. As he collected his winnings he kept a lookout for AA's snowy head. He bought a whiskey and wandered around the Grandstand but there was no sign of the man. He decided to search the car park. AA's vintage Armstrong Sidley was easy to spot. Byron got his car, drove down and parked diagonally opposite, reclining the driving seat so that he was partially hidden. After half an hour there were only about a dozen cars remaining in the park and still no sign of AA. Byron decided he'd give it another ten minutes then go and search the bars in case the old fool had drunk himself senseless. He knew AA rarely drove if he was drunk, preferring to sleep it off in some hotel or get a willing chauffeur. He boasted he had never got the slightest scratch on the cream and brown classic car.. Byron became so involved in admiring it that he didn't see AA until he walked past. His pace was very measured and deliberate with no hint of a wobble.

Byron was just about to open his car door when he noticed the two men. It was the way they kept looking behind them that made him instantly suspicious. AA was fumbling in his pocket by the driver's door when the nearest man ran up and dragged him around the back of the car. The other one, after a quick final look around also ran behind the car. Byron couldn't see anyone else nearby as he scrambled out of his car, pausing only to pick up the heavy metal steering lock from the passenger seat. He crept over to Armstrong Sidley. With the Steering lock raised he stepped quietly around the rear of the car. The men were so absorbed in punching their victim they didn't notice him. He brought the bar down with all his might on the head of the nearest one. For a few seconds nothing seemed to happen so Byron hit him again. The man collapsed so awkwardly in front of him that Byron was hampered in his efforts to get within striking distance of the other. The man pulled AA in front of him and locked his arm around the little man's throat.

"Drop that fucking bar or I'll break his neck" he snarled.

Byron let his arm drop to his side but he kept hold of the bar. The bloke was powerfully built but Byron could see the fear in his eyes. Byron checked that the man he'd hit wasn't moving before he said in the most relaxed tone he could muster; "I don't think you'll do that."

"Don't you? Just watch" AA's mouth opened wide but no sound came out as the man began to squeeze his neck.

Byron took a step closer as he said, "You're making it easy for me to hit you when both your arms are around his neck. If you do kill him you'll be done for murder. Think of all those years you'd be in jail. Do you really want that? Let him go."

The man snarled and dragged AA further away. "What do you take me for? Drop that fucking bar."

"All right. You let him go and I'll drop the bar."

The man looked around as if expecting help but Byron couldn't believe that it would have taken three men to mug AA. He held the bar out at arm's length.

"Throw it in them bushes."

Byron sized the man up. He was confident he could overcome him even without the bar. "You let him go. When he's taken two steps away from you I'll chuck this away. As I'm taking him to his car, you can pick up your mate and go."

Byron kept his eyes on AA's face rather than his captor's. He didn't want the thug to feel he was being challenged. He wanted to give him a way out. "Of course as soon as you let him go, if you choose you can bugger off. I've no interest in pursuing you. All I want to do is rescues my friend. However, if you do leave your mate, I promise you we'll take him to the cops. Think he'll keep his mouth shut?" He paused to let his words sink in before adding "You'd be safer taking him with you."

Suddenly the man released his hold on AA's neck and muttered "Two steps. That's all." AA didn't need a second telling. For such a small man he made two enormous strides. Byron tossed the bar away. AA reached his side in two more strides and Byron bundled him behind him as he mouthed "Get in the car." He made as if to follow him but as soon as he sensed the thug had reached his mate he turned and raised his right arm. As the man looked up Byron kicked him viciously in the left knee cap. His yell of agony was cut short as Byron chopped him backhandedly across the throat. When he hit the ground he kicked him twice in the side of the head: hoping he wasn't scuffing his best handmade English brogues as he did so. He was ready to deliver another kick when he became aware of somebody on his left. He whirled, hands pointed to attack, only the glimpse of a white head checked him.

"Not a Queensbury rules man eh?" said AA as he lowered the steering wheel lock that Byron had thrown away.

"Bit like yourself," Byron gasped, nodding towards the bar.

AA smiled. "What shall we do with these chaps? Not a case for the Law, wouldn't you say?"

Byron seized the chance to use a word he seldom got the opportunity to utter. "Indubitability."

AA uttered a high pitched laugh which was cut short as one of the bodies on the ground stirred. Byron bent over him and pressed his thumb hard into a pressure point on the man's neck. The body jerked a few times then crumpled.

"I don't think they'll remember us driving off" he said to AA. He was anxious that neither of the attackers had any chance of seeing his car's registration. He didn't want them or any of their friends to come looking for him.

"No I don't suppose they will."

Byron took his steering lock from AA. He thought of giving the men an additional tap on the head to make sure their brains were addled enough not to remember what had happened but the Armstrong Sidley's engine purring into life sent him scurrying to the driver's door.

"AA. Do you know the Lord Beaconsfield's Arms?"

"Of course. But I'm afraid I can't have another drink old chap. I know my limit."

"We're not drinking we're eating. I'm bloody starving. And we got a lot to talk about haven't we?"

The little man nodded sheepishly and drove smoothly away. Byron ran to his Mercedes and set off after him.

CHAPTER 42

Back at his desk Paul sat in a trance, shielding himself from the staff with his computer screen. All his years of service ending like this. It...the noise of the staff getting up and leaving alerted him to the fact it was lunch hour. He'd no heart to stay and eat his sandwiches in the office as he usually did so he followed them out. The light rain made it impossible for him to eat them in the park so he decided to keep them for his tea and made his way to a restaurant where he'd eaten on Friday. He had that day's "3 course special." When he'd finished, the rain had ceased so he went down to the riverbank and walked with measured steps along by the water's edge. Inside him was developing not a furious explosive anger but a cold calculating rage, a rage that demanded one thing above all others, vengeance. People would pay for the way he had been treated. By Christ they would. His thoughts were interrupted by the ringing of a school hand bell. Looking up he saw the children in the playground of the Primary School on the opposite bank beginning to make their way into school. He turned and made his way quickly back to the office. He had sufficient authority not to be accountable to anyone how long he took over lunch but he determined he would give no one at work any possible hint of his anger. He'd continue to be the model employee he'd always been.

Back at his desk he typed out his acceptance of his retirement terms and added the proviso that "Because I am a very private person I would very much appreciate it if there was neither any farewell ceremony arranged nor any retirement gift offered. I also wish that news of my departure be kept from all staff in the office which I have supervised for many years." They could stick their engraved pewter mugs "where the sun don't shine" as far as he was concerned.

Rather than do any more work for the Council he decided to spend the rest of the afternoon gathering all the information he could on "Sunset" and Byron Fuller and he also copied out all the steps the council used to trace people who had moved without paying their Council tax. He had for many years had his home computer integrated into the council's network. He constructed and keyed in a programme that would immediately notify him every time Fuller's name appeared on council records. Now he would always be able to find Fuller as long as he didn't move out of the county

At home after letting Kaiser out to play in the back garden he went to his computer and was glad to see it had received the Fuller information. When he took Kaiser for his evening walk he went past the top of Meldrum Avenue and was glad to see the shiny black car parked outside Sunset. At least Fuller was still in his sights. He walked quickly away down the hill and around to the back of a block of newly constructed council flats that housed single mothers. There were plenty of exposed living rooms with televisions flashing but no lights in any of the main bedrooms even though it was almost 11 o'clock. "If only these scroungers had to go to work in the morning perhaps they'd get to bed a bit earlier" he thought to himself. He walked on to another block where he'd seen a woman walking about naked from the waist up last year but drew a blank there as well. He consoled himself with the thought that when he was retired he also wouldn't have to get up early for work in the morning and could extend his sight seeing rambles until well after midnight.

Back at work next day he was glad to receive an e-mail from McHaddan that his "wishes would be respected" regarding his leaving. He was finding the office more and more oppressive and kept leaving it, either to go to the washroom or take brief walks outside. At lunchtime he ate his sandwiches in the park. Afterwards he strolled into a part of town he hadn't visited for years. Passing a car showroom something about the shape of one of the models displayed made him stop. Looking closely he saw it was the same car that was outside Fuller's. When he went inside to have a closer look he was at first pleased that none of the sharp suited sales staff approached him but his pleasure was quickly spoiled by the thought that perhaps none of them thought he was fit to be a prospective buyer. There were two models of the "Kompresser" on show. It shocked him to see that one was priced at £28,600 and the other at £30,200." Each cost more than half the lump sum he was getting after almost 30 years hard work. How dare a callous killer be able to afford such a car! He strode out of the showroom, ignoring the approaching Salesman.

He could not stop thinking about Fuller's wealth all afternoon. He did his work mechanically, signing form after form with only the barest scrutiny. Afterwards he could always remember when the word entered his mind. It was just after he'd put down a form with a note attached demanding "immediate payment." Blackmail. Rich people could be blackmailed. Fuller could be blackmailed. Not that an honest upright citizen like himself would really do any such thing but if Fuller thought he was being blackmailed and paid up what greater proof of his crime could the police want? It was the perfect trap.

CHAPTER 43

The Beaconsfield Arms was a four story red brick Victorian building that dominated the main square of the small town of Leggsworth. It had once been a coaching inn and a cattle market had for many years been held in the square in front of it. Now the only horns there were the blasts of angry motorists jousting for a parking place. The dining room on the second floor was always crowded on race days; AA & Byron were fortunate got get a table in the small overflow room. Service was much slower here but Byron didn't mind waiting. Portions were generous here and he'd plenty of questions to ask.

"Right, AA. Why were those two thugs trying to rearrange your features?"

"No idea. Just typical bullies picking on someone smaller."

"Really? Sure it wasn't because they saw you picking up all those bundles of notes you'd won by backing against Trumpeter?"

When he answered Byron noticed that AA didn't attempt to deny that he backed against the favourite. "I'm afraid I didn't win as much as I'd hoped, most of my cash was on Wonderful Will. Bloody myopic judges."

A waitress arrived to take their orders. AA decided to break his drink embargo and insisted on ordering a bottle of Pomerol Merlot to go with their roast lamb. He explained his change of mind saying "I think when she comes back I'll get her to see if they have any rooms available. This scuffle has shaken me up a bit. I don't fancy driving all the way back to London tonight. Besides I owe you a decent drink for your rescuing me from those thugs."

"Thanks old chap but if you really want to show your appreciation tell me how you knew Trumpeter wouldn't win."

"Shussh. You mustn't go around saying things like that."

"Look AA. I don't want to know all the ins and outs of the matter. Actually, I don't really want to know about Trumpeter. What I want to know is the next time a favourite is going to fail. I'm going through rather a bad patch at the moment and I can't afford to be backing no hopers."

"Abstinence, my dear boy, abstinence. Premium bonds are a better investment; I do very well out of them."

196

Byron's angry protest had to be aborted because of the arrival of the wine waiter. As he watched the old man go through a prolonged "tasting" ritual he decided he'd encourage him to drink to see if the Pomerol helped loosen his tongue. AA did indeed become garrulous but not in relation to losing favourites. Byron had to listen to vivid descriptions of the wild bets that were struck "in the mess" during AA's Service career. By the time their coffees had been poured, the only gambling AA had ignored was horseracing.

Leaning forward into the old man's face he whispered; "Listen to me AA. I've not brought you here to fart around. If you don't tell me what I want to know about nobbled favourites I promise you those stewards whose eyesight you impugned will soon be reading your name in an anonymous letter saying that I as an upstanding member of the sporting fraternity was horrified to be advised by you not to back Trumpeter today because you knew for a fact it would lose." He cut short AA's attempted protest about "no proof" by saying deliberately louder "It won't matter about proof. There will be more than one racing sheet tomorrow speculating on Trumpeter's poor performance. Once your name is linked with a doping scandal it will never be forgotten. You know what a clique the racing fraternity are. And how can you be sure that if there is an investigation that traces of whatever was given him to slow him down won't still be in his blood."

The old man looked at him horrified. "I never had you marked down as a sneak Fuller."

"Cut out that crap. This isn't some public schoolboy jape. I promise whatever you tell me my lips will stay as tight as a Scotsman's arse outside a paying toilet. So start talking."

AA drained his glass and held it out for a refill. After Byron had topped it up he had a couple of mouthfuls before he said "There's not really much to tell. I'm an old man who's been around a long time. People tend to regard me as part of the furniture, don't you know. What they don't realise is all my faculties, including my hearing are still A1. Occasionally I hear things I'm not supposed to. A while back at Cheltenham I happened to be near a couple of bookmaker chappies who were discussing how easily Trumpeter had won his last race and thanking God he wasn't going to win today's big handicap. When they realised I was there I pretended to be too inebriated to

197

comprehend what they'd been talking about. I thought I'd deceived them but evidently not. Somebody must have been watching my betting system today. I had some substantial place bets on Wonderful Will and a few savers on Bright Eyes. I can't think what else I could have done to upset them."

Byron waited while he took another drink assuming he'd continue but AA remained silent. Reluctantly he decided the old man was telling the truth. "So you're not part of a syndicate that targets certain favourites?"

"Fraid not old man."

"Pity. I was hoping to join you. I'd have made it worth your while."

"I'm sure you would" he paused, "so we'll forget about any penmanship on your part."

Byron nodded but said emphatically "Unless of course another favourite goes down that I know nothing about and I hear you've done well out of it."

"If any thing like that happened it would be pure coincidence."

"Yeah? Well I'm not a great believer in coincidences."

"When you've lived as long as I have you may come to think differently."

"If I do, I hope for your sake that I don't lose any cash in the process."

"I assure you it won't be my fault if you do. Now I think it's time for me to bale out. Still like my eight hours. I'll put this meal on my bill. It's the least I can do to thank you for saving my skin."

Byron didn't argue. He thought about taking a room for himself but decided to risk driving home. He couldn't be too far over the limit and it had been his lucky day hadn't it? He kept a keen lookout on the motorways and got home without attracting the attentions of the police.

As soon as he opened the door he knew someone was in the house. He was reaching out for one of the walking sticks in the hall stand he heard the chimes of Big Ben introducing the 10 o'clock news. Serena came running up the hall. The passion of her embrace forced him back against the door. As they kissed he was as always astounded how such a strong muscular woman could be so soft in his arms.

"I couldn't wait any longer. My car's three roads away. I..." He silenced her with another kiss... "I'm sure no one saw me come in. Where've you been?"

He led her into the lounge and sat her down on the settee. Standing over her he emptied his brief case and pockets; throwing down wad after wad of notes. She squealed like a schoolgirl as the money piled up around her. "You clever bastard" she gasped "How much have you won?"

"Oh...about £25,000 "he said with exaggerated nonchalance.

She screamed and grabbing four of the bundles began to juggle them expertly.

"Where did ...?" His question was cut short by the telephone. He moved over to the handset and stood irresolutely beside it. Serena let the notes fall to the floor and came over beside him. He had caller display and could see it was a local number but it was not one he knew. There was no one he could think of who would be ringing at this time of night. If Serena hadn't been here he wouldn't have answered it but he knew if he didn't she'd be quizzing him all night about who the caller might be. He picked up the receiver and said quietly "Hallo?"

"Mr. Fuller, after you hear what I've got to say I expect you will immediately want to put your phone down. But if you do I promise you my next call will be to the police. I just want to ask you a simple question. Have you still got the white chemical protective suit you wore that night when you strangled your wife?"

CHAPTER 44

"C.S" Bullerton joined enthusiastically in the applause. The touring opera company's production of *Cosi Fan Tutti* had been thoroughly enjoyable. He was glad he'd let his new girlfriend Helene talk him into attending the performance. He'd noticed her when she'd started working at the Path. Lab a year ago but only gathered up the courage to ask her out in the past nine weeks. This was their third date and her choice.

It was because of her that tonight he was "CS" instead of "Bully." She utterly refused to call him by what she said was "a disgraceful and utterly inappropriate epithet." She was a strong minded woman but hadn't so far been able to prise out of him what "CS" stood for. He wasn't yet that confident of their relationship

"Fancy a drink?" he asked.

She nodded. He led the way out of the theatre. However much provincial theatres needed support, he wasn't prepared to further subsidize them by paying their inflated bar prices. He'd gone to school in this town and took her to a nearby pub where he'd enjoyed many an underage drink because of his size and a tolerant landlord He ordered a pint of the pub's own real ale and Helene a mineral water.

"I told you you'd like it" she said as soon as they were settled in one of the cosy alcoves with their drinks.

"It was all right" he answered.

"What do you mean 'all right'? The music was magnificent."

"It was but the plot was crap. How could anyone be expected to believe those two girls couldn't recognize their boyfriends one day later just because the put on false moustaches."

"Oh no one ever takes any notice of opera plots. They're just vehicles for the music. That's what matters. I do love that parting melody *"May the winds be gentle."* It got to you too, didn't it. I saw your eyes glistening."

"Oh, you fancy yourself as a detective, do you?"

"Stop shilly-shallying. Go on, admit it."

"O.K. It did make me feel a bit emotional."

She snuggled closer to him and said gently "You know that's what I really like about you CS. You're such a big butch bloke but you're not afraid to show your feelings."

He felt himself blushing, "Thank you, Mamm"

"And you really did like it? You're not just saying so because I told you I'm an opera nut."

"No there is quite a lot of classical music that I like."

"Such as?"

"I suppose mainly the ballets."

"What? You like ballet? You'll be offering to show me your entrechat next."

"There was a time when I could have done just that."

"You're joking. No. You're not. You're not the type of man who would joke about a thing like that. You actually danced?"

"From about 10 to 14 I never missed a lesson."

"Christ CS. You're a brave man. Most policemen would rather die than admit they'd ever danced ballet."

"It wasn't bravery that made me do it. Just the opposite in fact."

"What do you mean?"

"Well, as you can guess I've always been a rather hefty chap. Even at ten I was big for my age so sports masters were always shoving me into the scrums. It was too dangerous for my liking and too bloody dirty."

"What happened?"

"Well after every match while I was trying to scrub the blood and mud out of my belly button I'd see these sparkling clean little wing threequarters already dressed without a hair out of place. I decided that was more my style. My sister Rosie went to ballet every Saturday morning and my mother and I used to meet her there after doing a bit of shopping. When I saw how quickly and elegantly she and the other kids moved I thought I'd have a bit of that. I hoped it would give me a neat swerve or a quick sidestep."

"And did you get to play wing threequarter.?"

"Eventually. I played a long time in the centre first."

"But you play on the wing now?"

"Yes."

"Enjoy it?"

"Occasionally. I still manage to stumble over the try line."

"Like you did twice in our lot's grudge match against the Met on New Year's Eve. Each time with three or four of their players trying to rip your balls off."

"How do you know that?"

"I was there watching. I've been watching you for quite a while CS."

"My God. No wonder the hairs on the back of my neck tingle when I see you. If I'd known I'd have asked you out ages ago."

"You're supposed to be the detective. I was waiting to see how good you were at it?"

He said "Thank God I did ask you to that dance" while vowing never to let her know he'd only done so to win a bet with couple of Rugby mates. To get off the subject he added quickly "Fancy another drink?"

"Only if you let me pay. Same again for you?"

When he nodded his assent she got up and went over to the bar giving him a chance to admire her from behind. He guessed she was about five foot nine. Her jet black hair usually scrunched up under an operating theatre cap, tonight hung down to her shoulders, softening the angularity of her face. . He rejoiced she had a bit of flesh on her. She came back with his pint and a balloon shaped glass of amber liquid.

He sniffed "Brandy?"

"Cognac" She paused before adding "It's a tradition in our family to drink it on special occasions."

His mind went into overdrive. "Tonight's a special occasion?"

She took a couple of brief sips of her cognac before answering "It can be....if you want?"

202

"Well, my dear Helene. Using all my highly trained deductive powers, sharpened by hours of burning the midnight oil memorising *How to be a Detective in Ten Easy Lessons* I conclude there is only one answer to that."

"Which is?"

"You're place or mine?"

They snuggled up close together while they quickly finished their drinks.

At the exit of the car park he halted "Right or Left? "

"Left of course. I'm less than two miles away from here."

"Oh madam. You've such a silver tongue. How can a poor innocent boy like me resist such logic?"

"You'd bloody better well not resist. I'm counting on you for the perfect end to a wonderful evening."

He'd no idea what speed he drove but they seemed to reach her address in seconds.

She led him straight to the bedroom of her flat. "Take your jacket and shoes and socks off but nothing else. I want to undress you. I won't be a minute." She hurried out of the room. He did as he was told and sat on the edge of the bed until she came back wearing only her bra, knickers, tights and high heeled shoes. Sensuously they undressed each other kissing passionately as each item was removed. She was completely naked as she pushed her hands down each side of his boxers and eased them off. They snagged on his penis for he was now as hard as a rock.

"Jesus" she said as she fondled him "It's true what they say about big feet."

He couldn't stop himself laughing.

"What's so funny?"

He moved his hands from her breasts and pulling her to him eased her gently down on the bed. "I'll tell you later. Talking time is over."

Afterwards as they lay in each others arms she asked "So what was so funny? That was a very guilty laugh when I mentioned your feet. Have all your girlfriends made the same comment."

He brushed her black hair gently with his free hand and kissed her. "All my girlfriends? I should be so lucky. No. I couldn't tell you because it would have stopped our passion stone dead."

"Why?"

"Because the last woman to say that about me was at least sixty years old."

She punched him playfully on the chest, "You pervert."

"No No listen." He told her about Dot and Van. As she relaxed back into his arms she asked "So what was she like this Van? Was she as observant?"

"If she was she had the good grace not to say anything. She was rather a nice lady as a matter of fact. Looking at her you'd say she was a typical Essex blonde but she wasn't the least brassy. She was really upset abut her friend Lucy being killed."

"What happened to her?"

"I'm afraid that's the 64,000$ question. Her death could have been an accident. In fact it probably was. But, to put it mildly the husband's a scoundrel. He could have murdered her. But there's no proof."

"What about the body? Did forensics not provide anything?"

"There is no body." Briefly he told her the circumstances of Lucy's death.

"So there are no witnesses. He could have killed her and pushed her over the side but he'd be taking a hell of a risk wouldn't he? Bodies lost at sea have a habit of resurfacing."

"That's what Dot is praying for."

"So apart from that happening you've nothing to help you convict this Byron."

"Nothing" he paused "Well, there is something but it's so ridiculous that it's no real help. We've had two reports, probably from the same person, swearing that they saw him strangle his wife in the back bedroom of his house the night before he and Lucy went to Greece."

"That's absurd...unless...she didn't go. You've got witnesses to prove that she left?"

"Yes. The next door neighbour saw and spoke to them both the morning of the flight. And of course Lucy spoke to Dot and Van several times while she was in Greece."

"So where does this fantasy about him strangling her come from?"

"Fuller's says he and his wife were randy after wineing and dining and had a bit of a bondage session the night before they left. It was a regular thing with them, according to him. He reckons some Peeping Tom must have been spying on them. The back bedroom curtains were never closed."

Helene thought for a moment then said "So you know for sure she went to Greece because of at least one eyewitness and the phone conversations. And ...photos. You've got photos?"

He shook his head. "No, no photos."

"But, people always take holiday snaps. "

"Fuller told the Greeks Lucy didn't like being photographed and that the camera was lost in the capsize."

"Why was she so camera shy?"

"Well. Lucy was a very well built girl. Her mother says that Fuller had made her so self conscious about her size that she never wanted her photo taken."

"Poor girl. You men are so bloody lucky. Look at you."

"Madam. As a trained scientist dealing daily with the human form I trust you will have noticed that this magnificent specimen you see before you is nearly all muscle."

"In your dreams CS. (She leant over and grasped the side of his waist between her right thumb and forefinger.) Pinch an inch? More like pinch a couple."

"Every body need a certain proportion of fat. It's a protection."

She was quiet for a minute, the said "You're right. But think about what that means. One thing a good layer fat will do is help its owner survive at sea. It's Nature's lifebelt. So how come well proportioned Lucy drowned so quickly?"

"That's the one thing that I can't get out of my mind. It was boiling hot all that week, on the day of the accident it was over 34 degrees. There is no way the sea could have been unbearably cold. Lucy should have survived quite a while under those conditions. But it does seem that there were quite strong currents where they capsized. They swept Byron unto a line of rocks. Why didn't they do the same for Lucy?

"Unless she panicked and swallowed a lot of seawater. Or she could have hit her head on something."

"Yes. He was certainly struck on the head by the metal boom. He reckons it knocked him unconscious. It couldn't have been for long otherwise he'd have drowned. Lucy might have hit her head on the hull as she surfaced. That's the curse of the whole scenario. No witnesses. If we charge him a good defence lawyer will suggest any number of possibilities for Lucy not surviving. No jury would convict him."

She nodded. "So it's the entire gospel according to Byron."

"Yes, he's another Da.Ponte. We've got to accept his story no matter how ridiculous."

"Da Ponte? So you do know something about opera."

"Oh everyone knows Da Ponte was Mozart's favourite lyricist."

"I don't think so. Anyway, I see Byron more as one of the seducers."

"Do you? Bryon the Albanian, there's a thought. He'd need a better disguise than ..."he stopped "disguise? No. That would be too far fetched."

"What would?"

"Oh, I just had a ridiculous idea that Lucy could have been disguised. Or rather I mean someone could have been disguised as Lucy."

Helene stared at him "You mean a mistress? Well, that certainly would explain the absence of any photos wouldn't it?"

"H'mm. She'd have to be a very good actress and a very good mimic."

"But, how would she know what Lucy sounded like?"

"It would all depend on how long he'd been planning to dispose of his wife. He could have made recordings of Lucy talking on the phone to her mother or this Van. And there's another thing. There had been a similar boating accident off that island a couple of years ago? He might have read about it and decided to repeat it, especially as one of the bodies has never been found."

"You think that's what gave him the idea for getting rid of Lucy?"

"Could be. But before we have him hung and quartered there is one other thing lacking besides proof, motive. We've looked in to his finances and he appears to be completely solvent."

"But a mistress could be the one making those phone calls."

CS shook his head "Yes, but what sort of woman would do that? She'd have to be besotted with Fuller and that's putting it mildly. He may be solvent but he's no millionaire. She'd have no really strong financial incentive to be a partner in murder."

"I hate to say this but some women will do anything to keep a man. You've heard of that terrible case of that woman in America who drowned her two infant children because the scumbag she loved didn't want them."

"I felt sick when I read about that. But men are just as bad. Look at how many kill their wives to be free to live with their mistress."

"You don't think that could be Fuller's motive for killing Lucy?"

"No, because he could have her and a mistress at the same time. Dot and Van said he'd had several throughout his marriage. Lucy was willing to put up with it."

"But what if this mistress wouldn't share? Told him it was her or Lucy."

"That's all very plausible but I don't really buy it. All he had to do was make sure Lucy went over the side. Could have got her legless first. Too much of a risk to involve someone else. Especially a woman. Cosi fan tutti, and all that"

"Balls. How come you think the story's ridiculous, yet you're pretending to believe the premise it's based on. Not very logical is it?"

"I agree. It's only the music that counts. So why don't we forget these fairy tales and make some more music ourselves?"

"Well, let me see if I can straighten this baton first."

CHAPTER 45

Byron slammed the phone down and ran towards the door, gesturing for Serena to follow him.

"What's up? Who was that? Where're we going?"

"We're looking for phone boxes."

"What phone boxes"

"C'mon, I'll explain as we drive along."

"Wait. Why haven't you dialled 1471?"

"Jeesus, yes." He ran back to the phone, dialled 1471 and listened. Jamming the receiver back he told her "Local, 854621 that's the one we want. You're a bloody genius Reena"

He ran out and down the path unlocking the car with the remote. Serena hadn't fully closed the door before they roared away.

"I know there's one just opposite the pub on the main road. Do you know any more?"

"No. What's this all about?"

"Some pervert is trying to blackmail me. He was using a public phone. "

"But he's not going to hang around, especially if he's threatened you."

"I don't know. He's got to phone again. Might do it tonight. But even if he doesn't, we'll have a better idea of where he lives if we find that number."

They drew up beside the pub; Byron got out and ran to the phone box. He came back shaking his head, "Not that one." He said as he slid into the driving seat. "I think there's some down in the precinct."

Serena pulled his hand away from the steering wheel as she said "Wait Bry. Wait. No good rushing around like a bare arsed baboon. We've got to think."

"But we have to find that box."

"Why? If you were blackmailing somebody would you use the nearest phone?"

Her words made him pause. She was right. What the hell was the matter with him?

"Did you hear any noise, any talk or music? Could he have been phoning from a pub?" she asked.

"I don't think so. I don't remember anything in the background except for a sort of echo. That's what made me think it was a box."

"So it could be anywhere."

"I know but now we're out I think we ought to drive around a bit and see if we can spot this bastard. I've got to find him."

"Why?"

"Because he saw me kill Lucy"

"What? That's ridiculous. How …?"

He cut her short. "He did because he's a fucking pervert. A peeping Tom. He was round the back of the houses. We've never drew the bedroom curtains because there's only open farmland behind us. He saw everything."

"Holy fuck."

"Now you see why I've got to get my hands on him."

"Too bloody right. But how?"

"I'll think of something. The most important thing just now is to find him."

"So what do you know about him?"

He couldn't tell her about the police. Instead he told her about what he'd seen from his front room window.

"This bloke definitely stopped did he?"

"Yes"

"Did you get a good look at him? What was he like?"

"Little fat git. Couldn't see his face. He had a tweed hat on."

"What about the dog?"

"No, just a lead, no hat."

She didn't laugh as he'd hoped. "Be fucking serious. I mean, did it look well fed or was it skin and bones?"

He saw immediately what she was getting at. "I only caught a glimpse of it but it looked well fed to me. Walked with its head held high."

"So why didn't he phone the Law straightaway?"

"Because he's a Peeping Tom."

Serena lapsed into silence. They drove around for a while looking for dog walkers and checking the phone boxes. They didn't find the number and the only dogs being walked were Labradors or Retrievers. Lamdon was that sort of town.

As soon as they got home he poured generous vodka for her and a large Jameson's for himself... She waited until they had topped up their glasses before she asked; "This bloke? You mentioned blackmail. How much did he want?"

He took a good sip from his glass before he answered. He wasn't going to tell her that the pervert had already told the police what he'd seen. It would, he knew, be sensible for her to make herself scarce for a while if the police came back asking questions. But for now he wanted her with him, not least because he needed her help to catch this pervert. "He didn't ask for money. Told me this was only a preliminary call. 'Just to introduce myself' was what the perv said. It's obvious he's trying to panic me but if that's what he thinks he's got another think coming."

"What are you going to do?"

"Move. We're out of here pronto. There's a place I've seen that's to rent. If we can't move in Monday we'll stay in a hotel until we can."

"Won't that just annoy him? What if he goes to the Law?"

"I don't think he will. He's a peeping Tom remember? There's a good chance he won't get in touch with the police because he's got something to hide. He must have."

"So why now? What's he up to?"

"I don't know. Most likely money. If he's suddenly found himself short of a few bob he might be thinking he'd be onto a nice little earner."

"You'd never give him money would you?"

"Never But I'd let him think I would. I've got to get my hands on him. We'll never be safe while he's alive."

"So why move? Why not stay here? Suppose he's so pissed off when he finds you've disappeared he spins some story to the Law. Just happened to be passing and looked up and saw you. You know something like that."

"Well, you could be right but there's also Lenny to consider. He could turn up here anytime."

"Christ, you're a real bundle of joy tonight."

"We've got to be prepared for all possibilities."

"Of course. But Lenny's a maybe. It's this Peeping Tom that's the immediate danger. You're sure it's a good idea to move right now?"

"Yes and I'll tell you why. I think there's a good possibility this pervert is an absolute arsehole. It could be he's been slow to get in touch is because he's not too bright. These perverts are damaged in all sorts of ways, aren't they? Anyway, when he discovers I've gone how's he going to find me?"

"Employ a private eye. Yellow pages are full of them."

"He might not have the cash to do that. As I've said it could be shortage of funds that's driven him to try and blackmail me. Even if he does it will take time. Give us a chance to work out how to trap him. Between us we should be able to come up with something."

"I'll be out of here bloody quick if we don't" she thought to herself. She thought he was taking a hell of a chance in moving. She'd no intention of being charged as an accessory to murder. Byron had said he'd take all the blame but he'd been rattled by just one phone call. How would he stand up to hours of being interviewed by the Fuzz? From now on she'd keep a bag with cash and her passport handy in her car.

CHAPTER 46

Paul was exhilarated. He was a genius; there was no other word for it. He unlocked his car and put the wash bag containing his "cleansing kit" in the glove compartment. He probably hadn't needed it; the phone box he'd used was in a very respectable village on the Southern outskirts of the town. He'd played for and umpired its cricket team for many years and they were all gentlemen. It wasn't the sort of place perverts or drug runners would use. Nevertheless he'd cleaned and disinfected the mouthpiece thoroughly. Better safe than sorry. The box was on the sharp S bend at the edge of the village, not a good place for any passing motorist to stop. It was also directly opposite the lane that led to the cricket club ground, so there was a good place to park.

He drove along humming "I'm the man. I'm the man." He was in charge. It had been well worth the two hours he'd spent earlier that night sitting in his car at the bottom of Meldrum Avenue under the stand of Silver Birches, watching until Fuller's Mercedes arrived. He thought he'd seen a woman go into Fuller's earlier but she'd moved so quickly he couldn't be sure whether she gone into *Sunset* or next door. It might be the mistress he'd speculated about. What a great mystery solving brain he had.

As soon as Fuller had gone inside he'd driven out here to the Cricket Club at the opposite end of town. Fuller might be driving around in a £30,000 car but he, Paul Montgomery Thewell was in the driving seat now. He'd put the frighteners on Fuller that was for sure.

It had more than made up for the humiliation he'd felt as he left his office for the last time. Not that he hadn't left with his head held high. If anyone had known he was leaving they'd given no indication. Mr. Oakshaw had quietly wished him well when they'd met in the corridor the day before. Not a word was said by anyone else to him as he left. That was what he'd demanded but it wasn't the exit he'd long envisaged. He'd expected a leaving worthy of whatever position he'd risen to by that time. Not only would all the other managers have been present as well as Mr. Oakshaw but in all probability the Mayor would have come along. He'd done so when the chief cashier McDermott had left after 40 years service. There'd been tributes and photos in both the evening and weekly papers. He'd been robbed of all that by a bunch of scheming woman.

One day when he'd exposed Fuller they'd realise how much they misjudged him. They'd go around boasting "I used to work with Mr. Thewell, you know." Now he'd got Fuller hooked he'd got to decide how to reel him in. He'd have to do it all himself. The police weren't going to be any help. If only he could phone the killer from home he'd be able to record the conversation and hand the incriminating tapes over to the police. But he knew anyone with a computer can trace your address if they have your phone number.

He though the best plan was to stick to his story that the screams he'd heard and reported in his letters had made him want to investigate further and how by diligent searching he'd found the tramp who'd told him what Fuller had done. It didn't matter that the police wouldn't believe him; they'd never be able to prove otherwise. He'd let Fuller stew for a few more days then phone him again. Tell him if he sold the house he'd better not leave without letting him know his new address. That was...he stopped...how could Fuller do that? There was no way Fuller could get in touch with him. Any link he established would give Fuller the chance to trace him. There was no way he could risk that. What could he do?

His biggest problem was how to keep track of the murderer. The ideal answer would be to fit something like a GPS bug to Fuller's Mercedes. He went to his computer and googled up Car Tracking Systems. There were plenty available but that they all had to link into a firm's or a police computer system. That was no use to him.

He consoled himself by thinking that now he didn't have to go to work he'd have time to study all the notes he'd made of the crime novels that had most impressed him. There might be something that would give him some ideas of how to deal with the killer. He'd start in the morning.

The next three days flew by. By the late afternoon of the third he'd reread five of his favourite crime novels and checked all his notes about them. At first he didn't think that they were going to be any help but after he finished the fifth and was giving Kaiser his major weekly grooming he suddenly realised that the final pages of all the stories had one thing in common. Once the criminal had been identified, each investigator would trap his suspect into making that final fatal mistake that proved their guilt beyond doubt. It seemed that all villains no matter how clever were prone to making complete miscalculations when they thought they were in immediate danger of being exposed. The only drawback was that in three instances the investigator had set up him or her self as bait. Paul had no intention of doing that. He could though put Fuller under a bit more pressure by phoning him again.

He drove to Meldrum Ave. There was no Mercedes parked outside *Sunset* but it as it was only a quarter past six he told himself it was too early for Fuller to be at home. He decided to come back every half hour so he drove to the town's big Tesco store and wandered around the aisles until it was time to come back. When he did there was still no sign of Fuller, nor was there any on the next three times he returned. The rain had ceased by then so he drove home had a leisurely coffee and two Bath Oliver biscuits and returned with Kaiser in the car. The parking spot was still empty and there were no lights to be seen in the house but he drew comfort from the fact that the FOR SALE sign was still up at the gate. He waited once more under the Silver Birches. Sitting there in his car watching made him feel like a detective or private investigator but after a while he decided that perhaps it wasn't a good idea to stay in one spot. Someone might have noticed him on the last occasion and wonder why he was back again. So he drove out to the village from where he had made the first call. He got his "cleansing kit" from the glove compartment, priding himself on his foresight in keeping it there. He wasn't going to phone until he'd taken Kaiser a few times around the gravel path that surrounded the playing fields but a preliminary check of the phone box showed it to be as neat and clean as ever. Nevertheless he "cleansed" the mouth piece half an hour later when he'd finished the walk. He checked his watch as he made the call, "twenty past ten" Surely Fuller would be home by now. He let the phone ring until it cut itself off. He was tempted to sit in his car for a while and phone again but decided against it. Instead he'd go out early in the morning and drive up Meldrum Avenue. If the Mercedes was there he'd use the phone near the police station. It was only about ten minutes from Fullers and druggies and perverts wouldn't be likely to use a box so close to the Law, would they? Also disturbing Fuller so early in the day might help panic him.

He was tense with excitement as he entered the Avenue at seven o'clock next morning. Immediately he saw that the parking space out side Fuller's was empty his tension vanished. He was so busy looking at the house as the passed that the harsh loud blast of a car horn almost made him swear as he jammed on the brakes. A black 4x4 with a large red faced woman scowling at him from the driver's window was alongside him.

"Why don't you look where you're going?" she demanded as he wound down his window.

"Sorry" he said apologetically "That FOR SALE sign, it distracted me."

"Huh! Well keep your eyes on the road in future" she said and she edged past.

"Supercilious cow" he thought to himself as he wound his window back up.

The house didn't look empty; there were still curtains at the windows. If only he could see inside but he couldn't risk meeting Fuller. He could come back at any time. He drove down to the supermarket and bought a coffee. The caffeine perked him up but provided no answers to his problem. He'd taken Fuller's details from the council files, including his e-mail address. There were plenty of internet companies that could find anyone's address from their email. But all he'd get from them now was the Meldrum Ave address. If Fuller had moved it would take time for him to establish himself at his new address. There was a good chance he'd keep his e-mail address. People weren't nearly as careful as they should be with computers. He'd find Fuller eventually. Unless he'd moved abroad? But he couldn't do that when he was still under investigation from the Greeks could he?

When he drove out of the supermarket car park he decided to go home past Fullers for one last look. As he expected Fuller's car wasn't there only the FOR SALE sign was...FOR SALE! What a fool he was. Why hadn't he thought of it before? Of course he could look all around Fuller's house. All he had to do was pretend to be an interested purchaser.

He went home and forced himself to have a leisurely breakfast and take Kaiser for a walk in the park. Then he put on his best suit and shoes and drove to the Estate Agent's. When he looked in the window he saw *Sunset* was priced at. £385,000 and in heavy print at the bottom of the display was "No Chain. Immediate Possession." He hurried into the shop. He was immediately disappointed when he saw only two of the four desks were occupied and that the occupiers were women. He'd hoped to discuss his business "man to man." If he'd managed to establish a good rapport with a male agent he might have been able to get him to tell Fuller's new address when he moved. The black suited well groomed woman who was smiling up at him looked much too efficient to let information like that slip.

"Good morning, can I help you?"

"Ah. Yes. You have on display a property for sale in Meldrum Avenue. I'd like to have a look at it."

"Certainly sir. What time would be convenient for you?"

"Now. I'd like to look at it now."

"Let me see..." She stopped and looked across at the other woman who had just given a small apologetic cough.

"Mel. If the gentleman's enquiring about *Sunset* I'm afraid it was sold last night. Douglas told me over the phone about half an hour ago."

"Oh. It's a confirmed sale is it?"

"Yes. Deposit paid and all."

The woman looked at him apologetically. Before she could speak he demanded "Why is it still in the window then?"

She didn't seem the least embarrassed as she answered "As I said I only knew about it half an hour ago and I've been very busy with work that has to be completed today."

"What if I offer more?"

"I'm afraid we couldn't consider that sir. One of the terms of this sale is that the house be withdrawn from the market. "

"Then why haven't you done so?"

217

"But we have sir. That's why we can't entertain any more offers."

The first woman who had spoken to him said "We have several other equally attractive properties in that area. If you...."

"No, thank you. I prefer to deal with competent firms." He turned and left before she could answer.

CHAPTER 47

"Jeezus. Look at all these books. It's like a fucking library."

Byron laughed, "It is a library. That's what this room's called in the inventory."

Serena shook her head in amazement. There were books from floor to ceiling all around three walls of the room and half way up each side of the fireplace. "She couldn't possibly have read all these or if she has she must be at least 100."

"I don't know how old she is. We're not to touch or rearrange them in any way."

She walked over and looked closely at the shelves "You won't find me curled up in an armchair with *The Victorian History of the Counties of England* on my lap. Is that what she is, a history teacher?"

"She's a professor. Gone to the some university in the States for six months. Gives us plenty of time to find to find the sort of place we want."

"Yeah. This is too far out in the sticks for me. Even from upstairs you can't see another house."

"Yet it's less than five miles to the motorway. So we've got the best of both worlds haven't we? An isolated house, not easy to find and easy access to a fast exit if we ever need it."

"Maybe. At least there is a way out for cars around the back. Otherwise this place would be a dead end. We'd be up the creek without a paddle. Lenny could do us in if he found us here and nobody would know for weeks."

"If he finds us."

She turned away and looked out at the big green tree in the middle of the lawn. She wasn't happy with Byron's attitude. For herself, she believed there was safety in numbers. She'd have preferred a place in the middle of a big town. Somewhere with pubs and bars and a bit of nightlife. Make friends with the right sort of people there and you've got backup if you need it. It was the same with his attitude to this blackmailer. Why was he so sure the pervert wouldn't go to the police? Seeing naked women was a bit different from seeing one murdered. The bastard might be having nightmares about it.

She turned back to him and asked "Bry. This pervert who reckons he saw you do in Lucy. Are you going to do anything about him? He's not just going to disappear is he?"

"He will, if I get my hands on him."

"But how? It's all very well coming out here where he can't find us but that means we can't find him don't it?"

He sat down on the big settee and patted it for her to come and sit beside him. "First of all girl, you're in no danger from him. He knows nothing about you" he said as he hugged her, "But I agree we've got to decide what's the best thing to do about the bastard."

"I think we should stiff him as soon as possible. We're not safe while he's alive."

"I'm not so sure if it's as bad as that. After all his story is ridiculous isn't it? Everyone knows that Lucy drowned holidaying in Letsos There are eyewitnesses who saw her board the boat and her own mother believes Lucy spoke to her on the phone from Greece doesn't she? So does her best friend. So what are the police going to think if this pervert gets desperate enough to go to them with his story of her being killed the day before she arrived in Greece? The first thing they're going to ask him is 'Where did you see all this happen?' Once they know he's a peeping Tom they're not going to take him seriously are they?"

"What makes you so sure they won't?"

He couldn't tell her that his certainty came from assuming that was what had already happened. The cops hadn't come back to question him further about the pervert's story so they couldn't have believed it. There was no point in telling her that now. It might make her think he didn't trust her. His biggest concern was to avoid Lenny. He reckoned they were safe enough from him out here for the moment. He was sure Lenny was still alive. People like him didn't just disappear. But he had to reassure her about this peeping Tom.

"Well, I can't be absolutely sure can I? But what I've been thinking is this. By moving quickly we've make it hard for this bloke to have us, right? Now, I think he's after a bit of blackmail. He knows the police won't believe him so he thinks 'I going to

220

have a nice little earner out of this'. If that's the case he'll make it his business to find us. If he does we'll know he's serious and we can set a trap for him. If he hasn't got the nous to find where we are then he's just so much piss and wind, right?"

"So we just wait until he gets in touch eh?"

"Something like that. Unless of course, we come across him by some stroke of luck or something. Then we'll deal with him straightaway. Always assuming he's worth the bother. There's no point in risking our necks on squashing a useless little pervert is there?"

"I suppose not. What about Lenny then? You think he's alive and back here?"

"I think that's a wise assumption. He's too dangerous to ignore. That's why I haven't changed my mobile number. I keep thinking Dot will be so excited when he turns up she'll phone and gloat about how he's back and coming after me." He'd convinced himself that Dot hadn't really yelled "Lenny's back" at the end of their last conversation.

"Unless he tells her not to."

"He could but I think she's so anxious to make me suffer that she'd ignore him. I doubt if her IQ's written in double figures."

"Sod her. But we need to take precautions. I wasn't joking when I said I could get you a shooter."

"Could you use it? Ever fired a weapon before?"

"What's to learn? You just point and squeeze."

He shook his head "It's not as simple as that."

"Give over. You don't like shooters do you? What have you got against them?

"Nothing really. It's just ...well, I think they're too easy to trace. A few years' ago a chap I knew rather well forgot once too often to pay his gambling debts and was shot by a hit man who was caught and convicted because they traced the gun he used."

"But it would be self-defence with us, wouldn't it? Nobody's going to do us for shooting Lenny if he's trying to kill us."

"Ah, yes. But the gun, you see; that could be trouble. You've no way of knowing what it's been used for before. It could have been used in some robbery or worse still a killing."

"Bry" she interrupted "that's so out of date. There are hundreds of guns from Eastern Europe being smuggled into this country that have never been fired before. Honest"

"Maybe, but how would we explain our possessing such a weapon? You know what villains the police are"

"Too bloody right. The propositions I've had from some of them! But never mind that now. If we did shoot Lenny, we could dump him somewhere. How would..." she stopped "Oh shit...Dot.... I was going to say how would his disappearance be linked to us, but Dot would tell the cops wouldn't she?"

He nodded. "Look, let's do a tour of the house and see where the weak points are as regards breaking in. There's no reason why we can't use the Purdy's against an intruder. They're legit. They're supposed to be under lock and key but we need to have them handy. It's just picking the right place to put them."

"One's going in the bedroom, that's for sure." When he just nodded she thought to herself what a complex man he was. Most men she knew would have made some filthy joke about a "weapon in the bedroom" but he was if anything rather prudish. That was one of the things that had first attracted her to him. Yet, he'd no conscience about defrauding or killing. Several villains she'd know were like that. Some wouldn't let men swear in the presence of women.

They'd not got very far around the ground floor rooms before it was obvious that there were too many windows and French doors where an intruder could easily break in. There was a burglar alarm but Byron said it was too obvious and could easily be cut by any competent villain. They concluded that their best defence would be to have weapons hidden where they were easily reachable. There were plenty of suitable hiding places for weapons. One Purdy would go under Byron's side of the bed and the other behind the heavy curtains on the first landing of the staircase.

Byron had brought a couple of baseball bats from *Sunset* but they decided they'd need at least another three. In the main living room was an open fireplace with a fancy brass fireside set in front of it. But what interested Serena much more was the long steel poker that lay alongside the fender. That could do real serious damage. She'd not forget it was there. The more weapons she could lay her hands on the better.

When they'd finished their tour Byron sat down with his laptop to study the runners and to get the latest information on the race meeting they were going to tomorrow. Serena decided to take a walk around the grounds. She had a lot of thinking to do.

CHAPTER 48

"And the next to go is Chelsea Heppenstall-Brown on Greysocks."

"Double or quits she has a clear round" C.S whispered to Helene. They were having bets on each of the competitors in the Pony Club Gymkhana and he was £10 down

She hesitated before answering "You're on."

Chelsea was his sister Rose's daughter and he knew she was a competent rider but more importantly he knew Greysocks was a clever jumper. Even so his heart was in his mouth all through the round for Chelsea was taking every shortcut the course offered. At the last Greysocks rear legs hit the bar so hard that it jumped out of its sockets but to his great relief fell back into them again.

"Jammy bugger"

"Not at all. Just a judicious piece of judge...."

A strong confident female voice immediately behind him made the words stick in his throat. "Clarence, you made it."

He knew it was useless to try and walk away as if he hadn't heard. Guiltily he turned around "Yes mother."

He breathed a sigh of relief when he saw she was wearing her new Jaeger tweeds. She was a substantial woman and like the oak trees of which she was so fond each passing year had added its girth ring. Her wide hips had assisted the smooth production of her six children, four in the first six years of marriage and two ten years later. All six emerged alternately in a boy, girl procession. Clarence was the youngest boy.

Before he could introduce Helene his mother said to her "You must be the young woman I've heard whispers about. I've been dying to meet you. Clarence's just like his father and brothers never says a word"

"Chance would be a fine thing" he said quietly.

"I heard that young man. I'm not as deaf as you like to think." Turning to Helene again she said "I'm Marge and you are?"

"Helene"

"What a beautiful name…and one you can't shorten. You're a lucky girl. I'm Margarite but every one has called me Marge for donkey's years. You'd better call me Marge like everyone else does if you're going to continue to keep company with Clarence. We're a rather informal family. You won't mind if we all you Helene straight away will you my dear?"

"No, not at all…Marge."

His mother's face lit up with pleasure, "Splendid. Now tell me, has Clarence been treating you well? I've tried to bring up all my boys to be gentlemen but I not sure I've succeeded. Mind you I must say Clarence has always been the best mannered of them all. He used to hate me for calling him Clarence. But it was my father's name and I knew he'd be the last of my boys so he had to have it. Threatened to change it by deed poll when he was a teenager. But he's a bit more mature about it now, aren't you darling?"

He didn't have to answer because Helene said, "Oh yes. It was one of the first things he told me about himself." He concentrated his gaze on the show ring. She'd make him pay for this later..

"Good. Now Clarence, what did you think of your niece and Greysocks? Still a first rate pony isn't he? I don't think anyone will beat her now; especially after the time she did in that clear round."

As if on cue, the announcement came over the Tannoy. "The winner is Greysocks ridden by Miss Chelsea Heppenstall-Brown." He didn't move quickly enough to avoid receiving a sharp dig in the ribs. "You cheat" Helene whispered.

When his mother asked "Shall we all go down and congratulate them?" he was the first to move.

Approaching the parade ring he gave Chelsea the thumbs up sign. The way she waved regally back reminded him vividly of her mother Rose and the many times she'd been a winner in these gymkhanas. Rose was his favourite among his sisters. He caught sight her standing further around the ring and directed his mother and Helene towards her. As they approached he became aware of a blonde woman just a few yards past his sister waving and beckoning him over. It was Van. He acknowledged her wave and signalled he would be with her after he spoken to his sister and

Chelsea. After hugging them and introducing Helene he excused himself and hurried over to her.

"I didn't know you were one of the horsy Bullingtons. I should have paid more attention when you told me your name."

"Oh, we're everywhere. It's nice to see you Van. How goes it?"

"Not bad. We can't compete with you toffs and your thousand pound ponies but we weren't so far away in third." She motioned towards a miniature version of herself sitting on a jet black mount among the winners that looked miles too big for her.

"Well done but I can assure you Greysocks cost nowhere near that."

Before she could answer the announcer began to read out the names of the first three finishers and the rosettes were handed out. When the applause finished and the ponies left the ring she said "If you've got a minute there's something I want to tell you."

"Certainly. I'll walk back to your horsebox with you."

They weren't able to talk much on the way to the horsebox because her daughter wanted to relive every stride and every jump with her mother. Eventually, the horse which was called "Snaffles" was unsaddled and as the girl groomed and watered him Van turned to him and said "You remember you asked me to tell you if I learned anything more about Lucy's holiday?"

"Yes"

"Well, last week I decided it would do me no harm to go back to Weightwatchers." She held up a hand before he could speak and said "Don't lie and tell me I don't need to. My arse is nearly as big as Snaffles."

"Mummy! Don't be so crude" came a reproving little voice.

"O.K. Goody two shoes. But don't interrupt again while I'm talking to this gentleman. He's a policeman. I've something important to tell him about Aunt Lucy."

"Her nasty husband drowned her didn't he? He's a wicked man." Looking up at him she asked "Are you going to arrest him?"

"Maybe." He answered softly.

"Can I be there when you…"

"Charlene, stop chattering and get on with your grooming. We haven't all day" interrupted Van but not unkindly.

"If he's here and he tries to run away I could go after him on Snaffles."

"Charlene!"

The girl gave a little pout and turned back to her grooming.

"Sorry about that Mr. Bullerton. Look; it might be something or nothing but the first person I met when I went back to Weightwatchers was a German girl called Helga. She knew Lucy very well and amazingly she was on the very same island the week Lucy was killed."

"Did she meet Lucy?"

"No and that's the strange thing. She met Byron but not Lucy. He was sat down a few tables away from her in a café and she says he acted very strangely when she introduced herself."

"How? Did he try to leave quickly or something?"

"Not exactly. When she asked him where Lucy was he said she was shopping in one of the nearby streets but when she wanted to sit and wait for her coming back he wouldn't have it. He insisted that they both go and search for her immediately."

"I suppose they didn't find her?"

"That's it. That's what so funny about it all. He made her go into the boutiques on one side of the road and said he'd search those on the opposite side. She says she'd only gone in and out of one shop before he'd disappeared. She stayed in the street for at least another quarter of an hour but there was neither hide nor hair of any of the two of them."

"Most peculiar. What do you think could have happened?"

"I don't know. It's beyond me. Lucy and Helga were friends from way back. There is no way Lucy would have not wanted to see her if she knew she was nearby."

He thought for a moment and then asked "Did Lucy say anything about this in any of her phone calls."

Van shook her head "There were no phone calls. Lucy drowned the same afternoon." Her eyes were glistening as she spoke.

He reached out and lightly touched her arm. She looked up and asked "Could this be important? It IS bloody strange isn't it/"

"Mummy!"

They ignored the rebuke. He held her gaze as he answered "It is. I can't think of any sensible explanation can you?"

"None, I've gone over and over it in my mind ever since Helga told me but I keep coming up with only one answer."

When she didn't continue he said "You mean Byron didn't want Lucy and Helga to meet."

"Yeah. But why? Why?"

"That's what we've got to try and find out. I'll ask him as soon as I see him. Do you think Helga would come to the station and give us a statement? Having it in writing when I confront Fuller would be a great help."

"I'm sure she would. I'll ask her as soon as I get home. I'm a bit too uptight to phone to her now. I've still got your card. I'll phone you as soon as I know."

He thanked her again and reassured her that he would follow up on what she'd told him. He walked back to his family.

"Quite a lady's man today Clarence" his mother called out (he thought unnecessarily loudly) when she saw him approaching. He made his apologies and lifted Chelsea and swung her around squealing when she ran into his arms. "Clever girl. We'll see you at Badminton one day." She blushed with pride. As he kissed her mother she said "She believes everything you say C."

"I hope you don't" his mother said to Helene.

"No way." She answered with a smile.

"Come on then Clarence" his mother demanded, "What were you talking so intimately to Vanessa Frost about?"

He couldn't hide his amazement "You know her?"

"Of course...and her lovely daughter Charlene. She and Chelsea are good friends as well as competitors. Her oldest boy Mark is a policeman isn't he? Is that how you know her?"

"Mother, someday I swear I'm going to get you to write out your interrogation techniques for a police training manual. How do you get to know so much about so many people?"

"Simply by getting them to talk about themselves...and listening when they do. Now, come on, what did you want with Vanessa?

"Subtlety has never been your strong point mother I'm afraid that I can't say much other than she's being very helpful in some enquiries we're making." He had to put up his hand to stop his mother speaking "No. Not about her. Her best friend Lucy Fuller was drowned recently and there are some circumstances about the drowning that need to be investigated."

"Lucy Fuller? ...The boating accident in the Greek Islands? Well, well. You won't believe me Clarence but as soon as I read about it I said to your father "There's something fishy about this.""

"What did he say?" Clarence asked.

"Oh you know him. Made some stupid remark like 'Well, there's bound to be when it happened at sea. Lot's of fish in those waters.' He's never grown up that man."

"And you wouldn't have him any other way, Mummy" said Rose.

"H'm, Well, the thing is; that husband of Lucy Fuller, Byron; he's a bad 'un. Known all about him for years. Never liked him; he probably murdered poor Lucy"

"Mother, keep your voice down. You want to be sued for slander? There is not a shred of evidence to substantiate what you've just said. It's just some things that need to be cleared up"

"Of course, dear. We all understand don't we?" she said conspiratorially to the Helene. "Tell you what; you have a word with your brother Henry. He's never been a fan of Fuller's. He knows things about his business dealings. It's such a pity for his father was a fine man."

He couldn't tell her he'd already spoken to Henry and other members of his family about Fuller. He congratulated himself that he'd had the foresight to make them swear not to breathe a word about what he was doing to their mother. His satisfaction vanished rapidly when his mother continued "I didn't know this poor Lucy Fuller was a friend of Vanessa's. I must phone her and give her my condolences."

He immediately thought he must warn Van not to tell any of her suspicions to his mother. But a few seconds later another thought occurred to him, would it be such a bad thing if rumours did start circulating about the "boating accident? " Anything that helped to rattle Fuller was bound to be a help, wasn't it?

CHAPTER 49

The removal lorry was outside *Sunset* and Fuller's Mercedes was parked behind it. Paul drove carefully past, glancing briefly at the scene just as any naturally curious passer-by would. He parked on the opposite side of the road about 50 meters past the lorry and adjusted his interior mirror so that he could watch what was happening. He thought it a good omen that he was facing the same way as the lorry and the Mercedes; he'd be able to wait until he saw which way they turned at the top of the Avenue before setting of after them. He was confident he could do so without being noticed because he'd studied how the police and private eyes did it in crime novels. He didn't think he'd have to wait very long for the lorry seemed to be already well loaded.

He had only caught a brief glimpse of Fuller before he'd put that big helmet on so he didn't really know what the man looked like. It would be the first time he had ever seen a killer in real life. He knew from his crime novels that murderers didn't look any different from other people. It would…, he sat up straight as a woman with a suitcase came out of the gate of Sunset. The first thing he noticed about her was her short blond hair was braided in what he privately sneered at as "Sambo Strings." Why white women wanted to copy African hairstyles was beyond him. The suitcase was bulging but she seemed to have no difficulty carrying it. When she stepped into the road he was afraid she was going to cross directly just in front of his bonnet but instead she stopped beside a red car opposite him, opened the boot and swung the case easily into it. He had a good sight of her face as she did it. She was noticeably freckled and her large amber eyes separated by a short broad nose gave her a slightly pugnacious appearance. Not a lady to be trifled with. When she closed the boot and strode back to the house she reminded him of Tracey the girl who was giving him his gym induction.

He was attending the gym because when he was being discharged after recovering from his beating in the car park, Dr. Hindes had mentioned that it might be a good idea if he lost "A few pounds." He'd not taken any notice of the doctor but two weeks ago he'd had a letter from the surgery telling him that he was eligible to participate in a free 8 week " gym and slim" scheme sponsored by his local Hospital Trust. As he was finding it difficult to find enough to do to fill the hours every day he had surprised himself by going along and enjoying the first session.

He wondered if he should get out and walk up the Avenue a bit in case the woman came back and came over and asked what he was doing sitting there. She looked very much the type who would do it. Just like those hard faced P.E. teachers who came over and stared belligerently at him when he happened to stop for a few minutes to watch girls playing netball at his old school. He could show her all his council papers but he knew he wouldn't feel comfortable with her. Women like her made him feel on edge and who knows Fuller might come out and want to see who she was talking to. He was gathering his things together when she appeared again with another case. He made sure he kept his back to her as he eased himself out of his car and kept his gaze firmly fixed on the houses beside him. A boot being slammed shut made him tense but there was no sound of footsteps approaching. Instead a powerful engine purred into life and he turned to see the red car leaving. It was moving very quickly but there was no squealing of brakes nor any undue engine roar. He had to force himself not to suddenly turn away when she glanced at him as she drove away. There was a Ford badge on the boot and one of those flat metal strips across the top of just like the Grand Prix racing cars on the Television.

As soon as it disappeared from sight he turned and got back in his car. After a few minutes three men in brown overalls came out of *Sunset* with a few small items on their hands and after stowing them started to close up the back of the lorry He decided to drive up to the top of the Avenue so that he would not be noticed starting off at the same time as the removers. If Fuller left at the same time as the lorry he would let both vehicles get around the corner before starting after them. He was confused when the lorry drove away and there was no sign of Fuller. It was out of his sight before he decided it would be much easier to follow than Fuller's Mercedes. In his haste he stalled the engine. He made himself take a deep breath before he put the automatic shift into "Drive" again and pulled away from the kerb without mishap.

There was only one other car between him and the lorry when they reached the main road and after ten minutes he was sure they were heading for London. He didn't find it easy watching the lorry and at the same time keeping an eye on his rear mirror for

Fuller's car as well all the other traffic. Tailing suspects wasn't like this in detective novels. At a major roundabout he was completely taken by surprise when the lorry carried on around it to the right instead of taking the London exit. Finding himself in the wrong lane he had to endure the angry blasts of car horns as he swerved after it. Two cars passed him before he'd got his wits together again. He almost missed seeing the lorry turning left. There was a sign saying CLEENDON INDUSTRIAL AREA at the corner of the road. There were rows of Factories behind high wire fencing on both sides of the road. Fuller wouldn't come to live here. The lorry must be taking a short cut. He was surprised when it slowed and turned into a gateway. As he drove past he saw it had stopped outside a building with THE BIG BROWN BOX STORAGE COMPANY in giant letters on its wall.

He drove on to the next roundabout and turned back. When he passed the lorry again it was being unloaded. He'd had a completely wasted journey. He pressed his foot hard down on the accelerator. Perhaps Fuller might still be at the house. Once back in the flow of traffic on the main road he kept a lookout to see if any approaching cars were Fuller's Mercedes. When he didn't see any it raised his hopes that Fuller would still be at the house but when he turned into Meldrum Avenue there was no sign of the Mercedes and the windows of *Sunset* were curtainless.

When he got home he didn't feel like taking Kaiser for a walk. Only the dog's pleading eyes and its refusal to leave his side persuaded him to go out. He made his way down to the canal and strode briskly out along the towpath impervious to the sights that usually delighted him. It was so unjust, weeks of watching all for nothing. He had missed a golden opportunity to corner his prey. He would have phoned Fuller the very next day. That would have shown the villain what kind of man he was dealing with. He kept thinking of all he would have demanded off him from his position of power.

It was some while before he noticed how far he had walked. When Kaiser looked up at him he could have swore there was a sly satisfaction in his pet's eyes. "You ruffian" he said softly "You let me come all this way without any warning." Kaiser wagged his tail and help up his right paw for him to shake. "All right your majesty. We'll shake on it but you're getting a much shorter evening walk than usual." He'd no heart to look in any windows tonight. Kaiser stood up and turned towards home. He let him off the lead so that he could investigate whatever took his fancy as they ambled back home.

In the morning Kaiser didn't show any sign of aching anywhere but Paul's back and thighs ached. It was the second day of his gym induction and he thought he'd give it a miss. But when he couldn't settle to read or concentrate on anything at home as three o'clock approached he decided he'd go to the gym after all.

The session with Tracy proved to be as enjoyable as the first. She showed him proper respect, calling him "Mr.Thewell" and she was very complimentary about his efforts on each machine. After he'd had his shower and dressed he decided to have a coffee before going home. The café was on the first floor of the sports centre and when he sat down with his drink he found he could look straight down into the swimming pool. Two lanes that were roped off were being used by school children but just below him was a smaller shallow pool where three young women were playing with their children. The bikini's they were wearing weren't scanty but their breasts were practically falling out of them as they bent over their charges. He could see one woman's nipples through her wet top. To think he'd lived in this town all his life and never realised such delights were available. Nobody could harass him for looking. The windows were there to let you see the swimmers weren't they? He stayed pretending to drink his coffee long after the cup was empty. Then a pregnant woman lowered herself into the pool followed by a blond curly haired toddler. He looked at her bulging belly in disgust; such sights should not be allowed in public. Sickened, he got up and left.

He was halfway down the stairs when he saw the woman who'd come out of Fuller's. There was no doubt about it. He had a clear view of her freckled face and her ridiculous African hairstyle. He followed her down the corridor and had to hurriedly to stop and pretend to look in his bag when he realised he would be immediately behind her going through the double doors that lead to changing rooms. But he needn't have bothered for she strode through the doors and let them swing back without any thought of who might be following. When she went into the Women's changing room he entered the Gents, waited five minutes and came out a gain.

He was sure she hadn't done any exercise yet so he went to the windows of the room expecting to see her but there was no sign of her. The room adjoined the main gym and had clear glass walls on two sides and he could see an exercise class setting up in it. As he walked back along the corridor a bunch of women hurried past him into the room. He turned and looked at a poster on the wall and was just turning back from it when he saw her going into the room where all the women had gone. He didn't have the nerve to follow and look through the door but sauntered past it into the gym.and hurried over to the drinks dispenser. As he slowly drank the cup of water he'd drawn from it he turned to the glass wall where the exercise class was now in full swing. They were all women, several had blonde hair but she wasn't one of them. Where the Hell had she gone? Perplexed he studied each of them again. Perhaps her blond hair was a wig. The women were moving in unison, their actions looked very aggressive; they were punching and turning and kicking out, first with one foot then the other. She definitely wasn't there. Perhaps it would be better to go and search the car park for the red Ford. He was just turning away when he caught sight of the class instructor. It was her! She was wearing a microphone attached to a broad black headband that obscured most of her blonde hair. God she looked dangerous. There was a sharpness and clear definition about her movements that few in the class could match.

He would have liked to stay and watch her but he knew that would draw too much attention to him.. As he walked out of the gym the reasoned that as the class had just started and allowing for her getting changed afterwards it would be at least another thirty minutes before she left. He went over to big metal dispenser and got a Mars Bar. If only that hippopotamus of a pregnant woman wasn't in the pool he could have gone back to the café and enjoyed himself there. He'd have to wait in the car park. Kaiser would be wondering why he hadn't come home to give him his meal but he'd make it up to him later. He'd wait for this woman even if she stayed until the centre closed at ten o'clock.

The Classic FM evening concert on his car radio was playing one of his favourites, Mendelssohn's Hebridean Overture. He regretted interrupting it when he moved into a spot near the exit that gave him a good view of her red Ford. Forty minutes later he congratulated himself on his foresight and tracking skills when she appeared and drove off immediately. He followed her out onto the dual carriageway. It as a 40 mph zone and he was glad to see that she was observing the limit. When she turned let at the last roundabout he assumed she was heading for the motorway but she turned left again after some fifteen minutes and went towards the coast. The road was narrow and went through three villages he knew well from his cricket umpiring. This local knowledge stood him in good stead after she left the last village for he knew the road forked sharply just around the bend ahead. He pressed his foot down hard on the accelerator of his Rover 25 so as to get there in time to see which fork she took. He was just in time to see the back of her car disappearing around the left fork. He let his speed drop for he was sure there were no side roads off this route for the next few miles. There were a series of S –bends that led to a mile long straight where it would be easy to keep her in sight. He didn't want to arouse her suspicions by getting too close to her. When he turned into the straight she was nowhere to be seen. Assuming she must have rocketed along it he had his foot hard on the accelerator when he caught sight of a flash of red on his right. It was through a driveway flanked by two massive grey pillars. His first instinct was to brake sharply but fearing that she might hear his brakes squealing he let the speed fall gradually. He had to drive on for several minutes before he found somewhere to turn. As he drove slowly back he saw through gaps in the hedge a three storied Georgian manor house. There was no sign of the red car outside so he assumed it must be parked around the back. He stopped well past the entrance and when he ran back to the pillars saw the name TREVELYN carved into them. There must have been large gates at one time for there were iron pinions on each of the pillars. He was standing musing over whether to creep up the drive and see if the red car was definitely there. Maybe the Mercedes Kompresser would be parked beside it. Suddenly he thought "Fuller might not be at home. He could come roaring along in his Mercedes any minute." He ran to his car and drove quickly away.

Paul was wrong about Fuller; he was most definitely at home. He was sitting at the massive oak table in the kitchen smiling at a wide eyed Serena. The table top was completely covered with ten pound notes.

"Jeezus Holy Christ," she said as she stepped forward and picked a handful of them up "Are they real?"

He nodded "All genuine and dutifully signed by the chief cashier of the Bank of England."

"Where, where did you get them? I mean did you win them? "

"I have these by permission of six mudlarks." Before she could ask he added "By that I mean six genuine horses who can slog through the mud all the way to the winning post. This is the Tote Jackpot from Pakenham"

"Jackpot! You' backed six winners in succession. How the hell did you do that? I thought you didn't take big risks? What's got into you?"

"Actually it was easy. I couldn't believe when I studied the race card. You know how wet it's been these last couple of days. It was pouring all the way up to the meeting. So I was looking out for mudlarks, horses that act well on heavy going. And do you know what? Out of all the runners in 6 races there were only nine that had any form at all in the mud. Three of the races had two such mud loving horses in them; there was only one mud lark in each of the other three. So all I had to do was cover each combination of two in the last three races with the three straight selections of the first three. Follow?"

"Let Hell I do. But what does it matter? You won"

"Indeed. But I wasn't expecting such a great return. Thought lots of the pros. would have worked it out. Actually, there were 15 of us left in the pot by the fifth race. Most of them must have backed a horse called Silver Sides who acts well in the mud and was the short priced favourite. He was well ahead when he fell at the second last. An old stayer Fred's Dream who hasn't won a race for years came roaring in. There were just five of us left after that. And just three, including yours truly backed the winner, Bride's Surprise in the last. The jackpot was over £180,000. We got over £60,000 each. This is going to be a lucky place for us Reena."

CHAPTER 50

Paul awoke early next morning and jumped out of bed. Life was good again. Last night, once he'd eaten, fed Kaiser and taken him for a brief walk; he'd used his computer to trace Fuller. Using the electoral rolls and a Reverse Phone Directory he'd no difficulty finding the phone number for TREVELYN and the name of the owner, a Dr. Maud Patten. He assumed that Fuller was only renting so he would have to keep the owner's phone number. Only the fear of his call being traced back to his home stopped him from phoning immediately. He stayed on his computer searching for mobile phone accessories and was delighted to find that he could buy a mini cassette recorder to attach to a mobile phone for less than £60. He ordered one plus a pack of ten micro cassettes immediately.

To pass the time before the shops opened he went for a long walk with Kaiser and when he got back gave him a thorough grooming. He decided it would be safer to drive into Cleendon and buy two mobile phones there rather than here in Lamdon. He'd get the cheapest possible; all that mattered was that he could attach a recorder to them. Using his computer he printed out two name cards with the false names and addresses he intended to use and put them in his wallet where he could read them as he was making his purchases. He wasn't going to risk not remembering his false identities. All went well and by mid-day he had both phones bought and fully charged. On the off chance there'd be someone at TREVELYN he rang and asked for Dr.Patten using a strong country accent. He got lots of laughs at cricket dinners with his rustic yokel jokes. He was delighted to be told she was absent in America. He assumed the woman who answered was the blonde fitness instructor. Now all he had to do was to plan what he would say to Fuller.

He had concluded that the one sure way to prove Fuller was a killer was through blackmail. It was a serious crime but surely the police would understand when he presented them with the recordings that his only motive had been to convict Fuller. He'd not spend a penny of the money, that would help substantiate his story wouldn't it? His other alternative was to send the recordings anonymously to the police as a "concerned citizen" and wait until Fuller had been tried and convicted in court. Then he could write an article for a Sunday newspaper (Probably *The Sunday Times*) revealing that he was the "concerned citizen" who'd exposed the killer. They'd pay him thousands for that without a doubt. He could then follow that up with a book. As long as he stuck to his story about getting his information from a tramp nobody could accuse him of being a "Peeping Tom." If the worst happened and people kept on with such an accusation he could move away to somewhere befitting his new status.

That evening he made the call.

"Good evening Mr. Fuller how are you?"

Byron signalled for Serena to get upstairs and listen on the bedroom extension. "Sorry" he said, "I think you've got the wrong number."

"I don't think so Mr. Byron Wesley Fuller. Late of *Sunset,* Meldrum Ave, Lamdon, where you strangled your ......"

"I beg your pardon" he interrupted loudly, as he thought he heard Serena picking up the extension.

Byron's authoritive voice made Paul jump. He'd expected to keep the upper hand throughout this conversation. He gritted his teeth and said with deliberate slowness "*Sunset,* where you strangled your wife Lucy while wearing a white chemical warfare suit."

"Nonsense" replied Byron, then after a pause, he asked in a relaxed conversational tone, "Why are you phoning Mr.... I'm afraid I don't know your name. You are?"

Paul had to fight back an impulse to give his name. He had to concentrate hard before he could say; "Who I am Fuller is the man who saw you kill your wife. That is all that need concern you Fuller." (Omitting the "Mr" twice. made him feel better.) He was in charge here.

"Very well,Mr. Mysterious. Would you at least tell me this? Are you married?"

The unexpectedness of the question shook Paul; "That's none of your business" he blurted out.

"Quite so, quite so" came the smooth confident answer, "I wouldn't normally dream of enquiring into your personal life old man, if it were not for the fact you are interfering with mine."

Before Paul could reply, Fuller continued quickly, "If you are married, I hope you enjoy as good a sex life. Lucy and I did. We liked to be rather adventurous and I'm afraid that's what you might have seen. One thing that really turned Lucy on was imagining she was being abducted by aliens. That's why I was wearing a white space suit."

Paul cursed himself for not turning the recorder on. He'd not expected Fuller to admit anything so quickly. He fumbled for the switch and clicked it on. The next two minutes would be crucial. "Did your wife also enjoy you putting your hands around her throat and choking her?" he demanded.

Fuller gave a weary sigh "I told you old man, it was a game."

"Is that what you told the police?"

"As a matter of fact it is and they believed me. So you're wasting your time old man."

"You think so? You won't mind then if I tell the police everything I saw…old man? I'm afraid I only gave them a very brief account and of course there is the matter of what you did with your wife's body. Going on holiday next morning didn't give you much time to dispose of it. She must be buried somewhere nearby, maybe in your cellar?"

"Absolute nonsense."

"I don't think so. I'm sure with what I could tell the police they'd make a thorough search all around where you used to live."

There was a long pause and when Fuller answered Paul was amazed by the change in his voice. In a weary pleading tone he said "Look, I'm afraid I can't stand much more of this nonsense. My dear wife is dead, lost at sea and I miss her very much. All that you are doing is destroying the happy memories of the life we had. I'm a reasonably wealthy man and I want you to stop. How much do you want?"

This was something Paul had prepared for; "What would you say was a reasonable sum?"

"£5,000?"

"That's insulting. Is that how little you valued Lucy?"

"All right. I'll give you £25,000 if you stop this nonsense."

Paul glanced at the tape recorder, it was still running "That's better" he replied.

The authority returned to Fuller's voice as he said "Right. But I want you to understand that this will be a one and only payment. If you ever contact me again I shall go straight to the police and that I assure you that is not an empty threat. If you attempt to bleed me dry what would I have to lose? Is that clear?"

Paul was tempted to immediately ask for more but he didn't want to risk ruining what he'd achieved. Fuller's offer was as good as an admission of guilt. That's was all he needed. "Understood" he replied; "Get the money ready by tomorrow night at the latest. I'll be in touch later to tell you how and where to deliver it." He switched the phone off before Fuller could reply. He'd got it all on tape.

Fuller was standing by the phone when Serena rushed into the room. "You're not serious are you? You're not going to give that pervert 25K?"

"Only bait, my dear."

"It's only bait if you catch him. Suppose you don't?

"I will. I didn't want to waste any more time bargaining with him. Besides he won't get 25K or even 10K."

"What?"

"Remember what you asked me when you came home and I had all that money spread out on the kitchen table like it is now?

"Yeah. Something about whether it was real or not."

"Exactly. Well that's what put the thought in my head as to how I'd deal with this peeping Tom if he phoned. Only the first £1000 or so will be real. I've been in touch with someone who swears he can get me thousands of good forgeries."

"But won't this pervert do his nut when he finds out? He'll turn you in."

"Not if we get him first. The only turning he'll be doing is in his grave. I'm sure he an amateur. He was too quick to accept £25,000. I mean if you had the chance of blackmailing a punter and he swore you'd only get one payment would you settle for that?"

Serena shook her head, "Now that you've said it no, I wouldn't. You don't think he's in cahoots with the cops and trying to trap you?"

"I wondered that but I don't think so. First of all I'm sure phone tap evidence isn't admissible in Law. And then there's entrapment. Any good brief would get that phone conversation thrown out if they tried to use it. Besides did I admit anything except my wife and I had a bit of sexual hanky panky? No. Don't worry. Nearly all blackmailers are caught through the handover. I'll think of some way of catching him."

"It had better be good."

"It will be. Whatever I think of I'll go over it with you. You've got a good criminal brain."

"O Mr. Fuller, you say the sweetest things."

He took her in his arms and kissed her. "It's true. We'll come through this together girl."

"You bloody bet. And if this bloke of yours doesn't come up with the fake dosh I know somebody who's a whiz with Spanish Euros. He's sure to be able to get you some notes with Lizzie's head on them."

"You do that. We'll see who gets the best terms. We'll make this pervert sorry he ever set eyes on me."

CHAPTER 51

D.I. Morrison winked as she said "You realise Bully you'll have to follow this up in mostly your own time? I've tried to get the brass to let us continue to look further into Mr. Byron Fuller's misbegotten life but it's a NoNo. As far as they're concerned if the Greeks are satisfied so are they."

"I understand ; I don't mind spending some of my own time on this. I'm seeing Helga tomorrow morning at Van's."

"All these women you're on first name terms with. I hope Helene knows about them."

"She understands the sacrifices I've got to make in the line of duty ma'am."

"You hope. That's what I like about you Bully, you're such an optimist. Now remember; when you get back if anyone asks where you were refer them to me. This is strictly SWOMO."

"SWOMO?"

"Strictly Word of Mouth Only."

"Certainly ma'am."

When he drew up at Van's ranch style bungalow next morning he couldn't help thinking as he'd done on his first visit that her spiritual home was the American Wild West. Even the name on the fence "THE HOMESTEAD" had a massive pair of Steer's Horns fixed above it. His thoughts were confirmed when she opened the door to him, wearing a blue cotton cheque shirt with her jeans tucked into a pair of cowboy boots

"Howdy Ma'am" he said in his best Cowpoke voice.

"Welcome stranger "she answered in a Wild West accent far better than his "Step right in."

A well upholstered blonde woman rose from a settee and shook his proffered hand.

"I assume you're Helga."

"Yes, Mr. Bullerton"

Before he could ask her anything she added " I don't know if Van's told you but I'm a social worker and I've had some psychiatric training. I think I am experienced enough to know when I'm being lied to and believe me Byron was lying his head off that morning in Greece."

He needed to ask very few questions as she told her story. Her constant smiling and her rather out-re style of dressing and a perfume he could only describe as" boudoir-ish" had made him think she'd be all girlish and flirtatious but she was if anything the exact opposite. Her English was excellent and she spoke directly with few embellishments. She made the whole scene come alive for him in that Greek square with the sun beating down on the gleaming metal chairs of the café and Byron, face flushed, trying to hide his eagerness to get rid of her. He agreed that Fuller's story about the mobiles being in the hotel was nonsense. She concluded, "When he shooed me into that first boutique I almost turned around in the door way and followed him into the one he entered. I wish I had now."

"And you can't think of any reason why he didn't want Lucy to see you? None at all?" he asked.

"No. Not a one. It's true Lucy and I hadn't seen each other for some months. But we'd not had a quarrel or anything. We'd both stopped going to Weightwatchers with Christmas approaching. We meant to go back in the spring but somehow never got round to it. I've thought and thought about this but I honestly cannot think of any reason why Lucy wouldn't have wanted to see me. It was Byron that was anxious to keep us apart."

"And this hotel where he said they were staying. Was that the truth?

"Well...I suppose it was. I'm sure he said he and Lucy were staying at the Legomandra but when my husband and I went there that night they'd no record of them. But they directed us to a hotel about half a mile away, The Legomandra Beach. That's where they were. Or I should say would have been if Lucy hadn't drowned. It was awful, you know. The hotel had no idea what had happened to them. We stayed hours in the bar waiting. It was pandemonium when the police came."

"It must have been a terrible shock."

"It was. Not only then but afterwards. Every day we were expecting Lucy's body to be found. It completely spoiled our holiday. "

"Did you go to see Fuller in hospital?"

"We did but they wouldn't let us see him. Said he was unconscious. We had to fly back the next day."

Bully returned to the matter of the hotel and what Fuller had told her.

"You're sure he didn't say 'Beach Legomandra?'"

She took her time answering "You'll understand I've had lots of time to think about that. But no matter how often I play it over in my mind I cannot recollect him saying 'Beach.' But it would be an easy mistake for him to make if he was upset wouldn't it? "

He nodded his agreement and asked her again about the aspects of Byron's behaviour that made her think she was lying.

Van had left the room and now returned with coffees and a cake she swore was "low fat" which started them off on talking about their repeated failures with diets. It was Van who brought them back to Fuller by saying "One of the things I hated most about the bastard was that he could eat as much as he liked and not put on the pounds. It was easy to see why women where attracted to him."

Helga asked the question that he hadn't the nerve to ask "You weren't, were you Van?"

She shook her head "No fear. He always seemed to me to be what my old mother used to say "Too sweet to be wholesome. Right from the start I tried to put Lucy off him. I suppose that makes me a prejudiced witness Mr. Bullerton but after the first couple of years of their marriage, Lucy began to tell me things that confirmed my view of him. Once, she was sitting where you are now Helga she said she wished to Christ she'd listened to me and never married him."

"She said as much to me" added Helga. "You know we well endowed girls get used to peoples snide remarks about our shape but Fuller was a sadist. He absolutely destroyed Lucy's confidence by his harping on about her being a 'lardie.' At one time we had to practically force her out of her house, hadn't we Van?"

"More than once. I think the worst times where when some of his get rich quick schemes or his bets went down heavily and he wanted money off her."

"Did Lucy ever say that he physically abused her?"

Van was silent for a moment before replying "Not exactly. Once or twice she hinted he could be a bit physical in the bedroom. But I never saw her face or arms bruised or anything."

"He'd have been too clever for that" said Helga "This type of man knows how to hit a woman where it shows the least."

The more he listened to her the more he wished this was an authorised investigation. As he was thinking this Van asked "The fact that you're here doing what you're doing. That means he's under investigation doesn't it?"

He didn't look at her as he nodded. "He is but we've got to go carefully. We're very much controlled by the Official Greek Inquest and we don't want to tread on their toes. Also if he suspects we're on to him he could make a very serious complaint and we'd be forced to show our hand. So we've got to go very softly."

Van said vehemently "He can't be allowed to get away with murder. I know you've got to have evidence and all that but I 'm sure he killed Lucy. Even a manslaughter verdict would be something. You won't let this drop will you?"

"No you mustn't" added Helga. "That man had something to hide, I'll testify to that anytime."

"I'll do all I can to make sure you get the chance to do that Helga."

He asked them again about the holiday. Van confirmed Lucy had been looking forward to it.

"If only we had photos of Fuller and Lucy on Letsos" he said.

"Why? You don't doubt she was there do you? I spoke to her at least twice" said Van.

He really wanted to ask if she was certain it was Lucy but thought that might offend her. Instead he said "And there was nothing funny, nothing unusual about these calls?"

"Not really. Well…except we kept getting cut off more than usual. We never got the chance to talk for long."

"I had troubles phoning home once or twice, all other times it was fine." said Helga, before adding "Mr. Bullerton, you say you would like photos. Well, our hotel had a photographer; he was a nuisance most times. They had a big board in the foyer where they used to put up his snaps. Maybe, do you think, Lucy's hotel had such a photographer?"

"It's possible. I'll ask but I suppose any photos they took then that weren't sold would be destroyed by now."

"What about the other guests?" asked Van, "If you contacted them they might have included Byron and Lucy accidentally in one of their snaps? They're bound to remember them because of the drowning aren't they?"

"That's a good idea." He answered although he couldn't see such a request being authorised easily. They talked a little while longer and then he thanked them and rose to go.

As she accompanied him to the door Van asked "By the way, are you sure Fuller's still at Meldrum Ave. I've phoned three times in this last week and got no answer. I need to talk to him about Paddy, Lucy's horse"

"I'll check as soon as I get back" he promised.

When he did he was surprised to learn Fuller had moved but he'd complied with his Greek bail terms and left his new address. He phoned it straight through to Van.

When she told Dot, she replied "I knew it. I knew that scum was bound to do a runner. If he thinks he's got away from Lenny he got another think coming."

"He's back?"

"Sort of. He has to stay out of London until he finds out if the Greeks still want him. He's up in somewhere around Glasgow just now. He hates it. Says the Scots can hardly speak a word of English and that they're always moaning. Mind you he's one to talk; he's a miserable bugger most of the time"

"You think he'll make Fuller give back Lucy's things?"

"Too bloody right he will. Fuller's shit scared of him."

"Only I don't know what to do about Paddy. When I phoned Fuller just after he got back he said he'd see to it but he's not been in touch. I …"

"I'll pay for Paddy, you know that" interrupted Dot.

"Yes, but it's not the money I'm worried about. It's his papers I'm after."

"Don't worry; I'll make sure Lenny sorts him out. He'll get you Paddy's papers."

"Thanks Dot."

"Tell you what, I'll phone Lenny and let him know what's what. He don't need to be living down here to give Fuller a going over does he? He could be here and back in a day on one of them Stanstead flights. Or he can stay a night or two with me if he has to suss out the lie of the land beforehand."

"Thanks Dot. Make sure he gives Fuller a couple of extra whacks for me."

"He will. Even if the bastard hands everything over smart like, Lenny's still going to give him a hiding he'll never forget."

"The sooner the better."

CHAPTER 52

Paul sat in his car with his two mobile phones locked into Fuller's mobile. On Saturday night he'd phoned Fuller and instructed him to put the £25,000 into a Tesco's everlasting Plastic bag and to be ready at midnight the next day to deliver it. He'd chosen the time and Sunday because he thought traffic would be much lighter then and it would be easier to see if Fuller was being followed. Fuller hadn't wanted to give him his mobile number but Paul had insisted. He was the mastermind of this operation.

He'd already directed Fuller into and out of the next county and on to this A road. He got out and looked over the side of the bridge where he was parked. If Fuller had done as he'd told him he should be passing underneath in the next four minutes. The traffic was as light as he'd expected; he should easily be able to see if Fuller was being followed by the blonde's red car or the police. If he was everything was off. He'd send his tapes to the police and if they didn't charge Fuller with Lucy's murder that would be their lookout. He could write a book about it, he'd already thought of a good name for it *Murder Home and Away*. He'd use a pseudonym but make sure the events could easily be identified with what had happened to Lucy. Fuller wouldn't dare sue him.

The lights of a lone car approaching at speed made him run to the other side of the bridge and set the night sight he'd bought from an Army surplus store in place. He wasn't taking any chances that Fuller might spot him as he approached the bridge. The car sped past underneath...it... was the Mercedes. Fuller was being a good boy. Now he had to wait and see if he was being followed. He heard another car approaching; it too was speeding. It was a white Transit type van, he just able to read "Ltd." on its side. That couldn't be anything to do with Fuller. He waited exactly another minute, only one more car and a lorry passed below but they weren't going at excessive speeds. He ran back to his car and contacted his quarry.

"Fuller, can you hear me? Fuller, answer me." He had to repeat his questions three times before Fuller responded. "Right now. Leave this A road you are on at the next exit,, turn around a complete 180 degrees and head back down the way you've just come. Report to me as soon as you are back on the A road. Understood?"

"Yes. Yes. How much longer are you going to keep me buggering about? Let's get this over with" came the angry reply.

"Patience, Patience. Fuller. Not much longer. Just do as I say."

When he'd turned around and informed Paul he'd done as instructed Paul give him the road number where he next wanted him to leave the 'A' road. Byron had the interior light on in his car and a local Ordnance Survey map opened across his knees. It showed the exit was about two miles ahead. He pushed the mobile that kept him in contact with the blackmailer under the folded blankets on the passenger seat and picked up another one. "Red One, come in. come in." He was answered immediately by Serena in the White Ford Transit which was keyed into his set.

"Right He's as good as told me we're near the drop." He gave her the road number of the exit and added "I can go either right or left when I leave, he hasn't said yet. When he does I'll repeat what he says loudly as if I can't hear him. You turn the way you'll hear me shouting, understood ?" Again the reply was an instantly affirmative. As he approached the exit Byron looked closely at the map. He realised that if he was told to turn left he would be on a road that ran parallel to the one he'd just left. Why was he being kept so close to it? Did the blackmailer intend to use it for his getaway? It would make sense to use the fastest route available once he'd got the money, wouldn't it? He smiled when over his mobile came the instruction, "Turn left, then left again immediately after you come off the roundabout." He was getting inside the mind of this pervert.

"I'm a gambler" thought Byron "can I risk it?" He decided he could. It would be one of the biggest gambles he'd ever taken. "Red One. Change of plan. Stop in the next lay-by. I think he's going to use the road you're on for his getaway. If I can see which way he goes I'll tell you. If he goes the opposite way to where you're facing it's just too bad. Just get as quickly as you can to to the next roundabout. But don't worry. He'd bound to head back to Lamdon eventually."

"Will do."

Back in Lamdon, Dawn and her partner were sitting her Silver Peugeot 306. in a car park just off the High Street which was only some 50 metres from the town's major roundabout. Byron was certain that the Alsatian dog walker must live in Lamdon and that he would have to return to it with his loot. That was why he'd stationed Dawn near the town centre. He would contact them on a third mobile once the money was handed over and they were to take down the registrations of all the cars that came through the roundabout after that unless he gave them specific information about a particular car. In that case they were to follow it. They didn't know he was being blackmailed about Lucy: he'd told them it was some disaffected punter who was threatening to expose all his "winning tips" scams.

His thoughts were interrupted by new instructions. "Fuller, slow down. You will pass two pubs on your left shortly. One is about half a mile after the other. You are to tell me the name of each in turn. Is that clear?"

"Yes. Will do." The first pub appeared only seconds after he'd answered. He had to brake sharply to get a sight of its name.

"The Rose and Crown"

"Correct."

He drove slowly on to the next pub.

"The Cock Inn"

"Good. Good. Now what I'm going to tell you next is very important. You must do exactly as I say otherwise all I have goes to the police. You hear me?"

"Yes."

"Take the next turning on your left, drive in about 100 yards and stop. Tell me immediately you've stopped."

"Will do." Byron smiled to himself when he saw that the road he was being told to turn into crossed over the "A" dual carriageway. It had to be the bastard's escape route. It took all his self-control to keep the satisfaction out of his voice as when he reported he'd stopped where he'd been told.

The voice that gave him his next instructions was muffled and the instructions perplexing." Drive on across the first bridge immediately ahead of you and on to the middle of next bridge. It is the brick one that crosses the railway. Get out of your car; take your phone and the money with you. Say 'out' when you're standing in the middle of it."

He'd noticed the railway ran alongside the motorway but not thought anything of it. The two bridges were only a few yards apart. He did as he was told, taking care to bring both mobiles with him. This time there was a lengthy pause before there was a response. It was muffled and very quiet as if the speaker was whispering.

"At your feet you'll find a black bin liner. Pick it up and say 'Found' when it's in your hands."

He looked down and saw a dark shape lying close to the brick wall. It wasn't very heavy. He had to stop himself from putting his hand into the liner in case there was a trap inside. When he said "found" he found that he too was whispering.

"Right. When I tell you what to do, do it quickly. No hesitation or everything's off. Understand?"

"Yes"

"Right. There is a rope inside the liner, on one end there's a snap hook. Attach the bag of money to it and lower it over the bridge on the same side that you found the bin liner. Do not look over as you do it. I have a gun and if I see your face I will shoot. DO IT NOW!"

He'd heard the last words without the aid of his mobile. The bastard was directly below him. The gun was a shock. He wasn't prepared for that. Nevertheless he looked quickly at both ends of the bridge but there was nothing but continuous thick hedges on either side of the road. There was no way down. He lifted the bag over the parapet and lowered it slowly, keeping well back as instructed. He was expecting to feel it being grabbed and the money lifted off as it got near the rails. It surprised him when he felt it land on the tracks. He waited almost a minute before pulling the rope up slowly. He got his second surprise of the night when the rope went taut almost immediately. The money hadn't been taken off yet. He waited and waited but the rope stayed taut. What was the bastard doing? Why hadn't he taken the money?

He went to look over the edge then froze. Was the bastard waiting for him to look down so that he could shoot him? Christ he'd not expected this. He stood perplexed not knowing what to do. He let the rope out and listened. Nothing. Gingerly he eased the rope up but again it tightened. He turned back to the car seeking inspiration. As soon as he saw his car's gear change he knew what to do. There was plenty of rope in his hands. Quickly he looped the rope around it, taking care to keep it slack. He tiptoed to the end of the bridge and squinted down. The bag of money was still lying between the rails. This was insane. He ran over to the other side of the bridge and saw a figure running away along the track. As he watched it turned and disappeared through a hole in the fence that separated the railway line from the dual carriageway.

For a second he stood perplexed not knowing what to do next. Realising it would take him ten or more minutes to drive down unto the carriageway he decided to retrieve the money first. He ran over to the car and jerked the rope away from the gear stick. Savagely he hauled it up. When the Tesco bag appeared he grabbed it, plunged his hand inside and felt… stones. The bastard. The fucking bastard. He'd been suckered. The man couldn't have risked filling the bag with stones after he'd taken out the money. He must have had this one ready and switched the bags. Dropping it he ran back and along to the road bridge and looked down in the direction the blackmailer had run. A car was just leaving a lay bye on his side of the dual carriageway but this stretch of road wasn't lit. He ran to the other bridge and leaned over it as far as he dared and waited for the car to pass. When it did he saw it was a dark coloured hatchback. Suddenly the rear of the car was caught in the headlights of an overtaking 4x4. He caught a glimpse of the slight overhang at the top of the rear window and the rear number plate. It was travelling too fast for him to read it but he clearly saw the chrome trim that surrounded it. There weren't too many cars styled like that. The blackmailer was heading north. That meant that unless he was doubly devious he'd come back to Lamdon from the North. There were only two roads he could use to do that but if the bastard lived in the North of the town he'd have no need to use the roundabout where Dawn was parked. He had to act fast.

.

He spoke to Serena and told her briefly what had happened. "Get to Lamdon as quick as you can. I think he's going to return to it from the North. Go to the second roundabout just before

Tesco's on the new by-pass. Leave now. I'll tell you more as you drive back. I'm going to drive like hell to Heathfield Rd. in case he comes into town that way. Go."

He ran back to his car. The road he was on was narrow and he had to drive for a couple of minutes before he found a gateway where he could turn. All the time he was racking his brains to try and identify the blackmailer's car. He recalled how well dressed the man was that he'd seen at his gate. Three-quarter length coat and a pork pie hat? Both probably tweed. Sort of things Volvo drivers wore. Careful buggers the lot of them. But the car he'd seen wasn't a Volvo; he was sure of that. What else? A Rover? Why not? The careful pronunciation and the clothes just screamed middle class English patriot. They just had to buy Rovers didn't they? The only British car maker left. And Rovers had that chrome trim around their rear number plates, he was sure of that. It was worth taking a gamble on.

"Serena, can you hear me? Come in."

"Yes Bry. Loud and clear."

"I think he's driving a Rover Hatchback. One of the small ones, a 25."

"Don't mean a thing to me Bry. You know all I care about a car is how fast it goes."

"Right, then just look out for a small dark hatchback. There's a bit sticking out from the roof over the back window and the rear number plate is surrounded with a chrome trim. You know what I mean?"

"I'm not that fucking stupid. I know where a car's rear number plate is."

"Of course you do. So look at the number plates on the back of every car that passes you. If you're passed by a car with a shiny bit of metal all round the number plate there's a good chance it's him. Right?"

"Right, and we're still not stopping him are we?"

"No, too risky. We want to find out where he lives that's all."

He relayed the same information to Dawn. She knew plenty about cars and assured him she'd have no trouble spotting a Rover 25. "Go now and park up outside Woolworth's in the main street.

You're bound to spot him if he uses the roundabout. Even if he's goes the opposite way to which you're facing it'll only take you a minute to get after him."

"Will do boss. Oh, how long do you want use to stay here? This is costing you, don't forget."

"Don't worry I'll see you right". He looked at the dashboard clock. "We'll give it another couple of hours, till say two thirty. If we haven't spotted him by them we'll jack it in. But if you see him and he doesn't see you on his tail there's an extra hundred for his address."

"For both of us?"

"Don't be so fucking greedy. Just get him in your sights, so no fucking cuddling or snogging. Right?

"Spoilsport. Don't worry Fuller. We've eyes like owls. If he comes this way we'll spot him even if we have our hands in each other's knickers."

It took all his self-control not to swear at her. "O.K. But keep your eyes open." As he spoke he had the terrible thought that if she did follow the blackmailer home she might ask for a lot more than an extra hundred before she told him the address. She was one wiley woman.

Once he turned off the A road Paul relaxed and slowed down to a steady 40. He'd done it. He'd got away with it. Fuller would be behind bars in no time. All his years of reading detective stories and true crime books had paid off. That's where he'd got the idea of the ransom payment being paid under the bridge.. But the swapping the bags had been his own idea. He'd even found out from his computer exactly how much £25,000 in notes would weigh. He'd thought of everything. Even the possibility that Fuller might have seen him drive away and consequently think he would return to Lamdon from the North. But he wouldn't do that. He'd drive for miles around the countryside and come back into the town from the East.

And he'd kept Fuller travelling all around the county until he'd arrived at the railway bridge just when there was a 40 minute period when no trains would be on the line. That had been the action of a master planner. Fuller was no match for him.

For the next hour as he drove he kept rejoicing in what he'd done and what he was going to do. He was so preoccupied with his plans that when he crossed the roundabout in the middle of the town he never saw the silver Peugeot turn and follow him.

Likewise, two hours later a tired but happy Byron did not see the watcher in the bushes as he followed Serena into TREVELYN.

CHAPTER 53

The DVD of The Darling Buds of May had just ended. "Clarrie" as Helene now called him in private got up off the settee to switch it off. The remote control had vanished a week ago.

"Wait. Don't switch off. That's it" she said excitedly.

"What is?"

"David Jason."

"What about him?"

"Don't you see? Him playing Pa Larkin. He doesn't really talk like a Kentish yokel. He's a Londoner. They don't say 'perrrrfec'"

"I know that. He's acting. What's got into you?"

"Clarrie- you're supposed to be the detective. Can't you see that what you've just said is the answer to how Fuller did it?"

He thought hard but no answer came. "Is this another of your Cosi Fan ideas?"

"Yes Yes. It's so blindingly simple. Can't you see that there is only way Fuller was able to kill his wife in England and also take her to Greece. He used an actress."

"She must have been a bloody good one. Lucy's own mother and Van believed they were talking to her."

"Yes, but isn't it the same with David Jason? He must have spent hours listening to tapes of the Kentish accent for his Pa. Larkin character, mustn't he? Think of all the different characters you've seen him play. He's had just the right voice for each of them hasn't he? Actors list all the regional dialects they can do on their CVs. Some make thousands of pounds a year doing the voices for commercials, don't they? Fuller got an actress to play the part of Lucy. I know I'm right. You wait and see."

He nodded "Oh good. Miss Sherlock. Now all we've got to do is prove it." She was going to answer him but he held up his hand to check her. "Listen."

"Yes master."

"Sorry. But see what you think of this. We've had no photos from Greece but lots of people must have seen and spoken to this false Lucy. We should be able to find them from the flight passenger lists and the hotel register. It might just be that some, especially those in the hotel have taken photos that accidentally included Fuller and his "Lucy.""

"He certainly wouldn't have posed for any."

He nodded. "People will most certainly remember the couple because of Lucy's drowning. Even if they haven't photos we can get them to tell us what they remember. Any discrepancy however small might give us enough evidence to arrest Fuller."

"Like height? It would be remarkable if he'd found an accomplice exactly matching Lucy's stature."

"That's it. But she would have made some attempt to look like her. Lucy was a rather ample woman."

"Well then, make sure you pay close attention to whatever any women who saw the couple tell you. Women notice what each other wear. It's second nature to them."

He nodded. "Of course what would be best would be if we could find this woman who acted as Lucy. It's most likely his mistress. I don't think he could possibly risk just hiring someone. He'd have to pay them stacks lot of money to take part in a murder."

"And they could blackmail him afterwards."

"True. I imagine that Fuller would either want this woman to disappear off to somewhere like Australia or else have her close by where he could keep an eye on her. We haven't paid much attention to the company he's keeping at present. Might pay him an unexpected visit in the next couple of days."

They didn't get much sleep that night. They kept waking each other up to tell of another possible aspect of the case they'd just thought about.

So it was a tired D.C. Bullerton who reported all their speculations to D.I. Morrison. He was too honest to claim every idea as his own. After questioning him closely she told him; "You could be on to something here Bully. Write it up and I'll present it to the Chief. In the meantime e-mail some photos of Lucy to the

Greeks and get after those passenger lists. And next time you report any bright idea to a superior keep Helene out of it. You'll never get anywhere in this or any other force if you don't know when to claim all the credit for yourself."

"Thank you ma'am."

"Right; get on with it. But listen; if one of your relatives turns up on any of those lists, don't you dare tell me."

"Well, actually ma'am…."

"Bully I warn you I'll scream if there are. I'm a fabulous screamer."

"Don't worry. I'd already know if any of our lot went to Greece at the same time as Fuller. So you can save your vocal gymnastics for another day. It's just that my cousin Henry is a travel agent. He has a couple of shops here in Cleedon, you probably know them. "Travelworthy's the trade name."

She only just managed to stop herself screaming. The bloody Bullerton's must have bred like rabbits for generations. Anyway, she had another bone to pick with him.

"Hellfire.! Now you tell me. Our family's already paid him in full for a holiday in Cyprus. You'd have got us a discount, wouldn't you?"

"I'm afraid he's not big on discounts, even for relatives. Says he'd be bankrupt if he let us all have our hols. a bit cheaper."

" Oh Tragique. That would never do would it?" she mocked. Then before he could comment she added "Your family's another bloody Mafia, a finger in every pie in this county. I'm going to have to try and be nicer to you Bully. I bet you've got connections right up to the Chief constable and beyond."

The chief constable did in fact hunt with the same pack as most of the Bullertons but no way was he going to let her know that. He shook his head and said carefully "Afraid not ma'am but Henry's also got a shop in Lamdon where the Fullers lived. They might have booked their holiday through him and if we're lucky some local people might have gone on the same holiday or a least the same flight. I could enquire if you like."

"H'm. There might be problems with Data protection but it would do no harm to ask your cousin. But try the official channels first."

When he looked at the files on the case he discovered there was only one full face portrait of Lucy in it. It looked about as natural as a passport photo so he phoned Van and she was only too happy to e-mail him his requested "half a dozen full face portraits." Within fifteen minutes there were twelve being printed out from the office computer with an accompanying message telling him to "nail the bastard." He admired the range of her selections; there were views of Lucy from several angles. She was certainly a well upholstered girl but it was her innocent good natured face that you immediately noticed rather than her rotundity. She looked happy in most of the photos but then Fuller wasn't in any of them.

Getting the flight passenger list was more difficult. He had to navigate his way through a whole series of security loops before permission was granted and no indication was given when it would arrive. He was glad he had Henry to turn to.

His cousin remembered the Fullers because of the drowning. He told Byron "I'm sure they booked with our Lamdon office. I'll get Betty who's in charge there to check to see if there were any other locals booked the same holiday. Mind you we'd have to get their permission first before we gave you their details. Betty's the very soul of discretion herself. If there is anybody and she says it's O.K. to contact them you can be sure she's got their permission. I'll give her your name and number. She'll phone you one way or another, you can be sure of that."

It was just over two hours later when she did. It was good news. Another local couple, John and Mary Bentley had booked almost the same holiday. They were on the Fuller's flight but had stayed in a different hotel. They were willing to talk to the police. Bully phoned them straightaway. The man who answered had evidently been fully informed by Betty about what he wanted because after expressing his sympathy about the drowning and telling Bully he was welcome to come and see him and his wife added " I don't think we'll be much use to you mate, we only saw the Fullers briefly on the plane." Nevertheless when Bully said he could visit them right away he raised no objection.

The Bentleys lived in a small village some 4 miles outside Lamdon. He had no trouble finding them for as John had said "You can't miss us mate. We're the second house just past the pub." Bully didn't have to knock for the front door was opened before he reached it by a young man whose tanned weather beaten face confirmed his outdoor employment. He was urged inside out of the rain and his coat taken and hung in the hall before being lead into the lounge.

The Bentleys were a cheerful couple in their early thirties. John was a compact five foot two whereas his lean dark haired wife Mary was almost six feet tall. Bully guessed from their accents they were Londoners who had come out here seeking cleaner air and more space for their children. After he was welcomed and settled down on their black leather settee Mary said, "It was terrible what happened to that poor woman on holiday. You never expect these things to happen where you are, do you?"

Before he could answer John said "Are you here because you think it wasn't an accident after all?"

Bully decided it was best to be truthful; "To be honest Mr. Bentley we just don't know? Officially we are just pursuing routine enquiries at the request of the Greek police. But we'd like to find out all we can about the Fuller's relationship with one another."

Mary repeated what her husband had already told him "I don't know if we're going to be much help to you, we only saw the Fullers briefly on the plane, didn't we, John?"

"That's all. They wasn't even on the same coach as us going to the hotels."

"Where you seated near them on the plane?" Bully asked.

Mary answered "Just two rows behind, but we were on the opposite side of the aisle."

"But we certainly got a good look at her didn't we doll?" said John.

They both laughed as Mary told Bully about the spilled drink and Lucy's sudden swearing.

"How did Mr. Fuller react? Did he get angry?" Bully asked.

"No, he was a real gentleman. A bit embarrassed like."

John added "Full of apologies to the air hostess he was."

"Mrs. Fuller was mortified," said Mary "She couldn't look anybody in the face as she walked down the plane."

Bully went over the incident again without learning anything further so he brought out the photographs of Lucy for them to examine. They both looked closely at them before both agreeing that "she looks like the woman on the plane." Mary was just about to hand them back to him when she hesitated and started to examine closely the largest portrait of Lucy. She held it out and turned it around several times and then started to compare it with several of the others before she said "There is just one thing Mr. Bullerton. These photos show Mrs. Fuller at different ages. In all of them her hair looks natural but on the plane, although her hair looks the same, it was a wig. Had she been very ill recently? Had chemotherapy or something?"

He knew that Dot or Van would have told him if Lucy had been seriously ill, "No, I'm sure she hasn't. You're sure she was wearing a wig?"

Mary nodded. "I'm a hairdresser. I only work part time now I've got two kids. Wigs are popular. I've got a blonde one myself that I wear for a laugh at parties. Why would anyone get a wig the same as their natural hair unless they'd lost it through illness? I mean, what would be the point?"

"Indeed. Please don't think I doubt your judgement Mrs. Bentley but what you've just told me could be very important. Are you certain enough that Mrs. Fuller was wearing a wig to be willing to testify to it in court?"

She looked at her husband before answering but there was no doubt in her voice as she answered "Yes, I would. I saw it plain enough. It was the first thing I noticed about her as she walked past. The wig was ever so slightly askew. It would have had to have been specially made for it to be such a good match and that ain't cheap. If she hasn't been ill why would she go to all that expense just to replace her own hair with the same thing all over again?"

"Why indeed" thought Bully "Unless it was being worn as a disguise?"

CHAPTER 54

Despite arriving home so late Byron booted up his computer. In no time at all they were watching the FIND FRIEND or FOE website reveal the name of the occupant of the address Dawn and her mate had seen the man enter. As soon as the name came up on the computer screen Byron read it out aloud. "Paul Montgomery Thewell."

"He lives alone" added Serena "there's no other occupants listed"

"Just what you'd expect of a pervert. We've got him girl. Mr. Paul Montgomery Thewell's days, or should I say nights, as a peeping Tom are over."

"We going to do him in the morning?"

"You bet we are. We can't give him time to contact the police. The sooner we take him out the better. Let's get a few hours' sleep first."

Next morning at the breakfast table they discussed the best way to abduct the blackmailer. Byron said "It would be nice just to go up to his front door, knock and barge our way in as soon as he opens the door but ten to one the bastards got a spy hole in the door. He's bound to have seen us before, so he'll know what we look like. He'll never open up once he sees us."

"You think not? I know a way that he will."

"What?"

"You'll see. You get on with the breakfast while I bait the trap. Start me another couple of slices of toast in ten minutes. The thought of a good punch up always makes me hungry."

Paul too had risen early; he'd been too excited to sleep for long. He had a leisurely breakfast and counted the money twice. It was £25,000 alright. He didn't like there being so many new notes but since he'd no intention of ever spending any of it what did it matter? His big problem now was how he could deliver the tapes and the money to the police without them knowing they came from him. He couldn't just go into the station and hand them over the counter. He supposed the best way was to send them in a parcel addressed to the chief constable. But sometimes parcels went astray. Or if they were suspicious they might get the bomb squad to blow it up. Even a small explosion could ruin everything. Perhaps if he addressed it to "THE OFFICERS INVESTIGATING BYRON FULLER" instead of the Chief constable it would be handled more circumspectly. But then he thought there might not be any investigation of Fuller going on. He certainly hadn't seen any signs of one. It might just be shoved aside and left unopened in a storeroom for weeks or months.

He decided he'd take Kaiser for a good walk over the heath and see if the fresh air helped him think of a way of delivering the evidence that befitted the magnitude of what he'd accomplished. He would have to write an appropriate accompanying letter as well. He'd be suitably modest of course but nevertheless he thought it only right that he should remind them that he'd told them months ago that Fuller was a killer.

Although no inspiration came: he and Kaiser enjoyed their walk. It was rather muddy after last night's heavy showers but Kaiser was in great form; twice he almost caught a rabbit. He was never discouraged by these failures and as usual he came swaggering back as if to say "I could have caught it if I'd wanted." All his charging about got him rather muddy and when they got back Paul decided he'd groom his pet before starting his letter. Kaiser didn't enjoy being bathed so Paul usually got the mud off with a stiff brush before starting the gentle combing that would return his pet's coat to its usual lustre. Then he trimmed it with the hairdressing scissors he's specially bought for that purpose. He had a coffee first and then set all his grooming materials out on the waterproof sheet he'd laid on the kitchen floor. He'd only made a few preliminary strokes with the brush when the doorbell rang. "Stay boy" he said and hurried to the door.

When he looked through the spy hole as he always did there was nobody to be seen. Hesitantly he opened the door with the safety chain still attached. There was no one about but there was a brown paper parcel on his doorstep. It had his name in large bold black print on it. Muttering to himself about the lax standards of the postal service he opened the door wide and bent forward to pick up the parcel. He'd just touched it when he was shoved violently back and a man and a woman rushed into the house. He immediately recognized the woman from the gym so guessed the man must be Fuller. Paul scrambled away on all fours as Fuller pursued him. The woman had stopped and was putting the chain back on the door. Somehow he managed to get to his feet and run towards the kitchen but he'd only got as far as the door when Fuller grabbed his collar and pushed him all the way across the kitchen into the sink unit. He was pulled away and was about to be rammed back into it when out of the corner of his left eye he saw Kaiser launch himself at Fuller. Paul screamed "bite him, bite him" as the dog's teeth sank into Fuller's thigh. The man's scream was one of the most satisfying sounds Paul had ever heard. Fuller pushed him away and grabbed at Kaiser's neck. But the dog twisted free and ripped its teeth down Fuller's arm and hand before savaging him again in the thigh. Fuller slipped and fell to the floor; bringing Kaiser down with him but the dog immediately jumped back up and onto his chest to begin biting at his face and neck.

When the woman came running into the kitchen Paul reached behind him and grabbed the largest saucepan off its rack. As he turned back he began screaming at the top of his voice "NO. NO." She had picked up the hairdressing scissors and was repeatedly stabbing Kaiser. Paul leapt towards her with the saucepan raised but before he could hit her she twisted sideways and kicked him in his left thigh. As he fell forward she elbowed him in the face. An agonizing howl from his pet gave him the strength to ignore the pain and the blood flowing down his nose. He aimed the saucepan at her head but before he could bring it down a punch to his throat knocked him unconscious.

When he came to he was lying across the back seat of his own car. Anger overwhelmed him. To steal his car as well as everything else! He'd have screamed except there was a gag over his mouth. His hands and feet were tied with rope. Struggling he knew would be useless but he tried nevertheless. Thinking of Kaiser helped him endure the pain. His wonderful Kaiser. Women had been the curse of his life but none of them had ever hurt him as much as this one. He squinted up and saw her blonde head. She was driving. There was nobody in the passenger seat. He wondered if he got up quickly enough could he put his arms over her eyes, make her crash. If he was killed what did it matter as long as she died too? But he'd only moved his hands a few inches when they jerked to an abrupt stop. The bitch had tied the rope under the driving seat.

The car suddenly swung left, banging his head against the door. Despite the gag around his mouth he bit his tongue. He'd hardly time to register the pain when the car braked violently and he was thrown forward. He heard her get out. A few seconds later she opened the door, pushed and punched him back so she could undo the rope tied under the seat, then dragged him out by the collar and let him fall onto the gravel. As he went down he saw the blue plastic Tesco bag on the passenger seat. He heard another car approaching and looked across to see Fuller's Mercedes halting behind them. When Fuller got out his left arm was tucked into his shirt which was wide open at the neck; Paul felt a flush of pleasure when saw the torn flesh around the man's throat. The woman ran over and embraced him.

"Mind my fucking arm" he shouted at her.

"Sorry, sorry Let me help you inside."

"I can manage. Open the fucking door."

She ran over picked up the bag of money and headed into the big house. Quickly reappearing, she helped Fuller inside. Paul lay cramped and uncomfortable; the gravel was digging into is face and he was choking on the gag. He kicked and struggled until he'd managed to roll over unto his back, making it easier to breath through his nose. Through the pain he forced himself to think of escape. He thought if he could get partly upright he might be able to hop away. Digging his heels into the gravel he inched painfully backwards until he was beside the rear wheel of the car. Resting his head against the tyre gave him brief relief. He was gathering his strength to push himself up backwards against the wheel when he saw her running towards him, the sunlight glinting on what she had in her right hand. He realised to his horror it was a large kitchen knife. As she loomed over him he tried to synchronise the raising of his hands and feet to kick her between the legs but she stepped easily aside and kicked him in the ribs. A red mist of pain clouded his vision as he tried to roll away to avoid the next kick. But it didn't come. Instead she grabbed his feet and started to saw through the ropes binding his ankles. Every thrust of the knife sent a wave of pain through his body. When the ropes parted the blood rushing into his feet hurt so much he prayed he might faint. She seized his shirt collar and lifted him to his feet.

"Move yourself you cunt."

He took a couple of short agonizing steps. The gravel cut into his stocking feet. The next thing he knew she had grabbed the back of his collar and the seat of his trousers and was frogmarching him into the house. He felt as if his balls were being cut in two. He was retching with pain as she forced him down a long passageway and into a room where she flung him down onto a stone floor which he hit shoulder first. He lay there letting the hurt seep out of his body. Only when the pain became bearable did look around.

He was in a large kitchen. Fuller was sitting facing him at the far end of a large table with a red plastic basin in front of him surrounded by an array of first aid materials. She was wiping his throat with a white cloth and saying "We've got to get you to the hospital for an anti- tetanus injection."

"I've had them. I'll be ...." He suddenly jerked away from her, his eyes wide with horror.

A harsh voice from behind Paul snarled "Well, well. Got yourself a proper little Florrie Nightingale, haven't you Fuller?"

Paul twisted around and saw a short powerfully built man standing in the doorway pointed a shotgun at Fuller and the blonde. There was silence for a moment until Fuller forced his features into a twisted smile and said hoarsely "Lenny. Good to see you."

"You lying smarmy bastard. I'd blow your fucking head off right now only I ain't got what I've come for yet. What's the matter? Cut yourself shaving?"

Before he could answer, Serena said pleadingly "He's been attacked by a dog. He's got to get to hospital."

"He's got to get to hospital" Lenny mimicked. "You crafty bitch. Do you think I'm deaf? I'll see that the both of you soon get to hospital, by Christ I will." Pointing the shotgun at Byron he added, "You're a careless cunt, Fuller; leaving a dangerous weapon like this under you bed. Or was you expecting me to come calling after midnight? "

Fuller coughed as he answered "No, No. Not at all. There's been a lot of burglaries around here lately, that's…"

"Stuff it. I'm not here to listen to your fairy tales." Nodding towards Serena he asked "You his tart?"

She shook her head "Just a neighbour. Look, you can see Mr. Fuller's been injured, he needs…"

Again Lenny interrupted "You're a lying bitch. I've seen your sleeping arrangements and your bathroom. Got over Luce very quickly, haven't you Fuller?"

As Fuller just shook his head in denial, Lenny moved crablike over to Paul and without taking his eyes of Byron and Serena, asked "You ain't no friend of these are you?" Paul shook his head vigorously despite the pain. A long thin knife suddenly appeared in the gunman's hand. When he raised it towards Paul's mouth he saw a heavy gold ring with a snake's head with two red stones for eyes on the man's little finger. He wondered if it was a sign of membership of some secret society. "Hold still mate" the man said as he slipped the knife under the gag. It sliced the cloth as if it were paper.

Paul greedily sucked the air into his lungs and gasped "Kill them. Kill them."

"It'll be a pleasure if I don't get what I've come for," said the man as he cut the rope binding Paul's hands. "Where are they Fuller?"

"Lenny listen. I can't make you believe me but I swear by all that's holy that I really did love Lucy. When she…she was taken so tragically away from me I couldn't bear to have all her memories around me. That's why I left Meldrum Ave. I…"

"I've told you don't give me that shit." As he walked slowly towards them he gestured with the gun to Serena "You. Bitch. Get in that far corner." As she edged around the room to get there; Paul saw he'd chosen the corner furthest from any door or window. "Right, stay there. If you take even half a step forward I'll blow your tits off." He moved behind Byron and said "Move the basin out of the way and put your right hand on the table in front of you, fingers wide apart."

Byron did as he was told.

Lenny moved the shotgun so that it was cradled in his left arm. "Wider, fingers wider" he ordered.

Fuller whispered "That's as far as I can..." Before he could finish Lenny had raised the knife with which he'd freed Paul and brought it savagely down into the back of the hand; pinning it to the table. Byron and Serena screamed in unison. Paul had to turn his head away. Somehow he managed to stop himself vomiting. Byron tried to rise but Lenny clubbed him about the head with his fist, forcing him back down.

"Told yer I've ain't got time to waste. Now I've got this other little helper wot will help you talk faster and do wot you ain't never done before in your miserable fucking life. Tell the truth." He held up a Stanley knife. "Bought this yesterday. Never been used so it's nice and sharp. See." He leaned over and drew it along the back of Byron's little finger. Paul was both delighted and astounded at the casual cruelty of the man.

Byron's face was distorted with pain. He started to speak but Lenny stopped him with another blow to the head. ."Listen. Here's the deal. It's dead simple. I ask you a question and you answer. If I think you're lying I'll cut off a finger. Then I'll ask you again and if I still think your lying I cut off another finger. Right? "

Serena suddenly shouted out "Lenny. Listen. Please listen. There's £25,000 down by the door. There in that blue plastic bag. Take it and let him alone."

He shook his head "Somethinks is more important than money, especially to a mother. My sister loved her daughter and she feels real bad not having her bracelets and rings to look at. I'll take the dosh but I gotta have more, ain't I Fuller?" He jabbed the point of knife into Byron's little finger and said "Where are they?"

"Lenny, I had to sell them. I'd no..."

"You fucking thief. They wasn't yours to sell." He started to saw the knife across Fuller's finger. Blood spread quickly from the cut. Fuller's scream died in his throat as he slumped forward. Lenny reached out to pull him back up.

"Wait. Please wait" Serena shouted, "He telling the truth, he got me to sell them but I've still got the best bracelet. I was going to keep it. It's got the little gold horse that she named after Paddy and lots of other charms on it. Honest. It's in my bag on the dresser there." She pointed to a dark oak Welsh Dresser and a large leather bag with a train of camels engraved across its top flap. "Please, I'll show you." She took a hesitant half step forward.

Lenny stared hard at her before saying "Quick then."

She ran to the dresser and picked up the bag and thrust her hand inside. She seemed to be taking a long time to find the bracelet but then with a triumphant smile she held up the bag and held it out towards Lenny. There was a series of soft "pop" pop" pops". Lenny jerked back. Paul saw holes appear in his jacket and shirt. He jerked his knife arm up as if trying to swat away an angry wasp. Then, as another hole appeared in his chest, with a deep animal roar he brought the knife down and across the back of Byron's neck. Serena threw the bag away and using both hands aimed a small silver gun at Lenny and shot him twice in the face. He managed to take two steps towards her before he fell awkwardly forward, the shotgun clattering away across the stone floor. She ran to him and pressing the pistol into his ear, pulled the trigger. There was only a faint click. She hit him viciously on the side of the head with it before throwing it down and rushing over to Byron.

Paul heard him moan as she grabbed the handle of the dagger and tried to pull it out of his hand. When he saw that even though she was using both hands the dagger wasn't moving he crept over and picked up the shotgun. From his time in the Army Cadets he knew how to fire a rifle but he'd never handled a shotgun. Afraid that she might hear him as he tried to find and release the safety catch he seized it by the barrels and swung it with all his might bringing the butt crashing down on the back of her head. As she fell forward over the dagger she let out a piercing scream. Its very intensity seemed to send a surge of power up his arms and he hit her again and again. With each blow he spelled out his pet's name K-A-I-S-E-R. He could feel the crunch of wood on bone as her skull shattered. He wanted her to scream in pain but all he could hear was himself repeatedly screaming his pet's name. Only when a long stuttering moan came from Byron did he push her aside and holding the barrels as far down as possible he swung the gun like the cricketer he used to be and smashed the flat of the butt against the side of Byron's head. No cross- batted six he had ever hit equalled the thrill of pleasure he got from this blow even though the impact knocked the shotgun out of his hands. Fear made him bend down and grab it again but when he looked up, the sight of the two shattered bloody heads made him retch. Still holding the gun he let himself slide down unto the floor and be sick.

He stayed there until he was able to crawl over to the doorway. Using the wall and the gun as supports he hauled himself up and surveyed the room. The bodies at the table lay crumpled together and Lennie hadn't moved. All that mattered now was to get home to his pet. Maybe, just maybe, Kaiser was still alive and he could get him to the vet. As he turned to go he saw the plastic bag. He staggered over and grabbed it. He'd spend it all to help his pet. But if Kaiser was dead he'd have the grandest ever black marble monument erected over his grave. When he got the doorway he noticed a pair of green Wellingtons. When they fitted he took it as a sign that everything was going to turn out all right. He ran over the gravel to his car. The keys were in the ignition! Throwing the money unto the passenger seat he jumped in and drove quickly away. Once out on the road he pressed his foot hard down on the accelerator. On the sharp bend at the end of the long straight he almost collided with a police car coming towards him. It appeared so quickly Paul hadn't time to react. Only the police driver's skill saved them from a head on crash.

When D.I. Morrison stopped swearing she congratulated the driver on his skill before asking "Did you get his registration?"

"Afraid not. It was all I could do to avoid the mad bastard."

"What about you Bully?"

"I only got EJ 53 that's all but it was a Rover 25."

"You're sure of that ?"

"Oh yes ma'am. Grandma drives one just like it."

D.I.Morrison waited until the car stopped on the gravel drive of TREVELYN before she screamed.